FOREIGNERS

CARYL PHILLIPS

Harvill Secker
LONDON

Published by Harvill Secker 2007

2 4 6 8 10 9 7 5 3 1

Copyright © Caryl Phillips 2007

Caryl Phillips has asserted his right under the Copyright, Designs and
Patents Act 1988 to be identified as the author of this work

First published in Great Britain in 2007 by
HARVILL SECKER
Random House, 20 Vauxhall Bridge Road
London SW1V 2SA

www.rbooks.co.uk

Addresses for companies within The Random House Group Limited can
be found at: www.randomhouse.co.uk/offices.htm

The Random House Group Limited Reg. No. 954009

A CIP catalogue record for this book is available
from the British Library

ISBN 9780436205972

The Random House Group Limited makes every effort to ensure that the
papers used in its books are made from trees that have been legally sourced
from well-managed and credibly certified forests. Our paper procurement
policy can be found at: www.randomhouse.co.uk/paper.htm

Typeset by Palimpsest Book
Production Limited,
Grangemouth, Stirlingshire
Printed and bound in Great Britain by
William Clowes Ltd, Beccles, Suffolk

For Omar and Jamal

I   Doctor Johnson's Watch   I

II   Made in Wales   63

III   Northern Lights   167

     Acknowledgements   261

I

Doctor Johnson's Watch

It was a cold December morning, and the bitter wind penetrated my black cloak with ease. However, the stubborn sun continued to shine brightly in the sky, although it failed to bestow any warmth on either myself or the two dozen sombre souls gathered outside of Bolt Court. I glanced about my person, realising that I was part of a bizarre congregation that represented both high and low society, but how could we be anything other than a queer assembly of misfits when one considered the personage who was to be buried on this melancholy English morning? London society was still somewhat amused by the gossip relating to the recently departed Dr Johnson's final exchange with the sour-natured Sir John Hawkins, an apparently abrupt conversation which had taken place only some few short days before the doctor's death. Understanding that his mortal time was limited, the doctor had demanded of his chief executor in that stern, almost impolite, tone that he had perfected, a tenor of voice which unfortunately masked his more cordial nature, 'Where do you intend to bury me?' When the news of the doctor's question reached the ears of the leisured gentlemen who recline in the smoke-filled coffee houses which constitute London's informal business world, the question served only to occasion much laughter from both those who knew the gentleman personally, and from those who knew of him by reputation. Indeed, what kind of a question was this? 'Where do you intend to bury me?' Apparently Sir John Hawkins maintained his countenance and answered plainly, 'In Westminster Abbey.' He might well have continued and punctuated his uncharacteristically civil answer with the rather less civil question, 'My good man, where else do you expect to be lain to rest?' According to Hawkins, on receiving this news the great man simply stared back and then, almost as an afterthought, he adjusted his inadequate wig. Although he was evidently drawing close to the terminus of his existence, the slovenly doctor still appeared to be insensible to the squalid spectacle that he presented. However, despite his shabby appearance, Samuel Johnson was undoubtedly the foremost literary scholar of his age, a man whom nobody would dare to deny his rightful place in the abbey next to Geoffrey Chaucer and John Dryden. Eventually, the great gentleman, as though finally understanding that his resting place was *indeed* to be Westminster Abbey, continued in a less stentorian voice. 'Then,' he whispered, 'if any friends think it worthwhile to give me a stone, let it be placed over me so as to protect my body.' No report was made of Sir John Hawkins' reply, if indeed there was any, to this plaintive, and surprisingly coy, request by the good doctor.

On the Monday after the doctor took his leave from this earthly world, we subdued mourners gathered on the narrow pavement outside of Bolt Court. Our gloomy congregation could not be accommodated within the modest confines of Dr Johnson's house and, I confess, at this time I was not a member of that privileged inner circle who strolled boldly from their carriages and knocked upon the door before waiting confidently for admittance. Sixteen years ago, I was little more than a minor literary wit in London society, but more properly I was regarded as a financial investor, a man of the City. My participation in Dr Johnson's wider circle was unquestioned, but good manners prevented me from attempting to assert a prominence which I had not yet earned. Accordingly, I stood with the less celebrated members of the Literary Club and first stamped my feet, and then rubbed my hands together against the cold, determining that I would remember every last detail of this momentous day so that I might set it down for those who came after me. I was sure that other, more accomplished, pens would eventually make fine prose from the events that were about to unfold, but I remained hopeful that my own modest observations might have some future resonance.

And then, at precisely twelve o'clock, with the sound of City bells pealing gaily in the distance, the door to Bolt Court was thrown open and out into the daylight emerged the grief-stricken figures of the Revd Mr Strahan and the Revd Mr Butt, both of whom were attired in their sootiest frock coats and whose faces were decorated with a grave aspect. While weak sunlight still conspired to brighten the mood of the day, these two imposing men looked all about themselves before standing to one side. Thereafter, the six stern-faced pall-bearers – viz. Mr Burke, Mr Windham, Sir Charles Bunbury, Sir Joseph Banks, Mr Colman, and Mr Langton – walked gingerly from the house with the burdensome body of the deceased carefully balanced at shoulder height, its weight evenly distributed between them. All eyes were upon these half-dozen men as they prudently inched forward and then deposited the doctor into the hearse, while others who had been gathered inside of the house now spilled out on to the pavement and began distributing themselves into the various coaches that were waiting to transport those afflicted with tenderness and sorrow to the abbey.

The procession departed promptly at a quarter after noon with the hearse and six in front, and the executors – viz. Sir John Hawkins, Sir Joshua Reynolds, and William Scott, LLD – taking up the immediate rear in an attractive coach and four. Behind them were arranged a further eight coaches and four, which provided transportation for the favoured members of the Literary Club and other close friends of the deceased. Behind these eight coaches were two more coaches and four, which contained the pallbearers, and behind them another two coaches and four which would convey a small group of gentlemen who had kindly volunteered to help in any way they could. Closing the procession were no less than thirteen gentlemen's carriages, which spoke to both the affection in which the doctor was held and to his high social status, all the more remarkable when one considers that this most distinguished of men had been born into undeniably modest circumstances.

I understood that I was to have the great honour of riding in one of the eight coaches that had been designated to transport the doctor's inner circle. Not wishing to press my suit, I waited until the last possible moment and was eventually ushered into the rearmost vehicle. Once there I was surprised to find myself sharing the coach with Dr Johnson's faithful negro servant, Francis Barber, and another man who appeared, by his slipshod dress, to be an English servant of some description who had fallen below even this low station of life. The man appeared to be uncomfortable, and he immediately stared out of the window, as though concentrating hard upon some person or object in the distance. I soon surmised that this was probably his way of disguising his embarrassment at having entered a place which made him feel inadequate. Either this, or his seemingly purposeful gawping was enabling him to stifle a grief that might otherwise grow uncontrollable. I soon turned my attention from this nameless fair-skinned lackey and fixed my gaze upon the polished sable exterior of the renowned Francis Barber. I had, of course, previously made the acquaintance of the doctor's negro attendant, most commonly when the negro ushered me into the doctor's house, and then, later in the evening, when he conducted me out of the same establishment. On other occasions the black man might accompany his master on the short journey to a tavern in order that the doctor might dine in the company of a small gathering of his admirers, myself included, and once present the negro would sometimes linger a while before disappearing into the night. However, these few encounters with Francis

Barber stimulated precious little in the way of conversation between us, save the normal pleasantries between superior and inferior that one might expect in civilised society. Nevertheless, I had formed a favourable opinion of the sooty fellow as one who remained quietly devoted to his master while exhibiting some occasional exuberance of personality such as one might reasonably anticipate from a member of his race.

There were others whose opinions of the negro were not so generous. Some intimates of the doctor's circle freely expressed their conviction that Francis Barber was, to their minds, a wastrel, a man who considered his master's needs only as an afterthought, and who was wont to freely spend the doctor's money in order that he might improve his own situation. My limited experience with Francis Barber rendered me incapable of passing an informed judgement on this matter, but to my eyes the negro Francis loved his master with virtuous affection and was always protective and loyal to the man under whose roof he had spent the greater part of his life. After all, his master had been a great champion of the negro people, and he had loudly expressed his opinion that slavery could never be considered the natural condition of man. Furthermore, the doctor had consistently thundered that the number of black men who still repined under English cruelty, at home and abroad, remained too great. But dissenting voices could be heard, and chief among the negro-detractors, and Francis Barber in particular, was Sir John Hawkins, the chief executor of the doctor's will. This peacock of a gentleman was known to hold an ungenerous impression of his fellow man, be they black or white, but it particularly galled him that during the doctor's life he was never able to dislodge Francis Barber from his high position in Dr Johnson's affection. And now, no doubt due to Sir John Hawkins' scheming, within three days of his master's decease here was Francis Barber riding in the last of the eight carriages rather than at the head of the procession where he rightfully belonged and, no doubt, where his late master would have insisted that he position himself.

Sad to say, I soon discerned that in the carriage there was an odour, and a not altogether agreeable one at that. Although I refrained from casting any accusative glances, it was clear that the negro, Francis Barber, was the source of the unpleasantness. Our third companion, who could hardly boast that he was the most hygienic creature in the kingdom, visibly recoiled at the smell and quickly fastened a handkerchief to his face. I soon realised that it was not the clothes of Francis Barber that were unwashed and troubling to the senses, but in all likelihood it was the badly matted wig that was causing the unfortunate aroma. Clearly the negro's wig had lain unattended and unpowdered for quite some time and the negro had most likely hastily snatched it up for the occasion. Despite my discomfort, I was prepared to forgive Francis Barber, for his late master had not provided him with a reliable example. The doctor's own great bushy wig possessed a hedge-like mass which suggested that a comb had never penetrated its interior, and this chaotic mess no doubt served as the negro's model for what was acceptable in a headpiece. Sensing my eyes upon him, the humble negro continued to stare intently at the floor of the carriage, as though reading some secret message that had been laid out there for him. Eventually, he raised his black eyes so that they met my own, and then he spoke in a clear English voice.

'I am sorry that we should meet again in such unfortunate circumstances.'

I smiled, and nodded slightly, as I replied.

'Indeed, the timing is unfortunate, but I am content to once again make your acquaintance.'

This being said, Francis Barber extended his hand and we shook firmly like two merchants sealing a trading deal, but beyond this opening exchange it was unclear where this conversation might ramble. Accordingly, we retreated to silence and joined our third companion in gazing idly out of the window as London occupied herself with the trifles of daily business, as though unaware of the fact that this day held significance that England would evermore be obliged to note. I thought about 'Dictionary Johnson' and the busy society tongues that were wagging with news of the recent autopsy that had been conducted at William Hunter's School of Anatomy, off Shaftesbury Avenue, where it had been discovered that although the doctor's liver, pancreas, and kidney were chronically diseased, the heart remained both large and strong. I would have liked to engage Francis Barber on the subject of this news, and discover his opinion of its significance, but the negro and I spent the remainder of our journey studiously ignoring one another until our procession reached the west door of Westminster Abbey, which it did at a little before one o'clock. Prior to disembarking I peered through the carriage window and was alarmed to see few members of the general public, and little evidence that more would soon be arriving to swell the numbers. But even as I looked on I could hear the fierce voice of England's great lexicographer reminding me that such worries were pure vanity, and that I should be putting my educated mind to better use.

The carriage door was opened by the tall footman, and a sudden rush of fresh air served only to remind me of the malodorous conditions that I had been forced to endure. The third man quickly took his leave, but Francis Barber deferred to myself and, keen to achieve terra firma and the ability to breathe freely, I seized the proffered opportunity and stepped nimbly from the carriage. The six stern-faced prebendaries of the abbey were there to greet us in their surplices and doctors' hoods, and they marshalled the newly arrived congregants into some semblance of order with the two vergers at the head, followed by the Revds Mr Strahan and Mr Butt, and then the body of the deceased on the sturdy shoulders of the six resolute pall-bearers. The rest of us followed, two by two, behind Sir Joshua Reynolds, the designated chief mourner, and his fellow executors, Sir John Hawkins, and Dr Scott. We proceeded slowly into the woefully empty abbey, and made our way to the south cross where the body was carefully placed with the feet opposite the elegant monument to William Shakespeare. Then, to the surprise of nearly all gathered, the Revd Dr Taylor began to perform what was clearly a simple burial service, not the full service that we were expecting. I later discovered that the executors had felt themselves justified in keeping the expense of the interment modest, and of course they intended no disrespect, but the general feeling of those assembled was one of distress that things were passing so quickly and without lights, music, or a little gaiety. It was noticeable that, once the initial shock had penetrated, some mourners glared disapprovingly at the presiding Dr Taylor, for most of those present held him responsible for the hurried manner in which England's greatest literary figure was being given body room in the abbey. Sad to say, the ceremony was as dull as it was rapid, and it was disturbing to realise how strikingly it differed from the extravagant service that had been held for the doctor's life-long friend David Garrick, who five years earlier had made his rest at the same venue.

During the proceedings I sat across the aisle from Francis Barber, who perched uncomfortably with his head bowed and who appeared to be genuinely consumed with grief. It was noticeable that few chose to sit near to him, but having shared a carriage with the said person I fully under-stood that the reason for their reluctance had precious little to do with his sooty complexion and everything to do with the human sensation of smell. I looked at this unmoored man, who had undoubtedly lost a champion and a defender, for all of Johnson's circle knew that they should never speak ill of Francis Barber while in the doctor's presence, but the sad negro had lost more than perhaps even he had imagined. He had lost his father and his anchor in this world, and although I understood that these days Francis now possessed some version of a wife and a family, sitting quietly by himself in Westminster Abbey this poor man looked to all intent and purpose as though he was suddenly alone in the world.

At the conclusion of the short and unsatisfactory service, it was understood that we members of the Literary Club would repair to a nearby familiar tavern in order that we might drink toast after toast in the doctor's honour until late into the night. Aside from rehearsing the details of the great man's life, there would be other subjects for discussion, including the controversial nature of the day's truncated ceremony, and the question of the will and the disposal of the doctor's assets. These subjects would undoubtedly keep myself and my fellow devotees of Dr Johnson happily occupied for many hours, but I knew full well that Francis Barber, without the protection of his master, would not be invited to join the company. As I stood to take my leave of the abbey, I looked again at this forlorn figure bent forward in the pew and seemingly reluctant to rise to his feet. It occurred to me that the Christian thing to do might be to approach the negro and offer him sincere commiserations for his loss, thereby once again extending the hand of friendship, but I had no desire to place the servant in an awkward predicament and so I cast him a final glance and strode purposefully down the aisle towards daylight, leaving this abandoned man alone in the abbey with his master and his dark thoughts.

Some sixteen years after the funeral of the good doctor, I found myself comfortably appointed inside a carriage that was bowling into Lichfield, a fair-sized city with a reputation bolstered by Mr Daniel Defoe's favourable comments in which he recorded that he considered Lichfield a place for 'good conversation and good company'. I had been led to believe that this low-lying city, surrounded by fields and woods and marshes, was principally distinguished by its fortunate location, situated as it is 110 miles north of London, and a mere 14 miles beyond Birmingham. This places the city in an advantageous position on the main coaching route to the north-west and Ireland, but I understood Lichfield to be also renowned for its beautiful, yet somewhat eccentric, cathedral that was long ago constructed out of faded red stone, and which displays not one but three spires. I had arranged to spend a single night at the Three Crowns, a respectable inn that I had been led to believe was situated close by the doctor's childhood home. Having arrived at my destination, I announced myself to the ruddy-faced innkeeper who quickly escorted me to my room on the first floor. He informed me that dinner would soon be served, and as my hunger had been powerfully aroused by the long journey I suggested to him that I would like to dine as soon as possible. He lowered his eyes somewhat apologetically as he informed me that it might take his cook a full half-hour to prepare my meal, but in the meantime he encouraged me to try some Staffordshire oatcakes and a jug of Lichfield Olde Ale, which I hastily declined.

I dined alone, but under the judicious scrutiny of a young drudge who had clearly been instructed to cater to my needs. I ignored the lackey and carefully observed the boisterous local folk, who noisily refreshed themselves with draught after draught of malty beer. Having finished my adequate, but by no means exceptional, meal I interrogated my simple host with regards to the origins of the city, at which point he asked permission to join my table. He told me that legend had it that around AD 300, and during the reign of the Roman Emperor Diocletian, over 1,000 Christians were martyred nearby. According to this man, the name Lichfield actually means the 'field of the dead'. My host refreshed my glass of port-wine before laughing out loud and conceding that there was no evidence to support this *fact*, but he knew it to be true and beyond contention. He also 'knew' that there were no thatched roofs in Lichfield because of the risk of fire, a peculiarity which set this city apart from most English centres to the north or south. Exulting in what he imagined to be his own pleasantry, he continued and informed me that Queen Mary had long ago made Lichfield its own county, so that while the city stands in Staffordshire it does not take part as a member of the said same county. And what, I asked, now warming to the task which had occasioned me to leave London and travel to Lichfield, of the city's prominent or notorious citizenry? At this my host was quick to laugh out loud and proclaim two names that he insisted would be familiar to any who held English to be his tongue: David Garrick and Samuel Johnson. As though this were too easy a resolution to my question he continued and, clearly relishing the heat of conversation and the close proximity to controversy, he lowered his voice and informed me that some 200 years ago the last person to be burnt at the stake in England for heresy was burnt in Lichfield. I nodded sagely and then bided my time before asking after negroes. 'Negroes?' The man seemed confused.

'Around here?' he asked. I said nothing further and waited for him to continue, and then I saw his pockmarked cheeks begin to flush. 'I see. I suppose a gentlemen like you must be asking after Frank Barber?'

I slept badly in the awkward bed, for the whole contraption seemed to be woefully misshapen from having no doubt supported the fatigued bodies of countless exhausted pilgrims. Being one who was not familiar with the turmoil of undertaking frequent excursions, leaving London constituted for me a great adventure of sorts. Having recently retired from my commercial business in the City, where I grew to despise the vulgar rapacity of the sugar and slave men of the West Indies, I had recently begun to contemplate some involvement in the Province of Freedom – Mr Granville Sharp's scheme for resettling blacks on the west coast of Africa in an efficiently managed colony – as a way of honourably investing my money for profit and charitably passing my days. This being the case, my ageing mind was forever returning to the disturbing image of poor Francis Barber all alone in Westminster Abbey, and I finally understood that before making any decision about my own future philanthropic investments it might profit me to revisit the past and try to discover what had become of the forlorn negro. I wondered, was he yet another example of a poor transplanted African whose roots had refused to properly catch the soil of our fair land? Or had life beyond his master's departure showered the negro with good fortune? It chanced that my late-night conversation with the lumpish innkeeper had helped to clarify the situation. Eventually the light of day began to spill through the shuttered windows, and I heard stirrings in the various rooms about the Three Crowns, but I did not move. Recalling the previous evening's conversation, I found myself caught in a web of indecision. Should I follow my host's suggestion and seek out the widow, Mrs Elizabeth Barber, or should I simply depart in the direction of London and admit defeat in my quest. I lay in bed while the day announced itself as a fine summer's morning, and then I heard a timid knock upon the door which I assumed would be the servant bearing water for my ablutions.

The carriage bounced its way unceremoniously down the rutted lane, and I was sure that the ancient driver was deriving childish pleasure from seeking the most difficult and bone-jarring route. The carriage window afforded a fine prospect, and I looked warmly upon the young English maidens labouring merrily in the fields who knew that at the end of their working day there would be liberty and freedom. How different a life it was for those who we forced to expend themselves in the tropical fields of the West Indies. At the end of their day, there was neither liberty nor freedom, but merely the expectation of more suffering unredeemed by any financial or material gain. I continued to stare at the young maidens, but soon realised that, despite their obvious beauty, I should avert my eyes and focus my mind on the task at hand. The previous evening my host, having conveyed the dreadful news of Francis Barber's demise, had continued and informed me that, to the best of his knowledge, the family of Francis Barber had last been heard of living in a place named Burntwood, a hamlet that lay only four miles beyond the city to the west. Having given me this information, the innkeeper had ceased speaking for a few moments as though his mind was tormented with some burdensome secret. 'You do understand,' he said, 'that this is not a place to which those such as yourself habitually journey. Truly, there is nothing there of any consequence.' Again he paused. 'Except, of course, that you will most likely discover Mrs Barber.' With this said the man once again topped off our glasses with wine, and thereafter we fell silent for what remained of the evening. Securing the services of the ancient driver and carriage had been relatively simple, for the innkeeper had made it his business to assist me. However, this morning, when my host informed the driver that Burntwood was to be my destination, the puzzled look on the face of the wizened man spoke eloquently to all that the innkeeper had suggested. It was difficult to ascertain if the aged driver was genuinely offended, or merely temporarily surprised, at having been instructed to undertake a journey to such a place.

We eventually drew up beside a tall, unruly, hedgerow that was clearly in need of some attention. Initially, I found it difficult to understand why my driver had stopped the carriage for I could see no sign of human life. However, taking the whip in his right hand, the ancient man pointed beyond the hedgerow to a modestly proportioned stone cottage which I now understood to be my destination. The morning sun had been kind to my bones and so I required no immediate assistance descending from the contraption, although the driver rightfully made his services available to me. 'Wait here,' I insisted, and then, gathering my wits about me, I walked gingerly towards the unprepossessing abode and knocked sharply on the door. The ominous silence was disturbed only by the pleasing sound of birds singing and a brook babbling somewhere in the distance. I knocked again, and this time shouted out loud in the hope that I might attract the attention of somebody within, but it appeared that I succeeded only in alarming my carriage driver, for the decrepit fellow left his vehicle and hastened to my side imagining that I must be crying out for help. On discovering that I was perfectly safe, and merely attempting to arouse the inhabitants of the dwelling, he rearranged himself and withdrew again to his carriage leaving me perfectly alone.

It was then that the door began to slowly open, the crying of the rusty hinges announcing the action, and a shadowy head soon emerged and stared up in my direction. A strangely coloured and clearly disconsolate child, with eyes as big as two saucers, stared up at me, but seemed reluctant to say anything. I bade the apparition a good morning and asked if its mother was hereabouts. The child, which I now determined to be female, shook its fuzzy head, which at least suggested an intelligence of the English language. I asked the girl if she imagined that her mother might show herself in the near future, but it appeared that this question stretched her comprehension a little too far, for the urchin simply stared back at me with frigid indifference and said nothing. Clearly I had arrived at the right place, for this dirty-looking child was obviously the product of a union between one of England's fair wenches and a negro, presumably Francis Barber.

However, it was evident that there was little point in trying to draw the creature into conversation for its understanding was clearly limited, and its mother had obviously absented herself for the day.

By the time I returned to Lichfield it was midday, but my curiosity was so piqued by the discovery of the child that I determined to see what more I might learn about the fate of Francis Barber from my host. It transpired that the phlegmatic innkeeper had absconded to Birmingham on an urgent matter of business, but his portly wife informed me that her husband would certainly return by the evening. I thanked her for the information, and then spent a good part of the afternoon exploring the modest city of Lichfield by foot. To my dismay, the place appeared to lack a coffee house where a man might settle into a snug and partake of some wholesome liquor while perusing the gazette or public papers and, in the convivial company of his peers, receive news and information pertaining to both business and pleasure. Lichfield lacked not only a coffee house, but the city appeared to be thoroughly devoid of that constant flow of humanity which characterises the unique vitality of any great city, and is so abundant in my own London. The great immensity of London which assaults the ears, nose, and eyes of any visitor, where wealth, commerce, and plenty dwell next to poverty, pestilence, and despair, and where fully one-tenth of the nation's population teem and tumble together, was altogether absent in this simple place. In fact, there was little in this Lichfield that I deemed to be worthy of my scrutiny. I did see one or two fine buildings, and the architecture of the twelfth-century cathedral allowed me to soothe my eyes for an hour, but this was the sum total of Lichfield's pleasures. On arriving back at the Three Crowns I discovered that my host had recently returned, and shortly before dinner he sent word to my room that he would very much like to converse with me for he had gleaned information that I might find useful. Perhaps, he suggested, we might take a drink together after the completion of my meal.

Again I dined alone, and with the same young attendant ministering to my needs, but the quality of the food appeared not to have improved. I signalled to the boy that he should remove my plate, and soon thereafter the innkeeper joined my table clutching a bottle of port and two glasses. He looked somewhat downcast, as though in possession of news that he was going to find difficult to convey. However, after some preliminary conversation about the beautiful day that we had enjoyed, he turned his attention to his own journey to Birmingham and began to sing the praises of the merchants of that town. I listened until his tongue stopped flapping, and the sheepish look on his face suggested that he was suddenly aware that he might possibly be exhausting my patience. He poured yet another drink for us both. 'I have,' he said, 'made some discoveries about your Mr Barber.' I presumed he had and so I simply waited for him to share with me the nature of these discoveries. 'The child you saw today is Frank Barber's daughter, but I know there are also other children. Apparently the wife, Elizabeth, attempts to keep their Burntwood schoolhouse by herself, although the place enjoys an enrolment of only four pupils, and it is said that it will probably close before the year is out for want of custom. Mrs Barber's skills as a teacher are not greatly in demand, but her fees are such that practically any pocket can afford her services. According to the intelligence of those who were prepared to speak with me on this sad subject, those in desperate need would today rather send their children elsewhere than to Mrs Barber, so it's inevitable that soon the school will be no more.' At this he paused, as though trying to impress the gravity of the situation upon me, but I said nothing and merely took a sip of my wine. 'And then,' he continued, 'there is the case of Frank Barber himself. His final days hereabouts in Lichfield were not easy, filled as they were with both illness and poverty. Apparently Mr Barber squandered the not inconsiderable sum of money that his master left to him in his will. Furthermore, if you don't mind my saying, the fellow did let himself go, for when I last saw him he'd lost all his teeth, and his face was severely marked with the pox. He was as sad and as broken as a man can be while still remaining with us in this world.' The innkeeper paused. 'Of course, his last offence was to insist on wearing his late master's clothes, although they had clearly long past all usage. It was a truly pitiful sight.'

I listened but chose to say nothing in response to my host's words, but of course London society had long been aware of Francis Barber's descent into financial difficulties. Following his departure to Lichfield, some two years after his master's death, many had answered Francis' calls for money, for the negro claimed to have incurred significant expenses due to his own failing health and that of his delicate children, and the poor man appeared to be permanently fastened into coils of debt and anxiety. However, having squandered the generous sum that his late master had left for him in his will, and having often displayed 'vulgar insolence' in his written communication with those who had tried valiantly to help him, there were soon few in the doctor's circle who felt either sympathy or concern for the negro's welfare. Within a few years of his arrival in Lichfield, the careless Barber had also, much to the dismay of his few remaining supporters, managed to fully deplete the capital which had been set aside to provide him with an annuity. The nature of his presumably unhappy life on Stowe Street in Lichfield remained a mystery to those of us who remembered 'London Frank', and this, after all, was partly why I had chosen to seek out the negro, in order that I might discover for myself the full story of his fall from grace. 'I am led to believe,' continued my host, 'that Mrs Barber will be at home tomorrow, for apparently today she travelled from Burntwood into Lichfield on a series of errands. I'm sure that she'll be happy to speak with a gentleman such as yourself, and particularly on the matter of her late husband. No doubt she can help you with information where perhaps I have failed your good self.' I stifled my contempt, for this outburst of false modesty on the part of my foolish host was perfectly transparent. He was asking me, in an indirect manner, what exactly was my business with Mrs Barber, but that, of course, was something that I would never divulge to a man such as this. It was then that I realised that the man was most likely in drink, and although

I desired his absence I reminded myself that he was my host and I should endeavour to tolerate him for a while longer. We sat together for an hour or so more, exchanging pleasantries about the seasons, and about London and Birmingham societies, before I finally tired of this man's prattle and retired to my room where I took to my incommodious bed and discovered that, once again, the innkeeper had not had the decency to at least venture to improve matters by applying a warming pan to make the devilish cot more tolerable.

Unable to immediately find sleep, I hoisted myself upright and squinted about the dismal chamber. Then I lit the candle and reached over and pulled the precious object from the pocket of my waistcoat. The tortoiseshell watch, which I had been led to understand the doctor had paid Mudge and Dutton the princely sum of seventeen guineas to purchase in 1768 had, on his death, been bequeathed by Johnson to his beloved negro. Apparently, as the result of a sale born of desperation, the watch had fallen into the hands of the Canon of Lichfield, at a time when the high and mighty of this city had taken advantage of the black's innocence and poverty and stripped him of all mementoes of his master. Two owners later, the watch had come into my possession at a sale of Johnsonian relics at a London coffee house, and for the past year I had kept it close to my person. I harboured some notion of presenting the watch to the negro in exchange for some testimony about the vicissitudes of his recent life, but it now appeared that the delicate timepiece would remain safely in my keep. I replaced the watch and blew out the

candle, and in the darkness I allowed my mind to rumi-
nate upon the strange case of poor Francis Barber who,
along with the late writer Gustavus Vassa, was, at one
time, probably the foremost negro in England. Sad that
this man should have come to an unfortunate end in a
place such as Lichfield, but it was possible that my curiosity
about the negro's later years might now be satisfied by an
audience with his widow. I cast my mind back to the
malodorous carriage ride that I had shared with Francis
Barber as we journeyed to the funeral of his master, and
I remembered our one short conversation. I thought then,
and on many other occasions previous to the day of the
funeral, that being dependent upon a negro was a remarkable situation for England's greatest literary man to find
himself in. Nevertheless, Dr Johnson remained a vocal and
vigorous protector of his negro, who he always treated as
a son as opposed to a man at his beck and call.

As far as I could ascertain this unique relationship had
begun in the middle part of the century when Barber, then
only a young boy, and not yet refined by a full exposure
to civilisation, arrived on Johnson's doorstep in London.
Some few years earlier, the eight-year-old piccaninny had
been sold on a plantation in his native Jamaica and brought
to England by a Colonel Bathurst. It is said that the boy's
original name may well have been Quashey, and it is understood that his value was most likely five pounds or there-
abouts. Bathurst and the boy arrived in England in 1750,
whereupon Colonel Bathurst chose to live in Lincoln with
his son Richard, a doctor of medicine. It was decided that
the young Quashey, newly named Francis, should be sent

to Yorkshire to attend the Revd William Jackson's school in the hamlet of Barton, where it was hoped that he might acquaint himself with reading and writing. The negro boy remained in Barton for two whole years, during which time he achieved some knowledge of the English language, and then the now cheerful, and surprisingly gentle, ten-year-old boy returned to Lincoln and began service as the younger Bathurst's servant. It soon became clear that Dr Richard Bathurst had no desire to use the boy as an exotic ornament and dress him as a negro page in bright satins and a turban; he was, instead, actively looking for some role in society that the boy might profitably fulfil. As it transpired, Dr Bathurst's closest friend was none other than the literary man, Samuel Johnson, who, around this same time, lost his wife Tetty to a lingering and painful disease, which left Johnson all alone in a large house in London with neither company nor help. Richard Bathurst understood that his dear friend regarded solitude as a horror, for his sensitive mind was dangerously vulnerable to morbid reflections. In these circumstances, the younger Bathurst thought it only proper to pack Francis off to London in order that he might make himself useful to a depressed Dr Johnson.

On first encountering his future master, the ten-year-old boy was shocked by the sight of this large, shambling man who seemed to twitch uncontrollably about the shoulders, and whose face appeared to be painfully contorted, perhaps to compensate for an obvious blindness in one eye. The scars around this man's throat were terrifying and formed a red lumpish collar, and young Francis found it difficult to tell when Johnson was speaking to him or simply muttering to himself, for there seemed to be little division between the two modes of expression. The nervous Jamaican negro boy entered the service of Samuel Johnson, who informed the dusky stranger that he imagined this Jamaica to be 'a place of great wealth and dreadful wickedness, a den of tyrants and a dungeon of slaves', but the poor boy could make no reply for his mind was now almost totally cleansed of memories of his birthplace.

Johnson took immediately to the young black child, who was now styled Francis Barber, but like his friend Dr Bathurst, he too had no desire to impress his peers by dressing the negro as a satin-clad page or forcing the child to wear livery of any sort. He was aware that ostentatiously attired blacks were now commonplace in London society, appearing in law courts, answering doors, marrying servants, running errands, sitting for portraits. In literature they were making minor appearances in the novels, plays, and the poetry of the age, but to Johnson's eyes the negro, generally through no fault of his own, often lacked a certain civility. Johnson set about the task of saving the young heathen's soul, teaching him to pray and providing him with some basic religious instruction, but the literary man soon discovered that the boy's spirit appeared to be resistant to being given information as to how he should conduct himself. The boy also displayed a lack of enthusiasm in applying himself to even the most basic of household chores, and this was a cause of some surprise to his master, although in most circumstances the general untidiness of his living quarters never seemed to trouble Johnson greatly. After all, Johnson was a man preoccupied with literary matters and he had little time to waste on domestic issues, but he *did* have some understanding of the possible source of Francis' reluctance to follow orders. Dr Bathurst's father, the planter and former colonel in the Jamaican militia, had recently suffered great financial losses which threw all of his affairs into disarray, and then he had suddenly taken ill and died. However, his will contained a clause which granted young Francis Barber his freedom and the bountiful sum of twelve pounds, which greatly pleased Johnson who was firmly wedded to the belief that no man should by nature be the property of another. Clearly this unexpected benevolence had fed Francis' sense of himself as being somewhat independent and beyond any jurisdiction, but Johnson's personality was such that he found it relatively easy to overlook the boy's rebellious behaviour.

It was during this period that Miss Williams, the middle-aged daughter of a Welsh physician with whom the doctor had become friendly, established herself as a permanent occupant of the house, and she made it her business to reign over the domestic arrangements with a fist of iron. Despite her blindness, she found little difficulty ranging up and down the dangerous stairs, from the kitchen in the basement to her own room beneath Johnson's study, which was located in the garret near the very apex of the house. Miss Williams was a strict disciplinarian who seldom ate more than plain bread with butter, but she drank copious quantities of tea, and she saw little reason why others should indulge themselves beyond her own rigorous diet.

Miss Williams was prepared to tolerate the doctor's peculiar, and sometimes offensive, manners, but she had little patience with any others who sought to resist her rule.

Upon her arrival, Francis immediately noticed that Miss Williams exercised considerable influence over his master, for the doctor became a little more careful in his dress, utilising metal buttons instead of twisted hair on his familiar brown suit, and silver buckles occasionally decorated his shoes. However, the influence was limited, for Johnson's wig remained large and greyish, his shirt plain off-white, his stockings black worsted, and he continued to eschew ruffles on his coat so that his white shirtsleeves were generally visible. In short, his master's rugged exterior was still likely to alarm the unsuspecting, and his physical convulsions and general irascibility remained very much in evidence, but Francis continued to feel happy in the company of this kind, if somewhat eccentric, man. However, coping with the daily presence of Miss Williams was proving to be a great trial, for the blind woman made it plain that although Francis might be a clear favourite of her employer, she viewed the Jamaican as little more than an idle black boy who had absolutely no notion of his own modest place in the greater scheme of things. She continually attempted to exercise her authority over Francis, and their rancour was generally uncivil and often bitter. Johnson seemed reluctant to adjudicate, and he habitually allowed Miss Williams to put her oar in and verbally abuse his negro without any attempt on his part to intervene and curb her demanding nature.

Sadly, from the young boy's vantage point, the situation

grew steadily worse until finally he could tolerate no more of this peevish woman. With a few pounds safely tucked away in his pocket, and confident of his new-found status as a free man, the negro exchanged his master's household for that of a Mr Farran of Cheapside, an apothecary of modest means, who employed Francis as his assistant. For two years Francis lived with Mr Farran, but he soon understood that he did not enjoy his duties as an apothecary's assistant, finding the work both menial and taxing. During this period Francis did not completely cut himself adrift from his former master, and the young man still visited Johnson, who continued to treat him with kindness and warmth. His former master often suggested that the negro join him for dinner, and the two formed an astonishing spectacle as the doctor slipped a heavy arm around the boy and lumbered his way to a tavern, clutching, in his free hand, a vast oak stick that was six feet in length and of such girth that even the massive hand of Johnson could not completely circle it. Eventually, when Johnson saw that Francis' unhappiness appeared to be incessant, he suggested to the boy that he relinquish his duties as an apothecary's assistant and return to live with him at his new lodgings in Gough Square, for he worried about Francis' frail nature and his susceptibility to illness. However, soon after his return young Francis realised that the miserable Miss Williams' tyrannical hold over domestic matters had not abated and so, determined to make his own way in the world, the sooty youngster resolved to run away to sea.

On 7 June, 1758, sixteen-year-old Francis Barber enlisted in the Royal Navy and was registered in the muster books as 'L. M.' – which identified him as a 'landsman' or a member of a ship's crew who was unfamiliar with the ways of the sea. The young negro boarded *The Golden Fleece*, which was the tender ship for HMS *Princess Royal*, and a few days later, on 10 June, the black boy was transferred to HMS *Princess Royal* which lay at anchor at Sheerness. When Johnson learned that young Francis had once again abandoned his household, but this time run off to sea, he was beside himself with anxiety for he was sure that the boy must have been used wrongly in some vile manner. Initially he feared that his negro may have been kidnapped and pressed on board, or – worse still – disposed of at auction in some coffee house or tavern and become the metal-collared, human property of some conscienceless brute and dispatched back to the West Indies. It was equally possible that young Francis might have become an apprentice to some cockney thief, and Johnson understood that Spitalfields and Whitechapel markets were places where one might buy a poor young child to train as a pickpocket, or beggar, or prostitute, and so he spent many an hour there questioning strangers about his Francis. His enquiries led him to conclude that the sea was undoubtedly the new 'home' of young Francis, and although he now understood that his servant had almost certainly volunteered, he worried constantly about the fate of his boy. It caused him some irritation that Miss Williams seemed to care little that Francis appeared to have exchanged the relative comforts of Gough Square for a life of adventuring, and Johnson's agitation with regard to his servant's new choice of 'career' was further fuelled by the fact that the literary man possessed a particular loathing towards seafaring, being sure that long confinement in a ship served only to narrow the mind as opposed to opening up possibilities of seeing the world anew. He was often quoted as having declared that, 'No man will be a sailor who has contrivance enough to get himself into a jail; for being in a ship is being in a jail, with the chance of being drowned.'

For sixteen long months, Johnson suffered daily anxiety about the moral and spiritual well-being of Francis, who he knew was not a hardy youngster. Information reached him that the boy had transferred to HMS *Stag* and, unable to endure any further torment, Johnson decided to contact a Dr Hay at the Admiralty and request that an order for the boy's discharge be issued. Months passed by without the order being acted upon, for apparently HMS *Stag* was spending a great deal of time at sea, albeit in English waters, but finally, on 8 August, 1760, Francis Barber received the unwelcome news that he had been discharged. Unhappy to be so quickly deprived of his new and independent life, Francis loitered about the ship for two whole months before regretfully disembarking on 22 October at Sheerness.

On returning to London, the eighteen-year-old young man discovered that his master had taken slightly more spacious lodgings at 1 Inner Temple Lane, where he had been joined by a strange widow named Mrs Desmoulins, who appeared to be a person of little merriment, and a Dr Levett, a shabby and silent physician to the lower orders. Francis reluctantly reassumed his previous role, busying himself answering the door, running trifling errands, attending at table whenever company happened to call, and fetching an occasional dinner from a local tavern. In addition, Francis was entrusted with the power of purchasing provisions. The greatest joy for the young man was his discovery that Miss Williams had remained behind at Gough Square, where she now occupied herself running a small boarding school. Her blessed absence afforded Francis considerable time to enjoy leisure about the house without being hounded by this wretched woman. However, concerned that the boy's general level of education remained in dire need of improvement, Johnson insisted that Francis keep pace with his studies, and to this end he eventually dispatched his Francis to a modest grammar school at Bishop's Stortford in Hertfordshire that was willing to take him in and attempt to enhance his literacy and speech, and familiarise him with Latin and Greek. Francis was placed in the charge of the late headmaster's widow, who rose to the challenge of this experiment, but the reports that his master received of Francis' 'progress' were, at least initially, discouraging. Johnson soon found himself in the embarrassing position of being the recipient of written complaints about his servant's ineptitude, but he continued to send money and in the end he expended nearly £300. When the young Francis returned to London, Johnson *was* gratified that his servant could read and write English with improved ease, although not with great fluency, and in addition the negro had indeed been able to add Latin and Greek to his learning. While it pleased Johnson to now have the company of the negro to relax with him by the fire in the evenings, it frustrated him that the young man chose not to ask any questions or put his new education to the service of spirited conversation. But it was enough for Johnson, who described himself as 'a hardened and shameless tea drinker', that he had *somebody* to sit with him late into the night as he pursued his vice.

It was during this period that sooty Francis began to fraternise with others of his own race who were living at various stations of life in London, and his master welcomed Francis' friends into his house whether he was in residence or not. Far from being intoxicated with liberty, many of these blacks were gainfully employed, and when keeping company with Francis, they were simply enjoying a temporary escape from their menial duties, which included waiting upon ladies of quality, carrying their trains, combing their lapdogs, or producing smelling salts when required. Some, however, found difficulty in obtaining employment and, prohibited by law from learning a trade, the negroes were often confined to living in squalid hovels with whores, beggars, and criminals. Whether employed or not, Barber's negro friends felt at home in Dr Johnson's house and they were able to sit together in the parlour and enjoy a few moments of merriment. Such behaviour was not to the liking of many in Johnson's circle, but none would dare to question the literary man's judgement. Such behaviour was also not to the liking of the irritable Miss Williams, who had once again joined the household, together with a Scotch maid who carried coals, washed dishes, and attempted to clean. The increasingly gloomy Dr Levett contrived to carry on an open conflict with Miss Williams and, in both action and word, he chose not to obscure his ill-feelings towards her. For Francis, this warring household was not a happy abode and he daily wondered if he should leave and perhaps set up home with some of his own complexion, for his friends constantly urged him to escape the tyranny of the blind woman. However, Francis' loyalties to his master ran deep, and having abandoned him twice, and being aware of the anguish that the good man suffered as a result of his running away to sea, he had resolved never again to abscond.

On my second morning, I woke early to find the Lichfield sun streaming through my window, but this peaceful and pleasant start to the day quickly soured as a tempest of raised voices began to emanate from a nearby chamber. I immediately recognised the voice of the innkeeper, and that of his wife, and I was not surprised to hear them squabbling for I had already noted a tension between the pair which seemed to extend beyond any individual act or incident. Clearly this couple failed to understand the distinct roles that the sexes were intended to occupy, roles which complement the different natures and capacities of men and women. I suspected the wife of shrewishness, and the innkeeper of being under the tyrannical rule of a petticoat government, and this unseemly cacophony served only to confirm my suspicions. Surely the foolish man understood that in law husband and wife are one person, that person being the husband, and unless a man rules these trifling creatures with benevolent determination then things will fall out of their natural order. It is difficult to respect a man who cannot control his wife's cantankerous nature for it is clear that such a man will have difficulty maintaining order in all things in his life. I lay still for some moments and attempted to block out these unfortunate sounds, but realising that there was little probability of achieving peace I rose from the disagreeable bed and began to prepare for the day that lay ahead. Breakfast was a quiet affair, although the shrew did cause me to become excessively irritable by attempting to stimulate meaningless conversation, however the woman soon realised that her efforts to engage me were in vain and she finally fell silent before eventually withdrawing altogether.

The journey out to Burntwood followed the same pattern as the previous day, and on this occasion the sun shone even more brightly in the blue sky. My host personally escorted me to the carriage and assured me that today I would certainly have the pleasure of meeting with the wife of the late Mr Barber and so my mind was lively with anticipation. The driver, who was the same ancient man as before, remained somewhat puzzled by the nature of my quest, but he knew better than to question my intent. We departed in the direction of the house of Mrs Elizabeth Barber, and once again I observed the strange low-lying fields and peculiar marshes of this completely foreign part of England. There was little hereabouts to remind me of the rolling hills and valleys of my native Kent, and as my excursion progressed I discovered myself staring at a curiously low horizon that was presided over by the odd ugly tree. If nothing else, this venture into the Midlands was providing me with an improved understanding of the many varieties of landscape to be found in my England.

It was shortly after nine o'clock in the morning when we arrived at the modest abode of Mrs Barber, and I slowly alighted and ordered the driver to wait until I was ready to return. I half-expected the impudent elder of Lichfield to ask just how long he would be detained, such was the look of petulance that decorated his visage, but he wisely said nothing and so I had no opportunity to remind him of his inferior station in life. The ramshackle cottage and overgrown garden appeared just as they had on the previous day, but I was set now upon my course and determined not to be distracted by considerations of architecture or flora. Before I could announce myself the door opened and the same child presented herself, but once again she chose not to speak. I scrutinised her tawny visage, but before I could formulate a question the mother appeared behind the child.

'I have been expecting you, sir,' was how the English woman began her address. I noticed a certain high-pitched common tone to her voice which confirmed her lowly origins. 'Won't you please come in?' I smiled in her direction, and then stepped around the child who presented herself as an obstacle that I was obliged to negotiate in order that I might gain entrance into the gloomy residence.

It appeared that the kitchen served a double function as both a place to cook and eat in, and as a chamber to receive guests. I sat carefully at the table and was soon joined by the mite who had a disconcerting habit of simply staring. A coal-black kettle was warming over the fire, and while Mrs Barber prepared tea, I looked all about myself and began to understand the limited means of the shabby woman. Empty crooked shelves decorated the walls, and then I saw a mouse flit nimbly across the floor, but the woman continued to prepare the tea as if nothing un-toward had taken place, and it occurred to me that perhaps she was familiar with this creature and his extended family. I turned my attention to the peeling plaster, and to the torn and filthy drapes in the window, before speculating that if she had brought me, a gentleman, to *this* room, then what of the other rooms in the cottage? How had it come to pass that the widow of Francis Barber, a man so well loved and handsomely provided for by Dr Johnson, could have fallen so low?

Mrs Barber placed a dish of tea before me and then sat quietly across the table. The grimy-faced child looked ruefully at its mother, and then some few words were exchanged between them, although I had no idea of what they were saying for it was as though they were speaking their own secret language. As they continued to jabber, I deemed it polite to lower my eyes and look away for it appeared that whatever was being said between the two of them was becoming increasingly animated and more urgent. Eventually Mrs Barber asked to be momentarily excused. When she returned to the table she did so with a plain piece of bread in one hand, which she passed to the child, clearly intending this *gift* to be some form of incentive to persuade the cub to remain quiet.

'I'm sorry, sir,' she said. 'I don't mean to delay you in any way, but you know what youngsters can be like.'

The truth was, being a bachelor of some standing, I had been spared the antics of childish misbehaviour, but I nevertheless bestowed a generous smile upon the woman.

'Mrs Barber, first I wish to thank you for agreeing to

see me today. I know that you are busy with matters relating to your schoolhouse and I also understand that you must be grieving over your recent loss. However, I wish to write a small profile for the *Gentlemen's Magazine* concerning your late husband and the unique position that he occupied from which he was able to witness the birth of some of our finest literature. I was, of course, hoping to speak with him directly, but this being impossible I thank you most sincerely for granting me an audience. I will endeavour to occupy only a small portion of your morning.'

The woman looked quizzically upon me, but she chose to say nothing. For my part I was surprised to see how much of an inroad nature had made into her complexion for, sad to say, she was pockmarked extensively, and her grey hair hung lank about her ears. This was not the woman that I had expected to encounter, but the elements have a way of destroying even the most beautiful objects in nature, and sadly it appeared that Mrs Barber had been quite brutally exposed to the vicissitudes of rain and shine for many years now.

'Does it trouble you my daughter being present?' She spoke quietly, but before I could answer, she continued. 'I can send her out if it will please you.' I smiled, first upon her and then in the direction of the mongrel.

'It matters little to me, Mrs Barber. As I said, I have no desire to disturb your day more than is strictly necessary.'

The common woman looked at me in a strange manner, and for a moment I imagined her to be perhaps impaired in her faculties. She began to grin, somewhat toothlessly, and I found myself trying to imagine this Betsy in her full glory a quarter of a century earlier when all of London was animated by the news of the *scandalous* developments in the great lexicographer's household.

In 1776, Francis announced to his master that he was somewhat persecuted by love and that he had discovered the girl to whom he wished to be married. Initially, Dr Johnson wondered if the *lucky* girl was with child, but he deemed it politic not to enquire. He knew of Francis' popularity with a variety of young females, and although he regarded the sable young man with paternal concern, he was reluctant to begin lecturing the negro on *any* aspect of his behaviour in case Francis felt pressured into once again absconding to sea. Dr Johnson asked Francis if he might meet with his bride-to-be, and Francis said that he would bring the girl to him at his master's earliest convenience. Francis also suggested that in order to avoid further conflict with Miss Williams, he would prefer it if after their marriage he and his wife might be permitted to establish lodgings outside of Dr Johnson's house. After all, in addition to Miss Williams there was also her Scotch maid, and the gloomy widow, Mrs Jesmoulins, and her recently arrived daughter, so his master would not be short of assistance. Francis made it clear that he intended to continue to serve his master, but in the interests of peace and harmony he seemed to have already made up his mind that this would be the most sensible course of action.

Two days later, Francis arrived at the house with a fresh-faced, twenty-year-old English girl in tow, her arm linked nervously through his own. He introduced the girl to Dr Johnson as Elizabeth, and she curtseyed gracefully, but then Francis immediately began referring to her as Betsy, which his master took as his cue to do the same. The older man inspected the young girl, who seemed slight of body but possessed of a natural bloom, and he then asked after her family, and requested intelligence of how it had come to pass that she had met his Francis. He listened to her shy and cautious words, and then he delicately asked if the couple had any immediate plans for a family, at which point the girl blushed a deep crimson. Again, it occurred to the doctor that the wench might already be with child, for he knew full well that Francis' adventures in the world of passion were extensive and freely reported. Apparently some women, particularly those among the lower orders, found his ebony complexion appealing, and he saw no reason why this Betsy should be any different from the others. However, anything short of a direct question was not going to resolve his private speculation, and knowing that it would be impertinent to pose the question the doctor resigned himself to ignorance. After all, nature would soon enough provide him with an answer.

For her part, Betsy looked upon the famous Dr Johnson and wondered just what services her soon-to-be husband provided for this dishevelled man, whose wig had clearly seldom been combed and whose clothes looked dusty and unwashed. She had heard from many who had witnessed the gentleman roaming abroad at all hours of the day and night, that the man appeared to be insensible to his squalid appearance, but nothing had prepared her for this degree of slovenliness. However, he seemed to be a kind man, and he habitually referred to her Frank as 'my boy' in a manner that was affectionate enough for there to be no doubt in her mind how fondly he regarded Frank. And then later, but during this same visit, Betsy came to understand why her husband-to-be had insisted that they find their own place of abode outside of Dr Johnson's residence. Miss Williams, upon being introduced to Francis' intended, simply snorted in disgust and turned on her heels, which prompted neither comment nor admonition from the head of the household. As far as Betsy was able to discern, this blind woman, who apparently knew her way about the house with a confidence and ease that most sighted people lacked, clearly considered herself to be the *queen* of the establishment, and she made no secret of her contempt for Frank. Her husband-to-be had already informed her that she liked nothing better than to rail against him, calling him 'this supposed scholar!', and now Betsy saw for herself the truth of the situation. It was not until the ill-tempered Miss Williams left the room that she once again relaxed and felt able to breathe freely.

On the day of her wedding, Betsy made an extra effort to appear alluring, and to those gathered at the church she presented a splendid sight. Dr Johnson had seen to it that all the arrangements were to the liking of Francis and his wife and, as one might expect, the list of invitees comprised of those occupying both elevated and lowly stations in society. Guests were encouraged to mingle and, although this experiment was not entirely successful, most enjoyed a tolerable event, although there were some among the invited who had come principally to gawp and speculate at the propriety of this aberrant union. For his part,

Dr Johnson looked upon the match as well made, but inwardly he worried with regard to the purity of young Betsy and her loyalty to his 'boy'.

It came about that the doctor soon had reason to be concerned, for not long after the wedding, at a party given by his friends the Thrales in their Streatham home, a party to which Francis and his new wife were cordially and generously invited, some of the male servants began to flirt openly with Betsy Barber. Perhaps unwisely, the newly wed 'lass' chose to do nothing to deflect the attentions of these men, and in a rage Francis flew from the house and determined that he would walk back to London by himself. Dr Johnson noted his servant's rapid departure, and when Mrs Thrale informed him that jealousy was the cause of Francis' anger the news appeared to somewhat exasperate the doctor. Later that same evening, while riding his carriage back to London, Dr Johnson came across Francis walking rapidly and with fury still apparent on his begrimed face. 'Are you jealous of your wife?' bellowed a disembodied voice. Francis stopped dead in his tracks not knowing exactly what was happening. He wondered if he was the victim of an attempted robbery, but he soon recognised both the person and the stern voice. His master did not give him time to answer and he asked Francis if the Thrales' footmen had kissed his wife in his presence.

'Why no, sir,' said Francis, 'I don't believe that any of them kissed my wife at all.'

'Well what, then,' thundered Dr Johnson, 'did they do with the woman?' Francis opened his mouth as though about to utter an answer, but he was too slow to please the doctor. 'Well, come along lad, what did they do to her? Nothing, I'll warrant, and you my boy are merely caught tight in the grip of that green-eyed monster, jealousy. You must learn to make clear the difference between your wife and other women you have known, for truly there is something particular about her person that you value and trust ahead of any others or you surely would not have married her, am I right?' Francis nodded. 'Then will you go back and fetch your wife instead of abandoning her like some woman of the night? Will you be a man and protector for the woman that you stood up for in church, the woman that you professed your love and affection for?' Francis lowered his eyes, as though momentarily ashamed of his behaviour, and then he slowly nodded his head. 'Well, be gone with you then,' said Dr Johnson, 'and make me proud of you, lad.' With this said, he signalled to the driver of his carriage to move off into the night, and he left Francis marooned between London and Streatham and with little choice but to turn on his heels and retrace his steps in search of his wife.

It was difficult for me to believe that the fair woman who had won the heart of Francis Barber, and the woman whose loyalty Dr Johnson eventually came to respect, bore any relation to the fatigued creature who sat before me as I drank my tea. What hardships this Betsy must have endured in the intervening years, for it was evident that the two children that she had given birth to before the death of the doctor, and the daughter that she had produced afterwards had, together with poverty and an excess of hard work, conspired to deprive her of what must once have been an enchanting aspect. For a moment I looked beyond Mrs Barber, and the child curled across her lap like a slumbering animal, and I peered out of the window to where the sun had momentarily hidden itself behind a cloud. Then, realising that having been granted an audience with this woman it was remiss of me to suddenly disengage and peer idly through her window, I returned my attention to Mrs Barber.

'Might I prevail upon you to answer some questions relating to your late husband? As I have mentioned to you already, I am hoping to assemble a short biographical sketch for the *Gentlemen's Magazine* in London.' I paused. 'I can assure you that this is a most respectable publication and a small entry pertaining to your late husband can only help his reputation.'

As I concluded my words I noticed that the woman appeared to be genuinely alarmed, so much so that she set her child in a chair next to herself, carefully making sure that she did not rouse the mite. She began slowly. 'Please sir, I'm afraid I don't understand. Or perhaps you know something that I'm not aware of, and if you do may it please you to share your news with me. You see, to the best of my knowledge, my Frank is not deceased, or at least not yet. He's alive, but ailing badly in the infirmary. The doctor said he could linger like this for a good while and we've no guarantee when he'll be relieved from his misery.'

Now it was my turn to appear amazed. Had the innkeeper given me false information, or was this poor woman simply unaware of her husband's recent demise? I asked when exactly was the last time that she had spoken with her husband, and on receiving the news that she had seen him only the previous morning I concluded that the intelligence of the doltish innkeeper must have been misguided.

'My Frank has suffered a great number of difficulties during these past few years, and he's not always been comfortable in mind and body. Life hasn't been very kind to Frank since we left London two years after the doctor's death, and then came up here to Lichfield. It was his master's idea. I know he meant well, as he always meant well for his Frank, but maybe we'd have been better off staying in London where we knew people and could always make a few shillings. But the doctor always thought that people up here in his home town would look out for Frank on account of Frank having been so faithful to his master, but it turned out that people didn't care that much. You understand, Lichfield is where the doctor's from. My Frank's from Jamaica, but I expect you already know that, don't you?' I nodded, but said nothing for I was eager for her to continue. 'It's not been easy with the children, and then there were those who cheated us. Lots of them. Eventually we came out here to Burntwood to open a school and pass on the gift of knowledge that Frank's master had given to him. We wanted to bestow it on common people who might otherwise have remained in ignorance. Reading and writing, reason and logic, the principles of self-expression and the knowledge of the Lord, this is what Frank felt he could share with the people, but it seems like most of them wanted to receive such instruction from a more visibly competent source, if you're understanding me. Then Frank's health began to turn for the worse, and so I don't know what else I can say. It was always his master's idea that we leave London and come to Lichfield, and eventually Frank thought alright, but I remember having reservations at the time. I suppose I still have them now, all these years later.'

Towards the end of Dr Johnson's life Francis' presence became increasingly necessary, for it was apparent to all that the doctor's health was failing rapidly. His household was now located at 8 Bolt Court in an alley off Fleet Street, and Dr Johnson was paying the reasonable sum of forty pounds a year for a tall house with a garden to the rear. However, these years were to prove difficult for the doctor as he entered a period of great affliction. Miss Williams, though still present, was increasingly enfeebled, while Mrs Desmoulins and her daughter had suddenly moved clear away. Mrs Desmoulins had been unable to endure any further bickering with Miss Williams, but she had also chosen to go into hiding in order that she might avoid an indictment for debt that had recently been served upon her. Despite her capacity to be as mean and petty as Miss Williams, the doctor mourned the sudden absence of Mrs Desmoulins and it served only to deepen his sense of abandonment. After all, he had recently lost both of his dear friends, the actor David Garrick, and the literary man Oliver Goldsmith, while his Scottish companion, Mr James Boswell, was practising law in faraway Edinburgh. Furthermore, there had been an unfortunate misunderstanding, and subsequent 'break', with Mrs Thrale which, though now somewhat resolved, had left a rift in their friendship that he understood would never be fully healed.

In addition to these tender sorrows, he also mourned the passing of his house companion of thirty years, the destitute and dishevelled Dr Levett, who, like Francis, could be relied upon to join him for fireside conversation from the early evening and, if necessary, continue clear through until dawn.

Sadly, the doctor's ailments were such that it was no longer possible for him to roam the narrow, dirty, streets off the Strand, places that were shadowy and populated with a full tide of beggars, thieves, and abandoned women. These were dangerous passageways where violence was commonplace, but the doctor was long accustomed to observing and relishing this low life. Those irritating fellows, the night watchmen who bawled the hour in every dark street and alley of the city, were entirely familiar with his immense bulk and greeted him almost as one of their own. However, being a man dedicated to the night, the curtailment of his roaming proved a crushing blow to the doctor's spirit. Confined now to Bolt Court, loneliness was fast becoming a mortal enemy of the doctor, and he bestowed the name 'black dog' upon his deplorable bouts of melancholia. He appeared to have even lost his tendency to become excessively distracted at what he insisted were his witticisms, but what others often perceived to be nothing more than very small japes. No longer did the doctor relish his own jocularity and send forth loud and uninhibited peals of laughter, and life at Bolt Court was rapidly becoming miserable for residents and visitors alike. 'When I rise,' said the doctor in a letter to Mrs Thrale, 'my breakfast is solitary, the black dog waits to share it . . . Dinner with a sick woman you may venture to suppose not much better than solitary. After dinner what remains but to count the clock, and hope for that sleep which I can scarce expect. Night comes at last, and some hours of restlessness and confusion bring me again to a day of solitude. What shall exclude the black dog from a habitation like this?'

Dr Johnson's only hope, as he understood it, was to attempt to avoid too much in the way of either seclusion or idleness, and so he was often discovered by his negro watering his tiny garden, or sitting at the stout mahogany table that decorated the drawing room and busily translating an obscure literary work, or writing long letters. However, even this pleasure was sometimes denied to him, for occasional inflammations of the good eye often made it impossible for him to read for days on end. At these moments, Francis' presence served to provide him with the opportunity of a few hours of much-needed conversation. And then, early one fateful morning, Francis arrived from his home on St John Street, Smithfield, and discovered his master sitting upright in his chair, which was not unusual for the doctor's bronchial asthma was so severe that he was generally afraid to lie flat at night. However, what made this occasion disturbing was the fact that when the loyal Francis entered, talking away as usual, there was no reply from his master. It was then that Francis noticed a hand-written note, and by this means he discovered that during the dead of night his master had become overwhelmed by confusion and giddiness, suffered a stroke, and subsequently lost the power of speech. Francis immediately summoned Dr Brocklesby, his master's physician and best friend, and over the course of the following two to three days, and after much dosing and blistering, Dr Johnson's speech eventually began to return to him.

During this period, Dr Brocklesby spoke privately with Francis and shared with the servant his worry that, aside from the doctor's various physical afflictions, his master was suffering greatly from an oppressive loneliness that would only be resolved by his actively seeking the company of others. Conversing carefully with the occasional visitor over dishes of tea, or keeping the peace among his squabbling household servants, was never going to be enough to satisfy the intellect, or truly arrest the isolation, of the great man, whose appearance had, even by his own negligent standards, become wretched. These days the neck of his shirt and his breeches were habitually loose, his stockings were in need of being drawn up, he wore his shoes unbuckled, and his unpowdered wig was comically small and precariously balanced on his oversized head. There were very few 'clean shirt' days. Dr Brocklesby was sure that only by forcing the doctor back into society might things improve and so, during the harsh winter of 1783, his friends, myself among them, advanced the idea of establishing a small club in Essex Street, as a place where the doctor might enjoy congenial company and good conversation.

We members of this new association were encouraged to dine three times a week and suffer a fine of three pence should we miss a gathering. The first meeting was held at the Essex Head Tavern and it attracted an enthusiastic crowd, but Dr Johnson was racked with asthma, and clearly struggling to breathe properly, so much so that he was too ill to return home unaided. However, the true drama of the occasion was the doctor's behaviour during the gathering. For some time now his friends had noticed that his severe humour and dogmatic manner seemed to intensify as his ailments took a firmer grip. At such moments he would become increasingly oppressive in conversation which caused many, including those who held him in the highest esteem, to grow first to fear, then to abhor, his unpolished and disagreeable irascibility. The doctor's favourite technique of argument was usually a flat denial of his opponent's statement, irrespective of how foolish this made him appear, followed by a grand assault of verbal brilliance such as one might expect from a man who had fixed the English language and succeeded in ridding it of cant. But sadly, these days those opponents whom he could not vanquish by force of his admittedly large intellect, he simply bullied into submission with a vile display of rudeness which seemed unrelated to any quantities of drink that he might have consumed. Thereafter, he often failed to make amends by raising a glass to the offended person's health or shaking his hand when he left the room, gestures which he had long been accustomed to offering.

After the first meeting of the new association, it was nearly two months before the doctor was well enough to once again venture out of his house. During this period, Francis and his wife Betsy and the children moved their household into Bolt Court. This caused the doctor's friend, Sir John Hawkins, some consternation, but he temporarily set aside his prejudices and simply urged the great man to put his affairs in order and immediately prepare a will. However, Dr Johnson was fearful that such a course of action might suggest a willingness to cease struggling with life, and as such he baulked at taking a step that, in his rational mind, he knew to be both sensible and natural. The very thought of his own dissolution and eventual death was intolerable to him, but the one issue that he admitted must be swiftly resolved was the matter of what would happen to Francis, who had served him faithfully for almost thirty-five years, and about whose future he agonised. The doctor had little confidence in Francis' powers of survival, for he understood his servant's weaknesses and he had laboured hard to both accommodate these faults and at the same time protect the man. One afternoon the doctor asked his friend and physician, Dr Brocklesby, what might be a proper annuity to bequeath a highly regarded servant, and he was told that fifty pounds a year might be considered a generous amount. Dr Johnson listened carefully, and then decided upon seventy pounds a year for Francis, whom he determined would be his principal legatee. He instructed Sir John Hawkins to draw up the draft of the will and to include the generous legacy to Francis, however, Sir John Hawkins left blanks where, in good time, he imagined Dr Johnson would insert the names of other legatees, but the doctor appeared to have no desire to do such a thing. Instead he named two more executors, Sir Joshua Reynolds and Dr William Scott, and charged them and Sir John Hawkins with the task of disbursing sums to a few others after his death, and then he reiterated his desire to give 'the rest of the aforesaid sums of money and property, together with my books, plate, and household furniture ... to the use of Francis Barber, my manservant, a negro ...'

Sadly, Dr Johnson's recurrent battles with asthma continued to prevent him from attending the Essex Street Club as regularly as he wished. In fact, as he became increasingly aware of the reality of his situation, Dr Johnson decided to travel to Lichfield and revisit his youth, but while there his ailments caused him to sleep long and often, and his suffering seemed only to increase. And then the doctor received news of the death of Miss Williams, who had, for some time, been languishing in helpless misery, and this loss left him desolate. He returned to London where he yearned for pleasant company and conversation, but most of his time was spent in a deep, but agitated, slumber that was inevitably punctuated by raucous breathing and the occasional yelp of pain. Francis continued to attend upon him daily, but as his master's condition worsened the negro made sure that he was also available for long nightly vigils in the sickroom in case the doctor's pain became intolerable. On the morning of Monday 13 December, Francis noted that the slumbering doctor's breathing had become difficult, and then his master awoke suddenly with a series of convulsive movements that alarmed Francis. Apparently the pain in his master's legs was so unbearable that the doctor snatched up a pair of scissors and plunged them deep into his calves causing jagged wounds. This afforded the doctor some relief, but also occasioned a loss of blood which startled Francis and Mrs Desmoulins, who had recently arrived at the house to offer what help she could. In fact, she had another reason for attending upon her beloved Dr Johnson on this day, for she wished to receive his blessings, which he was happy to give. Once the bleeding had stopped, the doctor slowly turned to Mrs Desmoulins and whispered, 'God bless you,' in a trembling voice. Francis waited and watched as Mrs Desmoulins fought bravely to hold back her tears, and then she rushed quickly from the room.

Later that same day the ailing Dr Johnson received a visit from a Miss Morris, who was the child of a friend of his. The young woman's unexpected arrival alarmed Francis, but he escorted her from the street door up the stairs to Dr Johnson's chamber, where he asked her to wait. He entered and informed his master that a young woman was here who claimed to be the daughter of a friend, and that she had asked permission to see him so that she might receive his blessings. Dr Johnson smiled weakly, which his negro servant took as a sign that he should usher this Miss Morris into the room, which he did. The doctor turned in the bed and looked carefully at the girl before pronouncing, 'God bless you, my dear.' With this said he turned away and Francis marshalled Miss Morris from the room. Soon after, Francis, together with Mrs Desmoulins, returned to Dr Johnson's chamber where they both realised that the doctor's breathing had become even more laboured, but there was nothing that they could do to alleviate his discomfort. Shortly after seven o'clock in the evening, both Francis and Mrs Desmoulins noticed that the painful breathing had ceased and so they quickly left their respective chairs and went to the bed where they discovered that the great Englishman was dead.

The woman poured her visitor more tea and then coughed loudly without resorting to covering her mouth. It was clear that, in common with her husband's late master, this woman had no passion for clean linen or immersing herself in cold water. The story of her time in Lichfield with her negro husband was now clearly uppermost in her mind, but it was apparent that this was not a joyful tale. If, as seemed to be the case, Francis Barber was still alive then what I most desired was an introduction to the man so that I might discover for myself why fortune had not smiled upon him since the death of his master. It was an indisputable fact that Dr Johnson had provided hand-somely for Francis, although Sir John Hawkins, among many others, had complained loudly of the imprudence of Dr Johnson leaving money to a negro. If the rumours of Barber's fall from grace, and his foolishly squandering the assets bequeathed to him, and thereby betraying the generosity of England's greatest literary mind, proved to be true then this would serve only to confirm Hawkins' estimation of Dr Johnson's folly.

The woman coughed.

'Lichfield has turned out to be a disappointment for me and for Frank, but I expect you can see that, right?'

I said nothing but again I looked at the squalor that surrounded me.

'After a couple of years trying to make a living in London, we came up here to Lichfield. Then we discovered that my Frank had borrowed so much money from Mr

Hawkins that not only was the annuity no more, but Frank was told that the sum of money that provided for it was all spent. Mr Hawkins claimed to have settled his account with my Frank. My husband's health was never that good, then we had difficulties with the children. It was hard to find anybody who would give us work or even welcome us. Three years ago we moved out here to Burntwood, and we used the last of the money to buy this cottage, but Frank's sadness drove him to drink more and so we had to start to let go of the doctor's pieces. We don't have anything left. My Frank, he used to take pleasure in a spot of fishing or cultivating a few potatoes, but even that's gone now and look where he's landed. The Stafford Infirmary, which isn't a place for a decent man.'

Again the woman coughed, and I deemed it an appropriate moment to ask the question that was now sitting somewhat impatiently on my tongue.

'Would it be possible for me to see your husband?' Mrs Barber looked blankly at me, but said nothing. I continued in my efforts to engage the uncultured creature. 'I understand that Mr Barber's health may not be perfect, but an audience, however brief, would assist me greatly with my biographical sketch.' I paused, unsure whether the dull woman was sensible of my words. 'I would appreciate your assistance, if at all possible.'

After what appeared to be an age, the woman nodded briefly and said she would conduct me to the infirmary, but she asked if first it might interest me to see the schoolroom. Clearly this is what she desired, and so I rose to my feet and followed both her and the mongrel through a plain door and into a darkened room. Books and papers were strewn all about, but it was unclear exactly how many pupils still considered this to be a place of learning that they might visit on a daily basis. Mrs Barber drew back the curtains to let a little light into the room, but the illumination served only to highlight the squalor of the place. Just as I was beginning to feel that precious time was being wasted on this gloomy ruin, the child began to cry. Gathering the gamine about her skirt, Mrs Barber announced that it was some months now since her Frank had been forced by ill-health to abandon teaching, but she attempted to attend to those pupils who still wished to learn, although she did confess that her own learning was somewhat rudimentary. As we made ready to leave, I cast my eyes around the dismal chamber and concluded that this place had probably not been used as a schoolroom, or as anything else, for the greater part of a year, and the morose English woman's claims to be, in the absence of her husband, a replacement teacher of some description were undoubtedly exaggerated.

I soon discovered the Stafford Workhouse Infirmary to be a place of great misery, as opposed to a haven of rest and recovery for those who were temporarily ailing. As the carriage came slowly to a halt by the tall oak doors, I noticed that the infirmary boasted a stony black façade, and the grounds all about were entirely treeless, which created a most despondent atmosphere. Mrs Barber and her child led the way into the vaulted interior, and they moved quickly along a seemingly endless corridor as though hurrying to an appointment. Then the grey-haired woman stopped outside of a rough-hewn door that was partially ajar, but through which I was able to spy a long row of tightly packed and fully occupied beds.

'Frank's in there at the end. The last bed but one. We can wait here until you've finished your talking with him.'

I was somewhat surprised by Betsy Barber's reluctance to enter the cheerless chamber and introduce me to her husband, but I imagined that perhaps there was some rift between them that I was not sensible of. Or perhaps she was simply fearful of once again encountering her husband in such a pitiful situation. On entering the miserable place, I decided that it was quite probably the latter reason, for I could not imagine any wife who would be content to gaze upon a loved one who had been reduced to such lamentable circumstances. Most of the patients appeared to be quietly suffering from grave maladies that would soon carry them off, while one or two thrashed about as though trying to free themselves from imaginary leashes, and as they gyrated they howled like beasts. I could see no sign of a physician, but I was soon accosted by an attendant who offered me a sponge soaked in vinegar which I immediately pressed to my nostrils for protection. Thereafter, I made my way to the bed as directed and was somewhat alarmed to see the tortuously aged face of a man I had not seen for sixteen years. Blacky's eyes were fastened tightly shut, but once I sat on the edge of the cot – there being no other place for me to deposit myself – he soon opened his peepers and stared up at me as though unable to properly discern with whom he had an audience.

'Do you remember me, Mr Barber?' As soon as I asked this question I felt foolish, for why should the negro commit to memory knowledge of a man he had not encountered for nearly two decades? It was a somewhat presumptuous enquiry on my part and I regretted that I had allowed it to pass my lips, but to his great credit Francis Barber did not seem at all troubled by my impertinence.

'Forgive me,' he whispered, 'but my mind is weak.' He paused and blinked vigorously, as though trying to regard me anew. I could see now that the man was toothless, and his decrepitude was far advanced. 'Sir, I am sorry that you should discover me in this state of disrepair.'

I assured him that there was no reason for him to apologise, and that it was I who should be begging his forgiveness for this unannounced intrusion. I explained that it was the woman he called 'wife' who had suggested that I might visit, and who had subsequently conveyed me to this place, and he simply nodded as though he had already guessed that this must be the case. Again his eyes closed, and I looked around at the other patients in the room, most of whom, like this negro, appeared to be idling close to death. And then I turned my attention back to Francis who, even as I sat with him, appeared to be already experiencing life racing quickly out of his body. In fact, his short, shallow breaths suggested that he was merely lingering at the door to the next world. A few moments passed, and then Dr Johnson's negro once more opened his eyes and a thin smile crept across his black face.

'I wonder,' he said 'if perhaps I have disappointed my master. Have you come to this place to accuse me of this

crime?' The negro paused and gathered his thoughts. 'My
master placed a great deal of faith in me that I might
resist temptation, do you know this? Towards the end he
often called me to his bedside and asked me to pray with
him. He never failed to point out appropriate passages in
the scriptures, for he feared that my nature was too weak
and that I might misuse all that he was about to bestow
upon me. He feared that some men might take advantage
of my character and so we prayed together that I would
find strength and not succumb to my fondness for drink
and frivolity. My master and myself, we often prayed
together, the two of us, long into the night.' The negro
paused and gasped for breath. I instinctively reached down
and clasped his black hand, and eventually his breathing
subsided, but I chose not to release this poor man's fingers.
'I lack dignity. Even coming to Lichfield was a fulfilment
of my master's wishes.' I looked at Johnson's dishevelled
negro, but I could find no words. 'My master provided
me with many advantages yet I still find myself in these
circumstances. I sincerely wish that he had used me differ-
ently.' The negro looked nervously all about himself.
'Perhaps,' he continued, 'I would have been better served
committing to a life at sea, or returning to my native
Jamaica. Perhaps it would have been more profitable for
me to have established for myself the limits of my abilities rather than having them blurred by kindness, depend-
ence, and my own indolence. And when presented with
real liberty—' He stopped abruptly, then sighed. 'Well,
look upon me, sir. Look liberty in the face. What see
you?' Suddenly, with this question, his eyes temporarily

brightened, but then without waiting for my answer they fell shut again, like a falling curtain, and this time it was clear that they would not reopen again this day. At least not for me. Dr Johnson's negro had withdrawn from the world, and I was left alone with his pitiful words ringing loudly in my ears. Surely liberty had never before appeared to any man in such a state of mournful ruination. It was true, this negro had most likely been destroyed by the unnatural good fortune of many years of keeping company with those of a superior rank, thus depriving him of any real understanding of his own true status in the world. I felt that I could answer his final question with some confidence, even though he would remain insensible to my thoughts on the matter. Yes, the black should have left our country and journeyed back to Jamaica or to Africa with Mr Sharp's expedition. In fact, all ebony personages should do so for I was now convinced that English air is clearly not suitable for negro lungs and soon reduces these creatures to a state of childish helplessness. In this sad, wretched moment, I had received confirmation of the wisdom of my own intention to invest in the Province of Freedom, and thereby help prevent this spectacle of negro abasement from becoming endemic in our land.

In the evening I dined alone at the Three Crowns. The innkeeper had timidly requested permission to join my table once I had completed my meal, and I agreed to his entreaty for I now understood that my acquiescence would enable him to temporarily escape the tedious presence of his wife. In the morning I would be returning to London, so this would probably mark my final exchange with this weak man, whom I had already corrected with regard to the status of Francis Barber's mortality. The innkeeper poured freely from what he termed a 'special' bottle of French claret, and he once again apologised for his error, but I assured him that the man's wife, though puzzled, appeared to have taken no discernible offence. The innkeeper had hardly received my words before he sought intelligence as to just how far Mr Barber had fallen from the lower rungs of the social ladder. I smiled back at this odious man, but resolved to say nothing that might assuage his curiosity. The situation soon became uncomfortable, and my host quickly changed tack, and asked after the negro's wife. I answered that she appeared to be experiencing difficulties providing for her children, for clearly the schoolhouse had been neglected since the onset of Mr Barber's illness. I reminded this foolish citizen of Lichfield of Dr Johnson's conviction that a decent provision for the poor, particularly those in the final season of their lives, is the truest test of civilisation, and I left the rest to his conscience. The effect of the wine had begun to diminish this man's speech and I feared that it had also made inroads into what remained of his judgement. I could sense the deep desire on the part of the innkeeper to ask again after the Jamaican, but my mind was made up. The fall of a man is not a pretty picture to behold, but the spectacle of an individual attempting to hide his indifference behind a thin mask of concern is an altogether unacceptable sight.

I looked around as the inkeeper's 'guests' continued to drink like horses and grow increasingly shrill. Some among them began singing and pulling caps, while others stirred themselves as though preparing to dance a jig. Who in Lichfield had truly tried to help the faithful friend and servant of the city's foremost son? While I was sure that Francis Barber's own failings had led him to death's door in that inhospitable infirmary, I was also convinced that others had conspired in his demise by simply standing to the side and looking on. Dr Johnson's favourite, deprived of the protection of his master, and exposed to the hostile apathy of first London, and then Lichfield, had lost his way. A biographical sketch in the *Gentlemen's Magazine* would most likely be met with the same combination of fascination and disdain that had blighted the pathetic negro's life. Climbing to my unsteady feet, I bade my host a good night before abandoning him to the enmity of his wife. I carried a candle to my room where I anticipated a few fitful hours of half-sleep before clambering aboard a carriage back to London. I already understood that this night would be long and difficult, and that it was most likely that my dreams would be populated by multiple sightings of a small Jamaican boy named Quashey, who would no doubt be helplessly extending an arm in my direction. I resolved that in the morning I would tarry a while at Burntwood and, without comment, present his English wife with Dr Johnson's watch. Whatever she might obtain from the local pawnbroker would go some way towards feeding her irregular children. The good doctor would, I felt sure, approve of his handsome watch being disposed of for this purpose.

II

Made in Wales

On the morning of 9 July, 1951, a twenty-three-year-old
mixed-race man stepped off a train at London's Paddington
Station and looked all around at the cavernous vastness
of the place. The youngster had visited London before,
but today there was something auspicious about his arrival
in the great capital city for the young man's name was on
everybody's lips. Randolph Turpin was born, and had
grown up, in the Midlands town of Leamington Spa, a
place which, until the rediscovery of the town's mineral
springs in the late eighteenth century, was little more than
a tiny village called the Leamington Priors. The visit of
Queen Victoria in 1838, to discover for herself the nature
of the healing and restorative powers of the waters, resulted
in the town being honoured and renamed Royal Leamington
Spa. However, by the mid-twentieth century there were
two Leamingtons; the elegant Georgian and Regency
Leamington, which was a haven for the genteel and the
elderly, and then an altogether less attractive working-class
enclave. Turpin was a product of the less impressive face
of the town. As the train which had deposited Turpin, his
older brothers Dick and Jackie, and Turpin's manager, the

reliable and strait-laced Mr George Middleton, continued to belch smoke, the four men stared at the press of people. A large crowd made up of journalists and the general public in equal numbers gawped back in their direction. The train was half an hour late, but Turpin's reception committee would have waited all day if necessary. A flash-bulb popped, and a newspaperman's voice could be heard above the roar of the station. 'Randy!' And then another bulb popped, and another voice was raised, and then the crowd began to surge up the platform towards the new arrivants. The coloured brothers looked anxiously at each other, while George Middleton looked beyond the rush of people and tried to find his contact. And then, just as the crowd began to swarm around the Midlanders, Mr Jack Solomons appeared, complete with trilby and chewing on a cigar, and he restored some order. 'Gentlemen, please. Step back and give Mr Turpin some room.' The self-proclaimed king of British boxing slipped a paternal arm around the shoulders of young Randy, and took charge of the situation. Jack Solomons was a man who, in the parlance of the times, liked to talk fast and plenty. 'Gentlemen, you know the procedure. You'll have all the time in the world to converse with Mr Turpin later on. Now come on, please. Step aside. We don't want to wear out the young man, do we?'

As Mr Solomons' car pulled away from in front of Paddington Station, a few newspapermen ran alongside the vehicle, and a lone photographer persisted in pointing his camera at the car window and snapping away. However, once they passed through the first set of traffic lights, the journalists were left behind. On the train journey to London, Turpin, his brothers, and his manager had taken breakfast together and Randy had spilled the salt. Randy wasn't a superstitious man, far from it, but the look of alarm that crossed Mr Middleton's face gave him pause for thought. He had watched as his manager took a pinch of salt and quickly tossed it over his left shoulder. As they now sped towards the West End of London, Randy stole a quick glance at Mr Middleton, who was staring calmly out of the car window, but his manager betrayed his inner anxiety by the fact that he was biting down hard against his bottom lip. By the time Mr Solomons' car entered Piccadilly Circus the crowds in the street had begun to multiply, so much so that the driver was forced to slow almost to a halt. Suddenly, it looked as though it might not be possible to get much closer to Jack Solomons' gymnasium and offices at 41 Great Windmill Street, but two policemen on horseback began to clear a way through the crowds and inch by inch the car made its way forward until it was able to deposit them all at the rear entrance to the building. However, even here crowds of autograph hunters were waiting, but Turpin could tell by the hurried manner with which Mr Middleton and Mr Solomons kept glancing at each other that there would be no time to fraternise with his fans. They both wanted Turpin calm and settled for tomorrow's date with destiny, and the legendary Sugar Ray Robinson.

The following lunchtime, Turpin's opponent, along with his retinue of handlers and hangers-on, arrived at the 'Palace of Jack', as Solomons liked to call his gymnasium and suite of offices. Sugar Ray Robinson was born Walker Smith in Ailey, Georgia, in 1921, and he grew up in Detroit, Michigan. As a teenage amateur he won the Golden Gloves featherweight title, and people were already talking about him as a potential great champion. However, just how 'great' he would become none of them could ever have imagined. He made his official professional debut in 1940 as a welterweight, and he soon won the 147 lb world title. He then stepped up to fight as a middleweight and he also won the world title at 160 lb. By 1951, Sugar Ray Robinson had fought 133 professional fights and lost only once, to Jake La Motta. However, this was a defeat that he soon avenged in a rematch. Ray Robinson was a worldwide celebrity whose very name conjured up notions of both invincibility and flamboyance, and his fame was such that only a few weeks earlier, on 25 June, 1951, he had appeared on the cover of *Time* magazine. Having dispatched all of his American opponents, Robinson had recently taken to trailing Europe for fighters who would provide him with big paydays and easy victories, and when Robinson toured he did so in style. He drove a huge flamingo-pink Cadillac convertible and he stayed in only the swankiest accommodation. His entourage of boosters included his manager, his doctor, a golf pro, a hairdresser, a spiritual adviser, and a midget comic, or 'good humour' man, named Jimmy Karoubi, among many others. Awed by legendary tales of the Sugarman's extraordinary skill, and by the evidence of the maestro's oozing confidence, his opponents were generally beaten before they had even ducked their heads through the ropes. Very few doubted that Robinson was, pound for pound, the greatest fighter who had ever lived, and at thirty he was at the peak of his career.

It was Jack Solomons, Britain's pre-eminent promoter, who had persuaded Robinson to add a final date to his latest European tour and cross the English Channel in order that he might fight young Turpin *and* put his world middleweight title on the line. Solomons was born in 1900 in the East End of London, but this Yiddish-speaking cockney was not the most popular man in British boxing, combining as he did the 'talents' of thuggishness and business cunning. However, Solomons was a man who could get matches made. Robinson was undertaking a series of non-title exhibition fights in Zurich, Antwerp, Liege, Berlin, and Turin, and initially the American had little interest in risking his title in London against an unknown, unless, of course, the money was right. Solomons travelled to Paris, where Robinson's entourage was resting before moving on to Belgium, and he asked Robinson to name his price. Robinson laughed and told him '$100,000 and not one cent less', and a disappointed Solomons returned to London. This sum, which was the equivalent of nearly £30,000, was unheard of at a time when the vast majority of British workers earned less than £5 a week. However, Solomons was a man who relished a challenge, and having been in the company of the great Sugar Ray he was now more determined than ever to make this match. Solomons worked and reworked his figures, and then persuaded Turpin's manager, George Middleton — a man who he described as 'one of the most reasonable men in the world to do business with' – to accept £12,000, which was less than half of what Robinson would earn. Finally, he returned to Paris with contracts in hand, and a smiling Sugar Ray Robinson signed to fight Britain's own Randolph Turpin for the world middleweight crown. Jack Solomons would be promoting the biggest bout in British boxing history, and the great Sugar Ray Robinson would be bringing his flamingo-pink Cadillac and flamboyant personality to post-war Britain.

Soon after Robinson's arrival, the Savoy Hotel in London had asked the American to leave, for the masses of fans that daily thronged the lobby and pavements outside of the hotel were making it impossible for the management to run the Savoy with the grace and decorum that their regular customers had come to expect. As a result the Sugar Ray Robinson party decamped to the Star and Garter public house in Windsor where the proprietors made every effort to accommodate the eccentricities of their coloured guests. On the morning of 10 July, Sugar Ray Robinson and his team departed for central London and the weigh-in. Once they reached Piccadilly Circus, Robinson's party were taken aback by the size of the crowds that had gathered in anticipation of the day's events. Crowds like this had not greeted him in France or in Belgium, or in any of the other places where he had displayed his flashy talents on his recent tour. It was clear that the somewhat depressed people of England, in their still bombed-out country, were in need of some kind of glamorous boost, and this being the case Sugar Ray was happy to provide this for them.

The weigh-in was scheduled to take place at just after

noon at 'Solomons Promotions', and this would mark the first time that Turpin would set eyes upon the legendary Sugar Ray Robinson. Turpin had once again struggled to make his way through the crowds and into Jack Solomons' gym, but the Leamington man understood that although people were thrilled that a British lad was getting a chance to 'have a go' at Robinson, the vast majority of those in the streets, and the lucky ones packed into the gym, were eager for a glimpse of the hotshot American. His involuntary exile to the Star and Garter pub in Windsor had deprived Londoners of the chance of seeing the world champion and his entourage promenading through London, or going through their paces in Hyde Park. This would be their first and last chance to ogle the American before the title bout, and most London fight fans seemed keen to seize it. As Turpin stood beside the scales and waited, he remained calm and he appeared, to those who looked on, to be patient and focused. As noise and confusion continued to swell all around him, Turpin decided to sit down and stare at the ground between his feet and ignore the shouted questions from the mob of journalists.

Most of the sportswriters were convinced that Jack Solomons, and his 'yes man', George Middleton, had, in their quest for money, foolishly overmatched the promising coloured fighter with a man who was not only going to roundly wallop him, but a man who might well inflict serious and permanent damage on the youngster. The bookmakers' odds of seven to one on for a Robinson victory, and twenty to one against Turpin being on his feet at the end of the contest, suggested a forgone conclusion at best, and at worst a cynical attempt on the part of Solomons to cash in on Robinson's brief presence in Europe by throwing a dusky English lamb to the slaughter. Even if the coloured lad from Leamington did manage to stay out of Robinson's reach for the early part of the fight, he had never gone beyond eight rounds in his life, while Robinson had regularly fought fifteen-round pitched battles against American men of steel. But this did not deter the public who, once the fight had been announced, snapped up the 18,000 tickets to the Exhibition Hall at Earls Court in less than a week. Jack Solomons soon realised that he could have sold twice as many tickets, which ranged from ten guineas at ringside, to one guinea in the rafters, and doubled the £80,000 gate by putting the fight in a larger venue. Robinson versus Turpin was not only the highest profile fight in British boxing history, it was destined to be the biggest single sporting event ever held in Britain. Young Randolph Turpin's part was already written: to take his punishment like a man and put up a good show, and the unusual nature of his preparation suggested that he fully understood the script.

A year earlier, in the summer of 1950, Turpin, together with his brother Jackie, moved temporarily from Leamington Spa to set up training camp in Wales. The fight with Robinson had not yet been made, but Turpin had got it into his head that by moving away from the distractions of his home town he could better concentrate on preparing himself for the business of championship boxing. A Wales-based businessman named Leslie Thomas Salts had recently purchased Gwrych Castle near Llandudno, which had been originally constructed in 1819 and over the years had fallen into some disrepair. However, it still remained a magnificent listed property with a view of the Irish Sea, a famous marble staircase, dining rooms, smoking rooms, a billiard room, and over 200 acres of land that included stables and extensive lawns. Intending to open the place to the public as 'the Showplace of Wales', Salts had installed rides and attractions for children, but it occurred to Salts that having professional boxers training and sparring on his grounds, and charging the public to watch, might well be a further source of income. And so it proved. His first boxer was the British heavyweight, Bruce Woodcock, but Salts soon realised that the amenable and charismatic Turpin would most probably be a better drawing card. Turpin was initially overwhelmed by his first sighting of the huge, stone-walled fiefdom, with its acres of open, rolling hills, and the castle presiding high up on a hillside. The spectacular estate possessed a verdant grandeur that exceeded anything Turpin had ever seen or imagined. He was safe in this private kingdom, in which he was the prince to Salts' king, and he could temporarily escape his upbringing, his past, and imagine himself to be a man free of the considerable pressure of being obligated to family and friends. However, Turpin's manager, George Middleton, was not happy with his fighter retreating to Wales for he did not regard Leslie Salts as a straight shooter, but he knew that once Randolph Turpin had made up his mind there really was little point in arguing with him.

In the late summer of 1950, Turpin fought a tough opponent, named Eli Elandon, and defeated him in under two rounds, and therefore the relative isolation of the castle as a training base seemed to have worked. Once the world title bout with Robinson was announced, Turpin decided to move back to Wales in order that he might prepare for the biggest fight of his career. This time, rather than have Turpin training up on the hillside, the opportunistic Salts moved Turpin's camp to the more spacious east lawn and put up a huge sign: COME AND MEET A BRITISH CHAMPION AT SUNNY GWRYCH CASTLE.

Come they did, and they paid two shillings to see Turpin jogging lightly towards the ring like a gladiator in his white robe, flanked on one side by his smaller brother Jackie, who carried his gloves, and on the other side by a sparring partner who would soon be given a thorough going-over. Salts was making good money not only out of admission fees, but from selling autographed souvenirs. The constant flow of sparring partners, including Turpin's brother Jackie, all felt underpaid and underappreciated, often having to go down into the town in order that they might find a decent meal. However, Salts had managed to work his way into the full confidence of Turpin, and the fighter's mind remained fixed on the discipline of training. In fact, Turpin was content to leave all business and financial arrangements to Middleton and Salts.

Britain in the early fifties was a desolate place whose urban landscape remained largely pockmarked with bomb sites. Derelict buildings and wasteland spoke eloquently to the pummelling that the country had taken in the recent war, but the government lacked the resources to do anything about this bleak terrain. Victory against Germany had been achieved, but at a price that some now considered simply too high. While Allied money flowed into Germany to help rebuild the defeated nation, six years after the war Britain appeared to have stagnated economically, its confidence shot, and its people suffering. Thousands of servicemen had returned after the war only to discover that there was no industrial machine for them to rejoin, and that jobs were scarce on the ground. The women who had manned the factories during the war found it difficult to readjust to their old roles as housewives and mothers, and those for whom privilege had been an accepted part of their pre-war life soon discovered that the introduction of a welfare state, with free health and education for the working classes, heralded a challenge to their assumptions of class superiority. Britain was depressed and good times seemed a long way off. The average Briton still utilised his ration book and had to remember to count each penny, and day trips to glamorous locations like Gwrych Castle were to be savoured. The opportunity of seeing boxers in action, particularly champion boxers like young Randolph Turpin, brightened up everybody's lives. When it was announced that Sugar Ray Robinson would be visiting Britain, and that a British lad would be given the chance to enter the ring and go a few rounds with him, this was a shot in the arm to the blighted confidence of the British people. Everybody was excited that the Sugarman, pink Cadillac and all the rest of it, would soon be in town.

After Turpin and Robinson shook hands and posed briefly for photographs, Turpin stripped off his shabby dressing gown and mounted the scales. At 5'11" and with unusually broad shoulders, he tipped the scales at 159 lb. His opponent, on the other hand, was 5½ lb inside the 160 lb limit. Robinson looked at the Englishman and found it hard to believe that this heavily muscled coloured lad was not at least a light heavyweight. The strapping lad was clearly as strong as an ox and in his autobiography Robinson was to describe his feelings at this moment. 'Right there, Turpin impressed me. His torso was like an oak tree. If he could box even a little bit I was going to be in trouble.' Of course, the British knew that their man could fight a bit. After all, he was the British and European middleweight champion, and he never seemed to worry unduly about who he was going to fight. In fact, this was his greatest asset, his ability to approach every bout as though it was no more or no less difficult than the one before. However, those pressmen who had bothered to visit his camp at Gwrych Castle would have seen how, on this occasion, his training had been geared specifically to cope with Robinson's fast combinations and the most devastating left hook in the business. One training partner in particular had been detailed to throw nothing but Sugar Ray-style left hooks, hard, fast, and non-stop. However, despite Robinson's private ruminations on seeing Turpin stripped to the waist, Sugar Ray knew that he was the champion, he was the draw, and tomorrow his European sojourn would be at an end and he would be counting his money and readying himself to depart back across the Atlantic Ocean in the direction of New York City.

The weigh-in ended with the British Boxing Board of Control doctor verifying that both the champion and the challenger were in a fit state to fight this evening over fifteen rounds for the middleweight championship of the world. For most of the proceedings, Robinson had effortlessly played to the crowd, who clearly adored him. Turpin, by contrast, had stayed quietly in the background enjoying the 'show' as much as anyone else. As the weigh-in concluded, and the Robinson entourage left noisily for a West End hotel, Turpin, his brothers Dick and Jackie, and George Middleton realised that they had a whole afternoon to kill and they were momentarily stumped as to what to do. It was Randolph Turpin who decided that the most important thing would be to get away from the hordes of people, and so he suggested that they all go and watch a film. After all, it would be dark inside the cinema, and nobody would recognise them so they would be able to sit down and unwind in peace.

George Middleton bought four entrance tickets and they all trooped into a West End picture house and took their seats. Within minutes of the feature beginning, Turpin was pushing Jackie and rousing him from his sleep. 'Wake up, Jack. This is a bloody good film!' Jackie tried to stay awake, but the warmth and comfort of the cinema won the battle and soon he was once again fast asleep. Randolph Turpin, however, paid rapt attention and he followed the whole story right down to the film's conclusion. As they stepped out of the cinema and into the light of a beautiful late afternoon in July, George Middleton looked nervously at his watch. It was time. They found their way to the nearest Tube station where George bought four single fares to Earls Court and handed the brothers their tickets.

Fight fans who were travelling from work directly to the Exhibition Hall at Earls Court could scarcely believe their eyes when they saw Randolph Turpin, his fight gear in a used carrier bag that was tucked neatly under his arm, riding to the biggest night in British sporting history on the same Tube as them. Whatever the outcome of tonight's fight, this man of the people was already a hero. Should he manage to survive even one or two rounds and put up a decent showing, this would be enough to get the celebratory pints flowing later on in the evening. Few could ever have imagined it, but on this particular night it was a coloured fighter on whom all British hopes were pinned.

British people have always held their prizefighters in high esteem, for their toughness and rugged durability represents, in their eyes, the very best of the British bulldog spirit. Boxing is also a sport which brings together those at either end of the social spectrum, with the bouts generally fought by working-class toughs under the supervision and patronage of blue bloods and aristocrats. For the upper classes, being able to box is a social skill which one often acquires as part of one's education, but actual prizefighting is considered best left to the lower orders. In the early nineteenth century, both the blue bloods and the lower classes came together when an outsider, a black American named Tom Molineaux, was scheduled to fight the British hero Tom Cribb for what would have been regarded the undisputed heavyweight championship of the world. The fight took place in December 1810 at Copthall Common just south of London, and thousands of people poured out of the city and gathered in a field to witness the *battle royal.* The black American was clearly getting the better of the Englishman, but unable to tolerate the notion of the championship being in the hands of either an American, or a black man, the crowd stormed the ring injuring Molineaux's hands. The fight was eventually restarted, but the 'ebony imposter', as the English had dubbed him, was incapable of defending himself and was eventually defeated. The championship title remained in English hands and the foreign threat was vanquished.

Eighteenth- and nineteenth-century bare-knuckle fighting eventually gave way to 'boxing' in 1867, when twelve rules for the sport were drafted and published under the patronage of John Douglas, the ninth Marquess of Queensberry. Fights were now to be 'a fair stand-up boxing match' in a twenty-four-foot ring, with rounds of three minutes duration and one minute of rest between each round. Padded gloves were to be worn, and there was to be no 'butting or wrestling', and should a man be knocked down he would be allowed ten seconds to get up. The first world title bout under these rules saw the heavyweight 'Gentleman Jim' Corbett defeat John L. Sullivan in 1892 in New Orleans. By the end of the nineteenth century, and on into the twentieth, the odd stout-hearted English fighter aside, American boxers ruled the roost at most weights. Wave after wave of new American immigrant – Italian, Irish, and Jewish – attempted to establish a place in American life by earning some respect in the ring. However, when it came to title shots black boxers were often deliberately left at the back of the line. The charismatic black boxer Jack Johnson, who held the world heavyweight title from 1908 until 1915, did much to stir up hostility and antipathy towards coloured fighters by the outlandish nature of his behaviour. Boastful, arrogant even, with a twinkling eye, a broad grin, and a succession of white women on his arm, Johnson was everything that 'white America' hated. When 'white America' finally won back 'their' heavyweight championship in 1915, they were reluctant to let any other uppity negroes take it away again. In the future their champions would be white, or black and humble, like Joe Louis. Sugar Ray Robinson fell into the category of the humble for, despite all his flash and his panache, he was a charmer who possessed impeccable manners. He was, in short, an acceptable negro, a person who most white Americans were proud and comfortable to see representing them.

In Britain things had been, until two years earlier, somewhat different. A clear colour bar had been in effect so that black boxers were prohibited from fighting for or holding the British title. They were allowed to fight for the British Empire title, but at all weights black boxers, even if they were, like Randolph Turpin, born and bred in Britain, were treated as foreigners and excluded from fighting for their own national championship. After the Second World War there was increasingly vocal opposition to the policy, and in 1947 the racist restriction was lifted. Fittingly, it was Turpin's eldest brother, Dick, who, in June 1948, became Britain's first black boxing champion, lifting the middleweight crown. He lost the title in April 1950, but a few months later, in October 1950, his brother Randy won back the title. However, a national title was not nearly enough to guarantee a lucrative payday. Fight fans tended to rally behind local heroes, and to some extent box offices depended upon a fighter bringing his loyal followers to a bout. Although many people in the Midlands did recognise Randolph Turpin as one of their own, there was no serious box-office support for a coloured fighter no matter how skilled or game he might be. There was no doubt that Turpin was popular and regarded as a man of the people, but the interest of the general public in the Robinson versus Turpin bout was generated by Robinson's presence, and by the David versus Goliath aspect of the clash. The British Boxing Board of Control may have relaxed their rules to accommodate coloured boxers, but the general public had still not fully warmed to the idea of black boxers being also British.

On the warm summer's evening of 10 July, 1951, 18,000 people were packed into the Earls Court Exhibition Hall, with many hundreds more milling about in the car park outside. In homes throughout the length and breadth of the country, over twenty million people were tuned into the BBC Home Service to listen to Raymond Glendenning's live radio commentary, including King George VI who was sitting next to the wireless in Buckingham Palace. Inside Turpin's dressing room, the young boxer sat calmly on a bench immersed in a comic book, which was often his preferred reading matter. Never one to panic or become overly agitated before a bout, there was something almost resigned about Turpin's demeanour which worried his Manchester-based Irish trainer, Mick Gavin, his brothers Dick and Jackie, and his manager, George Middleton. Eventually Turpin was encouraged to put down his comic book so that his seconds could slip on his gloves and fasten them tightly into place, and then his threadbare dressing gown was slipped around his broad shoulders and everybody was ready. In keeping with tradition, the challenger would enter the arena first. Shortly before 9:30 p.m., George Middleton opened the door to the dressing room allowing the clamour and noise to greet them for the first time. As Turpin shuffled past Robinson's dressing room, he could hear noise and laughter from within. The American was clearly upbeat and confident of an easy payday and a swift return trip home.

These days fighters tend to enter the ring to loud, thumping music of their own choice, with laser beams cutting through the air and a razzle-dazzle of a performance that is more akin to the circus than a sporting event. On this particular July evening, the lights were dimmed and the spotlights picked out Turpin as he entered the arena to nothing more than loud cheers of encouragement from those who were able to strain their necks and get a glimpse of the lad from Leamington Spa. Some spectators stood on their seats as the British champion edged his way towards ringside, and then Turpin ducked through the ropes and stepped into the ring where finally he was visible to the sell-out crowd. They noisily and enthusiastically cheered the coloured lad, and then the champion appeared and he, in great contrast to the low-key entrance of Turpin, seemed to revel in his self-assigned role of showman. His hair was slick and straightened, with not a single lick out of place, and he flashed a broad smile for the cameras. As he moved towards the ring, draped in a white robe with a blue silk gown on top, he bobbed and weaved as though eager to let everybody know that he was ready for business. Behind him, like courtiers traipsing after a prince, were his attendants, all uniformly pristine in blue and white tops with the words 'Sugar Ray' emblazoned on their backs. Having climbed into the ring the champion bowed respectfully to all four sides of the arena, and then he turned to acknowledge the challenger who was visibly sweating in his corner. As the announcer began to declare that the feature contest of the evening was about to commence, Robinson made a display of not taking his stool, preferring instead to bounce ominously from foot to foot in his corner, and bang his gloves together as though eager to get the proceedings over and done with. The prince of the ring stared at his English opponent, who appeared to have dead man's eyes, and Sugar Ray wondered if the Limey was yellow. Turpin sat slumped on his stool as though awaiting his fate. From where he was sitting he could see the Movietone cameras already whirring with activity for, whatever the outcome, the newsreel of this fight would soon be broadcast in all the major picture houses in Britain. The referee, an ex-heavyweight from Scotland named Eugene Henderson, signalled to the fighters to ready themselves, and Turpin drew himself to his full height knowing that there was now no turning back.

A little over an hour, and fifteen gruelling rounds later, Turpin slipped an arm around the American's shoulders and escorted him back to his corner in a gesture of respect. The fight was over and the 18,000 voices in the Earls Court

Exhibition Hall were raised as one, singing chorus after chorus of 'For He's a Jolly Good Fellow!'. The BBC's unashamedly patrician Raymond Glendenning, with his handlebar moustache and clipped received pronunciation, posed the rhetorical question to the whole nation. 'Who has won?' Those who were present at the fight had no doubt who had won, but Glendenning kept the whole nation, including the king, on tenterhooks. In the ring, Turpin congratulated Sugar Ray and his corner men, and a breathless champion patted his British opponent on the back muttering, 'Good fight. Good fight, kid.' Eugene Henderson saw that both fighters were in the American's corner and he knew that there was no need for him to consult his scorecard. He walked over and raised Turpin's hand, at which point Glendenning's words exploded across the beleaguered nation. 'Turpin has won! Turpin has won! Turpin, Randolph Turpin, twenty-three-year-old from Leamington Spa, is the new middleweight champion of the world!' George Middleton, Dick and Jackie Turpin, and Turpin's trainer, Mick Gavin, leapt across the ring and hugged the new world champion, while in the hall pandemonium broke out. The chorus of 'For He's a Jolly Good Fellow!' increased in volume as Robinson climbed his way out from the ring and shuffled in the direction of his dressing room, leaving Turpin to bask in the applause and cheers of the Earls Court crowd.

Once he reached his dressing room, the new world champion showered quietly and then got dressed. His brothers were clearly far more excited than he was, and they pressed him to tell them what Sugar Ray had said to him. Turpin thought for a moment and then said that Robinson had told him, 'You were good. Real good. Just like everybody had said you were.' Turpin knew that he had fought well, his seventy-four-inch reach keeping Robinson at bay, his wide stance allowing him to maintain his balance, and his upper body strength enabling him to bully the American in every clinch and inflict a wound over the American's left eye that would require fourteen stitches. In between rounds Turpin had remained calm and relaxed on his stool, his legs spread out before him and his elbows resting up on the ropes, but each time the bell rang he sprang to his feet and his superior conditioning and unorthodox crouching style eventually left Robinson battered and exhausted.

Randolph Turpin was now the undisputed 160 lb champion of the whole world, but he seemed temporarily bewildered, as though this title was not what he had been seeking, and the events of the evening had been a strange, unsolicited, consequence of simply doing what he enjoyed. As the Turpin group left Earls Court, they could hear those inside the Exhibition Hall still singing 'For He's a Jolly Good Fellow!'. Outside in the car park, and in all the streets leading to the Earls Court Tube station, there was cheering and joyous celebrations the like of which had not been seen or heard since VE Day some six years earlier. However, Turpin seemed untouched by all of the exuberance, and he simply smiled as though unable to comprehend whatever forces he had just released in the soul of the British nation. Meanwhile, a chastened Robinson, having had his stitches administered in the privacy of his own dressing room, sought to avoid the press by seeking out a nearby Earls Court bed and breakfast. In the morning he would leave quickly on the first boat train to Paris, from where he would fly home to New York City. He left instructions that his entourage should make their own way to France as soon as possible.

In the morning a practically unblemished Turpin awoke in his hotel room bright and early, and he decided to go out for a short stroll with George Middleton and try to walk off some of the stiffness in his muscles. The country had partied hard and long on the previous evening, but Turpin had avoided the limelight and got his head down for a good night's rest. This morning it was not so easy for the new champion to avoid the crowds, but Turpin and his manager, with the assistance of the hotel staff, managed to sneak out of a back door. Predictably enough, the British newspapers were full of reports of Turpin's almost unbelievable victory, and triumphant stories were blazoned across both the front and the back pages. In the United States, reporters were aghast, not only by the fact that Robinson had been defeated, but by the manner in which he had been so easily outboxed, outjabbed and outmuscled by, of all people, a Limey. The only possible explanation was that Sugar Ray's constant whirl of European social engagements, his nightclubbing, golf games, exhibitions for money, and constant travelling, had taken their toll on the great man. Surely there would be a rematch?

Back in Leamington Spa, the mother of Britain's new sporting hero had listened to the fight on the radio. When reporters eventually beat their way to her door in order to secure a quote, she gathered her wits about her, looked them straight in the eyes, and, reluctant to distinguish between Randolph and her two other fighting sons, she told them, 'I am proud of my sons. A lot of people thought they were nothing. Well, my sons have shown them.' She knew that all of Leamington Spa, and the nearby historic town of Warwick, where Turpin had spent some part of his childhood, was abuzz with excitement. Turpin's mother assured the reporters that either later today, or tomorrow, her world champion son would be coming back home. Before the fight she had heard her son cautiously suggest that victory might mean a new car and a new house for him, but with a mother's instinct she sensed that it would probably mean much more than this for her son. She worried, for she knew that young Randolph did not possess the business acumen to surround himself with the right people, and he was by far the most sensitive of her children, but why worry about this now? Maybe when he came home she might talk to him about things, but her youngest son could be strangely reserved and moody, and she did not imagine that he was about to change.

On 12 July, 1951, less than forty-eight hours after his dazzling victory at the Earls Court Exhibition Hall, Turpin was back in the Midlands where the mayors of both Warwick and Leamington Spa, the two towns that could claim to have produced the boxer, organised a joint reception. Turpin was seated in the back of an open-top black Humber limousine, democratically perched between the mayors of both towns, and he began his victory journey in the narrow medieval streets in the centre of Warwick. He had never heard of these men, but they certainly knew his name and they continually pumped his hand, and slapped him on the back, and posed with him for photographs. A bemused Turpin understood that this was likely to be the way for some time, but this was not a life that he was eager to get used to. The car was twenty minutes late leaving Warwick because, having just arrived from London, Turpin had decided to take a nap and he had overslept. This delay meant that they would be late arriving in Leamington Spa for the official reception, but the mayor of Leamington let the new champion know that he should not worry for they would just tell the press that the car had suffered a punctured tyre.

The journey did not take long, and all along the way people waved and cheered as the Humber limousine glided by. A somewhat shy Turpin followed the lead of the mayors and waved back, and as the car eventually turned into the centre of Leamington Spa the crowds became denser, slowing the Humber's progress almost to a halt. Clearly most people had taken the day off work, for over 20,000 cheering people thronged the streets. Bright streamers and banners were hung from every available place, a brass band was thumping out music, and up above an RAF jet from the nearby base was doing victory rolls and loops in the sky. This was the greatest day in the town's history, and all of this was due to the success of one man. At the sight of their all-conquering hero the crowd began to sing 'For He's a Jolly Good Fellow!' and their overwhelming adulation finally brought a lump to Turpin's throat. Surely all of this could not be for him? The limousine drew to a halt outside of Leamington Spa Town Hall, and Turpin looked up and read the sign that was hanging from the balcony: LEAMINGTON SPA WELCOMES THEIR CHAMPION RANDOLPH TURPIN.

Turpin stared at the banner and had to be prompted to leave the car. He entered the town hall, where the first man to greet him was John 'Gerry' Gibbs, the police inspector who had founded the Leamington Boys' Club, and who first saw promise in the fourteen-year-old Turpin. The new world champion warmly shook hands with his old mentor, and then made his way up to the balcony.

Photographs of Turpin on this special day show a handsome man in a double-breasted beige suit, a smart blue silk shirt, and dapper white shoes. However, Turpin appears to be a little confused. In almost every photograph he seems to be avoiding full eye contact with the camera as though hiding from somebody, or himself. Perhaps the most disturbing photograph of the day shows Turpin flanked by the two lord mayors in a wood-panelled room in the town hall. The mayors pose stiffly in pinstriped suits, while Turpin has his right arm draped loosely around his mother and he supports his young son in his other arm. A feeling of palpable discomfort radiates from the photograph, and nobody seems entirely comfortable on what should be a joyous occasion. The modest new world champion eventually stepped out on to the balcony of Leamington Spa Town Hall, and the roar from the crowd was almost deafening, as was the high-pitched drone of cine and newsreel cameras. The mayor of Leamington Spa urged him forward

('Go on, son') and Turpin took the microphone that was proffered. For a second he looked at the sea of white faces which swam out before him in all directions, and then he began to read from a speech which his manager had prepared for the occasion. 'It was a great fight on Tuesday and I am naturally very proud to bring the honour of the middleweight championship of the world back to England and Warwickshire.' Then Turpin stopped and looked again at the crowds of people before him. 'I must tell you how grateful I am to my manager, my trainer, my family and others who have helped me so much throughout my career . . .' Again Turpin stopped speaking, and this time he handed his speech to one of the mayors and addressed the crowds directly. 'Well, I'm not much at making speeches but you all know what I mean. Thanks.' He waved to the crowd and handed the microphone to somebody else. At this point George Middleton led an elderly Beatrice Manley, Turpin's mother, on to the balcony, and Turpin took her in his arms and gave her a kiss. Ailing now for some years, and suffering from a partial loss of eyesight, she was nonetheless the proudest woman in Leamington Spa and she had worn her best hat to prove the point. The coloured baby that, much to some people's disgust, she had given birth to twenty-three years ago in this very town was, on this day, the most famous man in England.

Randolph Adolphus Turpin was born in Leamington Spa on 7 June, 1928, the youngest child of Lionel Fitzherbert Turpin and Beatrice Whitehouse. There were already two older brothers, Dick and Jackie, and two older sisters, Joan and Kathy, but the cash-strapped family were struggling financially in a cramped basement flat in Willis Road. The new addition, who weighed in at 9 lb 7 oz, was the lightest of all Beatrice's children at birth, but he was still, by most standards, a heavyweight child. At a time when Beatrice and Lionel could barely afford food to put on the table the new baby was yet another mouth to feed and, to make matters worse, at the time of Randolph's birth Lionel was in hospital and ailing badly. The prognosis was not good.

Lionel Fitzherbert Turpin was born in Georgetown, British Guiana, in February 1896. He enjoyed a traditional British schooling in the sugar-rich colony on the northeast coast of South America, but the young lad had a yearning to see the world. He arrived in England as a merchant seaman on the eve of the Great War, and by the time Britain declared war on Germany in the summer of 1914, Lionel was ready to sign up. He was eventually sent out with the British Expeditionary Forces to the Western Front where he fought numerous campaigns, including the legendary Battle of the Somme. He survived the slaughter, but towards the end of the war he was badly wounded by a gas shell which burnt his lungs and left a gaping wound in his back. Lionel was shipped back to a hospital in Coventry, where they did all they could to help him before discharging the West Indian to a convalescent home near Hill House in the nearby town of Warwick. Although it was clear to the doctors that the mild-mannered coloured soldier was never going to fully recover, Lionel Turpin was eventually allowed to leave the convalescent home and he attempted to find work locally.

Lionel stood out in Warwick, for there were no other coloured people in the town, and he was regularly referred to as 'Sam', which was an abbreviation for the more pejorative 'Sambo'. He was equally exotic in nearby Leamington Spa, where the introverted West Indian veteran soon met a local teenager named Beatrice Whitehouse. Beatrice came from a rough, but tight-knit, local working-class family, her father being well known in the area as a bare-knuckle prize-fighter who plied his trade at the local Woolpack Inn. Lionel wasted little time in proposing to Beatrice, and although times were hard for everybody, they settled down and tried to raise their mixed-race family in a social atmosphere that was not always friendly or supportive. Later in life, Jackie Turpin remembered that 'there was a time when nobody would cross the road to speak to the Turpins. We was just little black kids as used to run around Wathen Road and Parkes Street.' However, Beatrice prided herself on having come from tough stock, so nothing was going to deter her from protecting and supporting her children, who were often taunted as being 'dirty' or 'khaki-coloured'. Sadly, as the family grew, Lionel's condition began to deteriorate, and it became increasingly difficult for him to hold down a job. He moved back and forth between the family's Leamington home and a hospital in nearby Coventry, until it was clear that the coloured veteran required full-time care and attention. He was eventually allocated a bed at the Ministry of Pensions Hospital in Birmingham, but on 6 March, 1929, nine months after the birth of Randolph, his fifth child, Lionel Fitzherbert Turpin finally passed away due to war injuries that he had suffered over a decade earlier. His funeral hearse was drawn by four black horses, with six soldiers as an escort, and the thirty-three-year-old former military man was buried in the Brunswick Street Cemetery, Leamington Spa, in a ceremony that was paid for by the Leamington branch of the British Legion.

At the age of twenty-five, Beatrice was left by herself to bring up five children: Dick, Joan, Jackie, Kathy, and Randy. She was entitled to a widow's pension of just under thirty shillings a week, which she could supplement with whatever she might earn cooking and cleaning for other people, but however hard she tried Beatrice could not make ends meet. As a result, she often sent her children to stay with different relatives; Dick frequently went to stay with his grandmother, while Joan spent time in Wales with her aunt. However, when circumstances allowed, Mrs Turpin would bring all of her children back together under one roof, but life was never easy for Beattie, and young Randy was particularly worrisome to her. As a three-year-old boy, Randy had contracted double pneumonia and bronchitis, and although he eventually recovered the diseases returned on two further occasions. On their final appearance, the doctor told Beattie that she should prepare herself for Randy's death, but she chose instead to sit up all night with her youngest child, sponging him down to keep his temperature under control, and feeding him to keep up his strength. Much to the doctor's surprise, and the family's relief, little Randy survived, and this served only to make Beattie all the more determined to keep her children together. She once again retrieved them from the relatives among whom they had been distributed and, having now decided to marry a local English man, in 1931 she permanently reunited her household.

As a child, Turpin earned the nickname 'Licker', a moniker that he would carry with him into adulthood and beyond. Although most people assumed that the 'Leamington Licker' was so called because of his ability to beat, or 'lick', his opponents, according to his brother Jackie, the name had nothing to do with his fighting prowess. Randy, Jackie, and sister Joan were all born in June, on the 7th, 13th, and 19th respectively, and when the birthdays arrived young Randy used to assume that because his birthday came first that made him the oldest. Apparently, Joan would shake her head and insist that he was, in fact, the littlest, to which he would shout that he wasn't the 'lickerest' he was the oldest. Sister Joan would mimic his pronunciation, telling him that he was just a 'licker boy' and if he didn't behave himself she would spank his bottom. The fiery Randy would inevitably rush at his sister with his fists flying, insisting that he wasn't a 'licker boy', and the family pet name stuck and became eerily appropriate for a boy who would eventually grow up to become a champion boxer.

Randy was not an easy child for his mother, his siblings, or eventually anybody to deal with. Headstrong and capricious, his family struggled to both protect him and avoid his occasional outbursts of anger. With so many children to cope with it was difficult for young Beattie to exercise any real discipline, and it was particularly perplexing for her to know how to handle her youngest child towards whom she felt a special affection. To make matters worse, while swimming in a river young Randy was trapped by weeds and his hearing was permanently damaged. He was, for the rest of his life, very much aware of his partial deafness, but he did not like to dwell upon it and would become upset if it was mentioned. However, he was a fearless child, and was always ready to attack no matter how big or implausible the opponent. Young Randy Turpin was quite prepared to strike out with just his fists, but if there happened to be a weapon to hand then he would happily seize it. He once chased his eldest brother Dick with an axe, threatening to 'chop his bleeding head off', but his weapon of choice was usually a knife. In one argument he actually stabbed his brother Dick, and despite Beattie's pleading with him to calm down it was clear to everybody that this child might well be on a collision course with trouble.

When he was five, Randy began to attend West Gate Council School, which was both understaffed and overcrowded. It was a school that was designed to provide precious little in the way of academic opportunities, being merely a place to hold working-class children until they could be processed out at the age of fifteen and enter the workforce. By the time Randy was twelve, the athletically gifted 'Licker' could beat any boy in the school with his fists, or with his feet. He paid little, if any, attention to his schoolwork, preferring to pour his energies into developing his well-earned reputation as both a sportsman and a 'tough nut'. He and his followers would 'persuade' boys to hand over money or sweets, and while his friends held their victim's arms 'Licker' would teach the poor lads a lesson by giving them a good pummelling. At home, his siblings were not spared his attentions. Joan remembers, 'He blackened my eyes for me twice. Once for my birthday, and once for telling my granny tales about him.' Sister Kathy recalls, 'If you didn't do what he wanted he'd clank you for it. He'd squeal to my mother if you hit him back and if you did anything he didn't like he came in and smashed all my dolls. I had some black celluloid dolls and he'd put his foot in them and break them.'

To some of the townsfolk of Leamington Spa, young 'Licker' Turpin was a bully whose mother clearly had no control over him. There were those who would not dare to make eye contact with him in the street, or even in the semi-darkness of the cinema, and nobody wanted to be in a shop when 'Licker' came in and demanded that you buy him something. Any challenge to his 'authority' might well be met with a torrent of verbal abuse, and it was also possible that the unfortunate person would be given a good kicking for their trouble. Many believed that being from the only coloured family in the town obviously informed the boy's delinquency. It did not occur to them that being the only coloured family in town meant that the Turpins, Randy included, *had* to be able to take care of themselves, and sometimes get their retaliation in first. In the thirties, most British people were unfamiliar with the novelty of living among people of another race, but given the evidence of the Turpin family, the novelty of living with coloured people was something that a number of the more narrow-minded townsfolk of Leamington Spa had concluded that they could do without.

In fact, black people have been present in English life since the time of the Roman occupation. There is very strong evidence that black Roman soldiers were stationed near Hadrian's Wall at the northern outpost of England, but the first really visible, permanent, group of black people in English life appeared towards the end of the sixteenth century. These Africans were brought to England in the wake of Sir John Hawkins' trading missions to Africa and the Americas, and were often treated as little more than exotic objects whose main function was to adorn the houses and palaces of the nobility and aristocrats upon whom the 'captives' were occasionally encouraged to serve. In 1601, concerned by the escalating numbers of coloured people in her kingdom, Queen Elizabeth I of England issued a proclamation ordering the expulsion of the 'blackamoors'. However, as the English trading mission transformed itself into the fabulously profitable business of slavery, hundreds of black people now began to find themselves adrift in England. By the late eighteenth century, England had a sizeable population of people of African origin, and these individuals were often able to form and maintain their own clubs and societies. In the nineteenth century, with the abolition of the slave trade, and the steady increase of instances of intermarriage, the black population began to decline significantly, and it was not to grow again in size until the late fifties and sixties with the advent of mass migration from the Caribbean. For most of the nineteenth and early twentieth centuries, there were vast sections of England where a coloured face had never been seen, and the appearance of an African or West Indian would be a truly alarming spectacle. This is how Lionel Fitzherbert Turpin must have appeared to the townsfolk of Leamington Spa in the early part of the twentieth century. After his untimely death, Lionel left a legacy of five mixed-race children in Leamington Spa, who not only constituted a truly unusual sight, but who were regarded by some intolerant locals as a social problem which they were ill-equipped to deal with.

By the time young 'Licker' Turpin reached fourteen, he was seldom attending school and it was clear that his life was in danger of taking a turn towards lawlessness. At the local Leamington Spa Boys' Club, a boxing section had recently been formed under the guidance of a local policeman, Inspector John 'Gerry' Gibbs, and an Italian former amateur welterweight champion named Ron Stefani. They both loved the physical skill and discipline of boxing, preferring the purity and dignity of the amateur ranks to what they perceived to be the chicanery and exploitation of the professional world. In 1942 they persuaded the young tearaway 'Licker' Turpin to come into the gym, and it soon became clear that the coloured lad possessed an extraordinary talent. He was quick, aggressive, and keen to learn, and he was also strong and eager to develop his strength by lifting weights. This was an unusual method of training, for traditionally fighters worried that it made them less lithe and supple; it was also believed that the new muscles might 'confuse' the boxing muscles, but the stubborn youngster continued to build up his strength with weights, a regime that he remained loyal to throughout the full length of his career.

The day young Randolph Turpin stepped into the Leamington Spa gym, boxing was already in his blood. His eldest brother Dick had turned professional as a two-pounds-a-bout boxer when Randy was only nine, and he was now establishing himself as a serious fighter. Jackie was also handy with his fists, but Gibbs and Stefani knew that the jewel in the family crown, and the kid who had everything, was young Randy. The following year, in 1943, when aged only fifteen, Turpin won the British junior 112 lb championship. In 1944 he won the British junior 133 lb championship, bringing even further glory to the name of Leamington Spa Boys' Club. However, with a war raging across the globe, nothing was going to be simple, including making a career and progressing as a boxer. His older brother Dick had joined the army and was on active duty, while Jackie had decided to join the Royal Navy. 'Licker' had now left school and was working as a labourer in a local builder's yard, but he decided to join the Royal Navy where he was assigned to duties as an assistant cook. This gave him plenty of time to continue to box, and in 1945 he achieved a unique double by winning both the junior ABA 147 lb British championship and the senior ABA title, which made him both the youngest boxer, and the first black boxer, to win an ABA senior championship. He also won the navy title, the Inter-Services title, and the following year the ABA senior middleweight championship. Those knowledgeable about the sport recognised the 'Leamington Licker' as the outstanding amateur boxing prospect in the country and the boy was still only seventeen.

After the war, 'Licker' returned to Leamington Spa and continued to fight as an amateur, but to him it made little financial sense, although both John 'Gerry' Gibbs and Ron Stefani were keen for him to remain an amateur and compete for an Olympic gold medal at the 1948 games in London. His brother Dick had already resumed his professional career, and Jackie, a promising featherweight, was also now ready to join the professional ranks and start earning some real money. In September 1946, eighteen-year-old Randolph Turpin became the third family member to box professionally, like his brothers before him, he did so under the management of a modest local businessman with round scholarly glasses and a pencil-thin moustache named George Middleton. With an outstanding amateur record of ninety-five victories against just five losses, all the London managers were clamouring for Randy Turpin's signature, but the teenager preferred to remain with a local man whom he knew and trusted, rather than sign with a big-name manager. 'Licker's' professional career began handily enough on 17 September, 1946 with a first-round technical knockout of a journeyman named Gordon Griffiths. The boxing press were convinced that the youngster had made a successful transition to the professional ranks and one of them wrote: 'The way Turpin leapt on Griffiths, like a bronze tiger devouring a tethered kid, battering him halfway through the ropes until the referee intervened in the first round, was enough to prove that a new middleweight menace had arrived.' Thereafter, young Turpin put together an impressive string of twelve victories in 1947, often appearing on the undercard of fights that included his better known older brother, Dick. His progress was extremely impressive, but at nineteen he was not yet old enough to fight for a British title. In fact, the rules had only recently been changed to allow a black boxer to contest for a British title, and both George Middleton, and perhaps more importantly, the Turpins' mother, wanted Dick to have first crack at a title fight.

Professionally, things were undoubtedly progressing well for Randy, but the teenager's personal life was beginning to show signs of considerable strain. The Turpin boys, Dick, Jackie, and Randy, known collectively in the boxing fraternity as 'the dark threats', all had an eye for a pretty girl, and they were tough, they were cocky, and they walked with a considerable swagger. Local girls found the boys attractive, particularly young Randy who, despite his youth, seemed to rule the roost. Among Randy's sparring partners at the Leamington Boys' Club was a young Irish middleweight named Mick Stack who, although he was destined to never make the top grade as a professional, already showed considerable courage inside the ring. 'Licker' Turpin was often short of sparring partners, not only because of his renowned skill, but because he didn't seem to know when to go easy on those of lesser ability. Any sign of weakness was likely to be met with a beating, but equally any sign of resistance was taken as an affront and the young fighter would begin to dish out punishment. In short, Turpin was as much a 'hard case' in the gym as he was in the streets, and beyond his brothers, Dick and Jackie, there were few who dared to tie on a pair of gloves and give him a workout. But not fearless Mick Stack, who could not only hold his own, but he sometimes extended Turpin in a manner that others seldom could.

The Stack family were immigrants from County Cork, and Mick's older brother Willie had already enjoyed a relatively successful career as an international amateur. They were a plain-speaking, working-class family, and it was the sister, Mary Theresa Stack, who really attracted Randy's attention. As he had begun to climb up the amateur ranks he had started to spend more and more time with Mary, looking to create with her the kind of domestic safety and comfort that was missing from his own turbulent upbringing. However, Mary Stack had grown up with two tough brothers, and she had learned how to raise her own voice and make clear what her own needs and demands were. In short, Mary Stack was no pushover, and while Randy may have intimidated some of the men and boys of Leamington Spa, Mary Stack had her own ideas on what she wanted and how she expected to be treated.

On 17 March, 1945, while still an amateur and on leave from the navy, and during his preparations for his first ABA final, seventeen-year-old 'Licker' Turpin was discovered in his mother's home collapsed on a sofa having clearly drunk some liniment. Beattie knew that her son had recently had a row with his girlfriend Mary Stack, but she tried not to get involved with his relations with girls. Beattie preferred to adopt the 'boys will be boys' philosophy and trust that in time all three of her lads would find themselves a nice girl and settle down. However, her youngest son was not only the most headstrong, she knew that he was also the most emotionally vulnerable. Seeing him lying semi-conscious on her sofa set off alarm bells that had been primed for years and she quickly called the doctor, and while she waited for his arrival she tried to revive Randy. Once the doctor arrived he realised that the patient was incapable of answering any questions and so he called an ambulance and had the young lad dispatched straight to the hospital. Questions as to how this 'accident' had occurred could be asked later.

Turpin was treated at Warwick Hospital, where they immediately pumped his stomach. However, once 'Licker' was left alone he sneaked out of the ward in his pyjamas and made his way back to his mother's house. The police soon arrived at Beattie's place to question her youngest son, but Turpin had once again 'escaped' out of a back window and into the night. After a short search, he was found hiding in a telephone box. Under interrogation 'Licker' admitted to the police that he had intended to kill himself by ingesting the liniment – 'I was fed up. That's why I took it.' The problem with his testimony was that prior to the Suicide Act of 1961 self-murder was a crime, and anyone who attempted and failed to kill themselves could be prosecuted and imprisoned. Irrespective of how depressed the young fighter might have been after a row with his girlfriend, he had, in fact, committed a serious offence. The following day he was charged at Warwick Magistrates' Court and remanded to appear the next week.

The few days' delay was absolutely crucial in terms of preparing a defence for the young fighter. His solicitor insisted that the first thing Turpin should do was to deny that there had been any intent on his part to commit suicide, and thereby effectively retract his confession. Thereafter, character witnesses were called to testify to the lad's stability and good nature. His former employer relayed how sorry he had been to lose young Turpin to the navy, while a representative from the Boys' Club insisted that success had not really spoiled the town's most promising sportsman. An officer from the Royal Navy, who travelled all the way from Portsmouth, was perhaps the most persuasive voice of all. He claimed that during his short service as an assistant cook, the young man had proved himself both reliable and modest. Furthermore, the boy was due to fight at Wembley in the ABA championships at the end of the following week. It made no sense that he would deliberately attempt to commit suicide when he had the whole world at his feet, and a bright and promising future before him. Mary Stack was neither called nor was she present in court, but despite the gravity of the situation Turpin felt at ease, for the pair of them had patched up their disagreement. Weighing all possible options, the bench decided that leniency was in order and, having issued a stern warning to Turpin, they bound the young fighter over to keep the peace and be of good behaviour for two years.

Two years later, in 1947, Randolph Turpin married Mary Stack. They were both teenagers, but their relationship had endured for some years and despite occasional irrational outbursts of emotion on both sides, to most locals they appeared to be well suited. After all, they had both grown up as 'outsiders' in the same town, they had many friends in common, and both families were familiar with each other. The Turpin–Stack white wedding took place at

Leamington Spa's Catholic Church out of deference to the bride's family's beliefs, but Randy was so befuddled by the details of the ceremony that when the priest placed a small stool before him at the alter, he shifted it behind him and sat down. This caused his brother Jackie, who was seated in the front pew, no end of laughter, but Mary and her family were not amused. The priest took charge of the situation and leaned forward and whispered to the squatting bridegroom, 'You kneel on it.'

How well Randy and Mary were *actually* suited to each other was something that others, including Turpin's brothers, had their own ideas about. There was only one way of doing things to Randy's mind, and that was his way, and this had always been his modus operandi since he was a small child. However, as most people know, marriage involves both compromise and accommodation of the other person's views, but whatever else Randy felt for young Mary, he was sure that her first duty was to obey him. She soon became pregnant, and a son, Randolph Junior, was born in 1948, but by this stage things between the newly-weds had become increasingly ugly. Mary had already left her husband on a number of occasions, and fled back to her mother's house alleging assault and abuse. In June 1948, following a flare-up between Turpin and his mother-in-law, Mary left yet again and this time took a job at the local Marlborough Hotel, claiming that as far as she was concerned her marriage was over. After his wife's departure, training for professional fights, with all the focus and intensity that is necessary for success at this level, became increasingly problematic for Randy. He could dominate in the boxing ring, but outside of the ring he appeared to be just another voice among many to whom his wife seemed to pay attention. George Middleton and Randy's brothers worried that these days so much of 'Licker's' emotional energy seemed to be being spent trying to control Mary. It concerned them that perhaps this marriage might eventually cost him his boxing career, but they chose not to say anything to 'Licker', for any criticism was likely to be met with either silence, or abuse, or both.

A month later, on 12 July, 1948, Mary and Randy reconciled and she moved back into the family home on Wathen Road in Warwick. Her mother and her brothers, Willie and Mick, were disappointed with her decision, but they knew full well that their sister was as headstrong and difficult as any man and there was little point in arguing with her. Obviously it was her wilful personality that had, in the first place, attracted Turpin to Mary, however, as is so often the case, the very thing that drew him close to her eventually grew to frustrate him the most. Less than a month after their reconciliation, on 9 August, 1948, Turpin was summoned to appear at Warwick Magistrates' Court where Mary claimed that on 24 July he had viciously beaten her and caused her actual bodily harm. According to Mary's testimony, on that day the couple had attended a funfair in Leamington, but Mary had decided to catch an early train back to Warwick at 9:35 p.m. She then waited up for her husband to return, but she became increasingly concerned by his late arrival. According to her testimony, her husband eventually rolled in at 5:30 a.m, and when she asked him where he had been he took up a broom and beat her with it until the handle broke. Screaming that he should stop hitting her for she was pregnant with another child, his wife claimed that Turpin then began to kick her repeatedly in the stomach saying that he would 'soon fix that'.

The following morning the doctor visited, and having examined Mary Turpin he treated her for bruises to her stomach and groin. After the doctor's departure, Mary told the court that she did not immediately flee the house for Randolph Junior was unwell and she made a decision to wait until her son felt better. Once her son had regained his health she called a taxi and left Randolph Junior behind with a note which read: 'Dear Randolph, I am leaving you with the baby because you can look after it better than I can. I prefer being out at work and having evenings free. I can't be at work and looking after the baby at the same time.' According to Mary, the strange tone of the message can be explained by her claim that her husband had forced her at knifepoint to write the self-incriminating note before allowing her to flee the house. She characterised him as a habitually violent bully who never hesitated to use his fists upon her to settle any arguments that they might have. According to Mary Turpin, he was a man who might be the pride and joy of sports fans in the East Midlands, but behind that quiet, self-effacing exterior was a violent, insecure man who had never learned how to curb his temper or face up to any responsibilities.

When it was Turpin's turn to speak he told the court that he had once hit her, but he insisted that his wife had spent the greater part of their time together goading and baiting him. According to his testimony, she tried to make him lose his temper by accusing him of seeing other women, or by throwing things at him or, on one occasion, actually threatening him with a knife. Turpin steadfastly denied having had any affairs, although the evidence was overwhelming that he was a habitual offender, and eventually Mary felt that she had no choice but to produce a letter that was allegedly written by a girl named Pam. 'My own darling Randy,' it began, 'Just remember I love you and I will prove how much when I see you again.' It was signed 'Your ever loving Pam.' Turpin's solicitor claimed that although his client knew of the girl, he denied that Turpin had ever seen the letter. He then quickly changed the subject and claimed that it was a known fact that men who made their living hitting people knew how to keep their tempers in control out of the ring. He concluded that all the evidence pointed towards nothing more than a strained relationship between two young and inexperienced people. The magistrates, having examined the evidence, felt inclined to agree with Turpin's solicitor and they dismissed Mary Turpin's case against her husband.

Unfortunately, Turpin's victory in the courtroom was not matched by his performance in the ring. In the middle of this turbulence, in April 1948, having amassed an outstanding record of eighteen wins and one draw since his professional debut two years earlier, Turpin lost on points to a relatively unheralded journeyman named Albert Finch. The newspapers claimed that Turpin fought as though his heart was no longer in boxing, and they speculated that although his older brother Dick was his next logical opponent, it appeared as though there was some kind of agreement that the two would not fight one another. In fact, it was their mother, Beattie, who had drawn a promise from both Dick and Randy that they would never 'go at each other' for money, but his reluctance to fight his brother had not contributed towards Randy's loss of form. Those close to Turpin knew that the real reason behind the fighter's shocking capitulation to Finch was Turpin's frustration at his inability to persuade his wife to accede to his demands. In every other area of his life Turpin was able to insist that people follow his line, but there was something humiliating about his failure to control young Mary Stack, and it caused him anguish to the extent that he was incapable of fully concentrating on his boxing career.

The loss to Finch in April 1948 was followed by an easy victory over an unimpressive opponent, Alby Hollister, and then in September 1948, as the contentions court case with his wife drew to a conclusion, he turned in possibly the worst performance of his boxing career against a modest fighter named Jean Stock. To those who looked on at ringside it was barely conceivable that the man they were watching was the feared 'Leamington Licker'. For the first four rounds Turpin was continually bullied, beaten, and knocked over, and at the end of the fifth round, much to everybody's astonishment, he simply gave up and retired. As in the case of his shocking loss to Albert Finch some five months earlier, career obituaries were prepared for him, but most pressmen acknowledged that it was Turpin's fragile mental state, not his physical prowess, that was the source of the crisis. In fact, in the dressing room, before the bout against Jean Stock had even begun, Randy had told his eldest brother that he did not want to fight and he would not be at all surprised if he lost. Dick tried to pull Randy together, as did Jackie, but they both understood that the humiliation of Mary having been awarded custody of Randy Junior earlier in the day was weighing heavily on their brother's mind. As it transpired, the result of the fight was an even greater embarrassment than the earlier loss to Albert Finch and, for the first time in his life, Turpin decided to take a prolonged break from boxing in an attempt to make sense of his personal life and gain some peace of mind.

After a five-month layoff, Turpin returned to the ring in 1949 determined that he would avenge his two defeats and re-establish himself as a championship-class fighter. He fought and won convincingly eight times in 1949, and then four times in 1950, before being once again matched against Albert Finch, who had recently beaten his older brother, Dick, to become the British middleweight champion. On 17 October, 1950, a dominating victory over Finch established Turpin back at the top of the British rankings. Peter Wilson's report in the *Daily Express* reflected the general enthusiasm which greeted Turpin's victory. 'Turpin, shaven-headed, his sleek brown body gleaming, his black-gloved fists weaving a deadly pattern of destruction through the smoke-scrawl over the ring, looked like some copper-coloured warrior of the Frontier days . . .' Just over four months later, on 27 February, 1951, in an astounding display of menace and brutality, Turpin defeated the Dutchman

Luc Van Dam in only forty-eight seconds to become the European middleweight champion. The ferocity of Turpin's assault was such that the Dutchman was unconscious in the ring for a full ten minutes, and the doctor had to attend to him where he lay. Turpin then knocked out his former adversary Jean Stock in five rounds, thus avenging his earlier defeat, and he quickly followed up this victory with three more sensational knockout wins. It was clear that there was nobody left in Britain, or Europe, who was a match for the twenty-two-year-old from Leamington Spa, and talk now began to turn to the possibility of Turpin moving up in weight. However, before this idea could be seriously considered, the London promoter Jack Solomons hit upon the unlikely idea of the young coloured boy tackling the great Sugar Ray Robinson.

After the mayor's victory reception at Leamington Spa Town Hall, Randolph Turpin stayed 'home' for a few days. He and Jackie would often take a purposeful walk down to the Cassino Milk Bar, where crowds of girls would gather around to bask in the aura of the town's most famous son. Although to many, particularly some of the older townsfolk, Randolph Turpin would never be anything other than a coloured bully, his unexpected success meant that he now walked tall in Leamington Spa. The weekend after his victory he fulfilled a promise to a friend, Charlie Hickman, by putting in an appearance at his fairground boxing booth, which was visiting nearby Kenilworth. All three Turpin brothers had, in common with most fighters of the period, earned extra 'illegal' money taking on allcomers at the boxing booths. The heavy drunks provided smaller 'pros' with a chance to hone their evasive skills and practise 'dirty' tactics such as butting or elbowing, or hitting in the 'breadbasket' so that they could keep these bigger men at bay. When Turpin appeared at Charlie Hickman's booth the crowds were astonished, and could scarcely believe their luck that they were being presented with an opportunity to witness an actual world champion who, although he did not box, refereed two bouts. But Turpin's days of levity and indulgence, which revolved almost exclusively around casual encounters with 'birds' and triumphant public appearances, soon came to an end when George Middleton informed his fighter that Robinson had inserted a clause in the contract which guaranteed that, in the unlikely event of a defeat, there would be a rematch within ninety days. Having consulted with Jack Solomons, the two men had decided to honour the clause and had therefore signed to fight a rematch in two months' time in New York City. They could have simply ignored the clause and taken a few easy title defences in Europe before eventually agreeing to meet Robinson, but George Middleton felt duty-bound to honour the contract and the money being offered for the rematch was astronomical by any standards. It was proposed that Turpin would be paid $207,075, while Robinson, despite being the challenger, would receive the larger amount of $248,491.

Almost immediately, Turpin returned to train at Gwrych Castle in Wales where Leslie Salts quickly erected a new sign which read:

COME AND MEET A WORLD CHAMPION
AT SUNNY GWRYCH CASTLE.
HAVE YOUR PHOTO TAKEN WITH RANDY TURPIN

Visitors arrived in their thousands, and after long days working out, Leslie Salts sometimes had Turpin autographing photographs late into the night. Salts claimed that all of the money from the sale of Turpin's photographs was going to the Blind Institute, although both Jackie Turpin and George Middleton had their doubts. Turpin was a good trainer, and he was always out of bed early and ready to do his exercises overlooking the Irish Sea and, much to George Middleton's relief, it appeared that Turpin's relative isolation in Wales was enabling him to refocus his mind on the task at hand. Every few days the press would appear at Gwrych Castle and Turpin would tell them about how he had been relaxing by spending time in the petting zoo at the castle, or amusing himself with some knife-throwing or archery. He said that in the evenings he listened to music or went to the local pictures, or simply read his Tarzan comic books. What he did not tell them about were the young local girls with whom he amused himself, and the vast number of photographs that Salts encouraged him to sign. However, despite the official, and unofficial, distractions in the castle, Turpin remained an assiduous trainer and towards the end of July he even fought an exhibition bout in Portsmouth on a bill that was topped by his brother Jackie. After a month's intensive work, the Turpin entourage was ready to sail to the United States where Britain's middleweight world champion would make his first title defence.

On 15 August, 1951, the *New York Times* announced the departure of Turpin from Britain. 'Wearing a black beret at a rakish angle, the quiet, smiling champion waved goodbye to cheering crowds as he boarded a train for Southampton. Tomorrow he will leave England on the *Queen Mary* for New York. In an unusual outburst of oratory, Turpin told fans, "Well, I'm on my way at last and I will not let the British people down. I'm going to win."' The passage on the luxury ocean liner was largely uneventful, but because they were travelling in first class the Turpin party were made to feel extremely comfortable. Both Dick and Jackie Turpin were among the fighter's team, along with George Middleton, and Jack Solomons and his wife, but Leslie Salts had decided to fly to New York. Everybody, except Turpin himself, seemed to feel that things would be better if the irritating Leslie Salts had stayed at home in Britain, but fearful of upsetting Turpin's mental state nobody had dared to make the suggestion. The *Queen Mary* possessed a fully equipped gymnasium and so, after doing 'roadwork' on the deck early each morning, Turpin was able to keep up his training routine. Flying, of course, was not a possibility for Turpin, or any fighter, for since the tragic death of the French boxer Marcel Cerdan, as he crossed the Atlantic on an ill-fated flight to New York, promoters had insisted that boxers minimise all travelling risks. The afternoons on board the *Queen Mary* dragged, and formal dinners with evening gowns for the ladies and tuxedos for the men were an interesting novelty for the Turpin boys, and they took great care to make sure that they were always immaculately dressed. After seven days, on 22 August, 1951, the *Queen Mary* docked on the West Side of Manhattan and Randolph Turpin set foot on American soil for the first time.

On reaching New York City, the Turpin group checked into the Hotel Edison on West 47th and Broadway, an acclaimed and opulent hotel close to the lights and glamour of Times Square. The art deco luxury palace, which featured an elegant marble and steel lobby, was a hotel that was familiar with the rigmarole of accommodating sporting celebrities. To Turpin's great surprise, it appeared that all of America wanted to know about this 'Limey' who had defeated the great Sugar Ray Robinson in London, and both radio and newsprint journalists immediately descended upon him with questions about how he had managed to beat Robinson in London, and how he regarded his chances in New York. Despite his convincing victory in their first fight, the bookmakers had Turpin pegged as a six-to-four underdog, but not wishing to antagonise his hosts, Turpin was careful to appear only modestly confident. 'The Battle of Nations', as the fight was advertised, would take place at Harlem's famous Polo Grounds at 155th Street, the home of the New York Giants baseball team, and a place that was also a popular boxing venue. In 1923, Jack Dempsey had knocked out Luis Firpo in front of 90,000 fans at the Polo Grounds, and the 61,370 tickets available for the Robinson–Turpin rematch had sold out almost the instant they went on sale. American interest was huge, and the projected gate receipts of $767,626 had already shattered the record for a non-heavyweight fight.

Jack Solomons and George Middleton limited the

fighter's exposure to the press and Turpin soon settled into a disciplined training routine at Grossinger's training camp, where the public could pay two dollars and come and watch 'The Man Who Beat Sugar Ray Robinson' sparring. Grossinger's was situated about one hundred miles north of New York City, high up in the Catskill Mountains. It was a country-club-style hotel, with a golf course, a restaurant, and extensive acreage and outbuildings, including an airport hangar where a ring had been constructed. An impressive Turpin punished his four American sparring partners and it was clear that he was in first rate physical condition and, if anything, even stronger than he had been for the original bout. Despite the manifold temptations of New York City, Turpin appeared to be resisting the lure of the city's nightlife and applying himself to his work but, as the fight drew nearer, there *were* worries in Turpin's camp about the fighter's mental state and, once again, the main problem was women.

Relations between Turpin and his wife Mary had irretrievably broken down, so much so that they were barely on speaking terms. It was not just her allegations of Turpin's violence towards her that had driven a wedge between the couple, but she was unable to cope with the humiliation of Turpin's persistent infidelity. Her tight-knit family rallied to her side and opinions in Leamington Spa were polarised as to the behaviour of the 'hero' Turpin towards his wife. There were still some people who had not forgotten how young Turpin would occasionally harass any who crossed his path, and no amount of public glory or sporting achievement was going to change their low opinion of him.

When his wife's allegations of violence became public, many people shunned both Turpin and his family. However, there were also those who regarded the Stack family with some suspicion, and although they knew that the Turpins, like all families, had their faults, they had no desire to see them vilified. Whatever the rights or wrongs of the situation, Mary Turpin had clearly taken all she could endure and Turpin had boarded the *Queen Mary* for New York knowing that at some point in the near future he was going to be faced with very public, and undoubtedly expensive, divorce proceedings.

That Turpin would be unfaithful to his wife was hardly a surprise to any who knew him. After all, he had not even been faithful to Mary Stack while they were courting, and his reputation as a fit, handsome man who liked to chase, and be chased by, the ladies was well earned. However, 'managing' women was something that a man with a controlling personality like Turpin's was unsuited to, for he could hardly expect to exercise authority over every woman that he was involved with. His manager worried about his interest in women for different reasons, for it had long been assumed that too much sex sapped a fighter's strength and made him vulnerable in the ring. Most fighters were encouraged to stay away from 'female temptation' for at least five or six weeks before a bout, the belief being that this pent-up frustration would result in a ferocious outpouring of energy when it was time to fight. However, Turpin's normal schedule of regular fighting, plus his inability to pass by a pretty girl, meant that this theory was never really tested in his case. Sugar Ray Robinson, on the other hand, not only believed in the theory, he practised it. In his autobiography he wrote, 'One of the big sacrifices in being a champion is sex. If you're a fighter, you need your energy. You can't leave it with a woman, even if she's your wife.' He believed that abstinence gave a fighter both a physical and a psychological advantage. 'In abstaining from it, you're not only stronger, but you *think* you're stronger. You're meaner because your nervous system is on edge. And when you walk into the center of the ring for the referee's instructions and stare at your opponent, you dislike him more than ever because he's the symbol of all your sacrifices. But for a weak one, a sneaker, as trainers call them, sex works the other way. When he goes into the ring, he's got a guilty conscience. He doubts his stamina. He believes that his opponent is better conditioned than he is. Mentally, he's beaten before the bell rings.'

George Middleton's biggest fear was that the alluring sights and sounds of New York City would prove an irresistible distraction for his fighter, for after all Manhattan was a world away from the drab, run-down, post-war East Midlands. Initially, Turpin seemed to be handling things with level-headed maturity, fielding journalists' questions and saying all the right things about the training facilities and his American sparring partners. However, as the fight drew closer things began to change. When they had initially checked into the Hotel Edison, the Turpin party had been greeted by a high society coloured lady who seemed to specialise in facilitating negro celebrities and making them feel at home. She informed George Middleton that the following morning there would be a reception in Harlem with food and entertainment where the negro 'smart set' would like to meet Randy. Although George Middleton cared little for such distractions, and would have preferred his fighter to skip the appointment, the Turpin brothers and, more importantly, Jack Solomons, were keen to oblige. Solomons feared the negative publicity if it ever leaked out that Turpin had snubbed coloured society, while the Turpin brothers were simply curious to see how coloured Americans lived. The following morning they arrived at the grand Harlem brownstone to discover that, even at this early hour, a party was already in full swing. The society host was keen to introduce the world champion to everybody present for, after all, he was the guest of honour, but she seemed particularly keen that he should make the acquaintance of a strikingly attractive young coloured woman in her early twenties called Adele Daniels, who, according to the hostess, was particularly excited to meet the world champion. Dick Turpin looked on and mentioned to George Middleton how attractive the young woman was, but Middleton's reply neatly summed up his concerns. 'A bit too good-looking,' was all he said. During the course of the next few days, Turpin appeared to be focused and the move to the Catskills took place without incident. However, George Middleton's concerns appeared to be well founded when Miss Adele Daniels began to appear whenever his fighter made a public appearance, and then, much to Middleton's consternation, Turpin began to leave Grossinger's and accompany her on private shopping trips when he had finished his daily training sessions.

On the evening of 10 September, 1951, less than three weeks after Turpin had stepped off the *Queen Mary*, hostilities with Sugar Ray Robinson began anew. After the first fight in London, Robinson had candidly declared, 'You were real good. I have no alibis. I was beaten by a better man,' but Robinson had absolutely no intention of allowing this to happen again. Having been bullied and outmuscled in London, Robinson weighed in 3 lb heavier for this fight and was determined to master the Englishman's strength and awkward crouching style. He remembered Turpin as being 'built like a heavyweight', and he never understood how a mere 160 lb were packed into his body. 'He should have weighed 190,' said Robinson. This time Robinson was prepared for Turpin's 'ruffian' tactics and, like the 61,370 people packed into Harlem's Polo Grounds, he was convinced that he would recapture the world title that he had 'accidentally' relinquished at the end of his gruelling European tour. His confidence was reflected in the bookmaking which, despite his being the challenger, made him a heavy favourite. As referee Ruby Goldstein signalled the fifteen-round championship bout to begin it soon became clear that, although Turpin was moving well, Robinson was now in first-class condition. His punching was crisp and his attention was fully focused on the task at hand. As the rounds unfolded it was apparent to George Middleton and the champion's brothers that Turpin's work rate was not what it had been in London, for his tempo kept dropping and he was occasionally taking breaks on the ropes and simply bobbing and weaving to avoid Robinson's precise punching. An early vicious left hook by

Robinson had shaken Turpin to his boots and, unlike the fight in London where Turpin had continually pressed the attack, he was spending the greater part of this fight covering up and counterpunching.

As the fight moved into the tenth round, the bout remained even on the referee's scorecard with four rounds for each man, and one round drawn, but the partisan crowd were now beginning to show signs of worry for it was clear that this Limey's victory had been no fluke. Turpin was a hell of a fighter, and the crowd soon received further proof of this fact when midway through the tenth round a swinging right from Turpin caused a cut over Robinson's left eye that began to gush blood at such a rate that it seemed inevitable that the fight would soon be stopped and Turpin would retain his title. Sensing his chance of regaining the world crown slipping away, Robinson cut loose into Turpin's body with hard punches and then followed up with right and left hooks to the head. Instead of backing away and defending himself, Turpin unwisely tried to meet fire with fire and was caught by a swinging right cross which sent him spinning to the canvas. The crowd roared and the referee began a count which Turpin could clearly hear. He rose at seven and shook his head as he tried to regain his senses, but he was immediately pinned back against the ropes by another ferocious assault by Robinson, who slashed at a sagging opponent who was suddenly proving to be an easy target. Normally a referee might have allowed the fight to continue to the bell, thereby giving the champion time to have a breather and come out fresh for another round, but on this occasion – Robinson having hit Turpin thirty-one times in just twenty-five seconds – Goldstein waved his hands in the air and stopped the fight with a mere seven seconds of the round remaining. The ferocious baying of the Polo Grounds crowd, and the referee's awareness of the recent death in the ring of a fighter named Jose Flores, probably encouraged Goldstein to draw proceedings to a halt. Randolph Turpin's reign as world middleweight champion was over; it had lasted just sixty-four days.

After the fight an unhappy Turpin claimed, 'He should not have stopped it. With only seven seconds to go I was perfectly keen.' It is certainly possible that a revived Turpin might have emerged for the eleventh round and opened up more damage on Robinson's badly cut eye, forcing the referee to stop the fight, but the referee had made his decision. Randolph Turpin was no longer champion of the world, and Jack Solomons began to immediately negotiate for a deciding fight, insisting that this was something that both fighters would welcome. However, most fight fans knew that Sugar Ray Robinson would be in no hurry to once again risk either his reputation or his title against a warrior like Turpin, at least not in the foreseeable future. Back at the Hotel Edison the Turpin party licked their collective wounds, while in the streets of Harlem thousands of revellers celebrated long into the night. A few days later, as Turpin, with newly straightened hair, made ready to board the ship that would take him back across the Atlantic Ocean, those in Turpin's party noticed that a beaming Adele Daniels was standing at dockside eagerly waving off the former world champion boxer. Nobody said anything to Turpin about the woman's presence, although it was clear that not one among them either approved of, or trusted, this coloured American woman who may well have disrupted Turpin's preparations more than they had initially realised.

Before Turpin had left Britain for the rematch with Robinson, George Middleton had already arranged for his fighter to undertake a nationwide tour of music halls and theatres on his return home. There was no provision in Turpin's lucrative contract for the tour to be curtailed, or the money altered, in the event of Turpin losing his world title, so this was a piece of shrewd business on Middleton's part. When the defeated champion returned home, he was relieved to discover that his popularity had by no means been adversely affected by his recent setback. In fact, there was considerable excitement when both George Middleton and Jack Solomons announced that not only were they still trying to negotiate for a third Robinson bout, but there was the distinct possibility that in the meantime Turpin would challenge the American Rocky Graziano for a huge sum of money. American bouts aside, Turpin remained British and European middleweight champion and the British public were clearly still willing to spend money to see their sporting hero defend these titles.

Soon after their arrival, Turpin made it clear to George Middleton that he was not altogether keen on the theatrical tour, but he could not argue with a weekly income in excess of £1,000 for barely breaking sweat. The main staple of the 'performances' were exhibition bouts with either his brother Dick or Jackie, and perhaps a little work on the punchbag and a display of his prowess on the speedball. In each city an appeal was made to promising fighters to come out and spar a few rounds with the champion, but after a near-tragedy in Birmingham few took Turpin up on his offer. During the second performance on a midweek night at the Birmingham Hippodrome, a local lad went two rounds with Turpin, but on leaving the ring he suddenly collapsed. In the end the young man recovered, but members of the public were now very cautious about risking their health against Randolph Turpin. Moving from town to town, doing little more than shadow-boxing alongside singing and dancing acts, clowns, and even pet acts, the novelty of this way of making money soon wore off. Luckily, by the time December rolled around the tour was over, for most of the theatres needed their stages for pantomime season, and Turpin was once again free to turn his mind to the more pressing business of his boxing career. In June 1952, having decided to temporarily step up a division, Turpin won the British and Empire light-heavyweight title, stopping a gallant Don Cockell in the eleventh round despite the fact that his opponent outweighed him by 12 lb. However, by this stage, it was becoming evident to those close to Turpin that the fighter was experiencing serious difficulties managing his finances.

Although Turpin had recently made plenty of money by appearing on stage, in addition to the large sums that he was earning from boxing, the fighter was spending his income at a reckless rate. After the Robinson defeat in New York, Turpin had informed a surprised George Middleton that in future he wished to take total responsibility for his own financial affairs. Up until this stage in Turpin's professional life as a fighter, George Middleton had countersigned all of Turpin's cheques and made sure that the boxer's accounts were kept in order. When Turpin informed him of his intentions, Middleton was alarmed, but he knew that he was dealing with a grown man and the last thing that he wanted to be accused of was being overly interfering or, even worse, stealing from his fighter. George Middleton knew that he had done his best to instil in his charge the idea that a boxing career is relatively short, and that it can all be over with just one punch, therefore Turpin should be prudent with his money. And Turpin had listened, but Middleton was unconvinced that his words had done little more than pass in through one ear and out through the other. George Middleton agreed to Turpin's demands, but he once again suggested to Turpin that he save his money in the bank, or invest it properly, but he chose to say nothing further and simply made the arrangements for his fighter to take charge of his own financial affairs.

After the Robinson rematch Turpin suddenly realised that he was a rich man. Unfortunately, with his new-found wealth came friends and hangers-on who fed Turpin's ego and whom he, in turn, was able to help out by allowing them to share in his fortune. If a virtual stranger needed a car, or a 'loan' to escape from pressing debt, or money to buy a pub or a business, Turpin was able to put his hand in his pocket and oblige. His own family were given houses and cars, and he bought himself a pair of pet monkeys and a big house in Warwick. If he felt like a break in the south of France or Spain, he would take family and friends, paying for their flights and accommodation, and picking up the bill for everything. His sister Joan, who was a frequent recipient of his generosity, often warned her younger brother to be less extravagant and to remember that it was his money and not anybody else's. However, casually tossing handfuls of banknotes into the air, 'Licker' would remind her that yes, he knew that it was his cash, which was why he would do with it exactly what he pleased.

Turpin did make one investment with his money, but it was hardly one which made George Middleton feel any sense of comfort. In the autumn of 1952, Turpin went into partnership with Leslie Salts, and the two men paid £7,500 each and together purchased a nine-bedroom hotel set on fifteen acres of land situated on a windswept, and somewhat isolated, headland just outside of the town of Llandudno in North Wales. Originally constructed as the Telegraph Inn, from where messages were relayed to Holyhead and Liverpool announcing the impending arrival of ships, it had later been rebuilt as the Summit Hotel and had served as the bar for those who used the Great Orme Golf Club. The golf course had closed in 1939 and become a sheep farm, while the hotel had been allowed to languish and fall into disrepair. The two men had the idea of transforming the hotel, which during the war had been requisitioned by the RAF and utilised as a temporary radar station, into an international sporting centre and tourist attraction and cashing in on the seaside trade. Neither man could have been thinking too clearly, for not only was there little in the way of public transport to the venue, known locally as the Great Orme complex, there was just one, woefully inadequate, telephone line. The view from the summit was undoubtedly panoramic, and the steep slopes flowed down from the hotel on all sides like an attractive green cape. But, in truth, the place offered the visitor little more than a laborious climb on foot, or an ascent in a lumbering tram, to the view. The hotel still sprouted a dense forest of aerials and antennas from its signalling days, and the building appeared to be permanently in transition. Visitors quickly surveyed the rolling hills, wide open sea, and the sumptuous scenery, before realising that it was time to return to Llandudno and, of course, the only way to leave the Great Orme was to descend on foot or by the same inelegant tram. George Middleton had little faith in Turpin's investment, and he had, by this time, conducted a private investigation into Leslie Salts and his business practices, and uncovered a whole series of wrongdoings. Once again he had made clear his reservations to Turpin, but Turpin's mind was made up.

The Great Orme complex opened on Easter Monday 1953 in a blaze of publicity, with telegrams of good luck and congratulations from British sporting heroes such as Dennis Compton and the boxer Freddie Mills; even Sugar Ray Robinson sent a telegram to his old adversary. Turpin's sister Joan and her bricklayer husband, John Beston, were put in charge of the complex, but they had no experience of running such an enterprise and the place was soon leaking money. The situation was not helped by Turpin's habit of turning up with friends from London or the

Midlands and insisting that nobody should pay any bills. The Welsh boxing champion Jimmy Wilde, who between 1916 and 1923 held the world flyweight title, and who was popularly known as 'the ghost with a hammer in his hand', opened Randy's Bar at the centre. However, despite Turpin announcing that he would be spending a good deal of his time at the centre training for his next fight, in the hope that the fee-paying British public might therefore be persuaded to put their hands into their pockets and pay to see him going through his paces, money continued to flow out of, as opposed to into, the venture. An advertisement for the Great Orme Holiday Centre in a 1953 programme for one of Turpin's fights suggests the scale of Salts' and Turpin's ambition. 'Visit Randy's Bar. Fully Licensed. The most unusual bar in Britain! Snack bar, Music, Sports, Exhibitions, Miniature Railway, Little Theatre. See the British Crown Jewels in replica.' The bottom of the advertisement proudly reads 'Owned by Leslie T. Salts and Randolph Turpin (the famous boxer)', and just in case one is still unsure, there are two large headshots of both men smiling intently. However, Turpin was soon asking George Middleton for a loan, and then he turned to Jack Solomons, and although both men were alarmed by Turpin's spending they agreed to help him out knowing full well that there was little point in talking further to the boxer about his cavalier attitude to money.

In the early summer of 1953, the two biggest British news stories were the coronation of Queen Elizabeth II, and the triumphant ascent of Mount Everest by a British expedition led by a New Zealand mountaineer, Edmund

Hillary, and his Nepalese guide, Sherpa Tensing Norkay. Most people were also excited because television, or the 'goggle-box', had become the latest status symbol and the new invention was beginning to change family and social life. However, the vast majority of the British public still got their 'visual' news from the cinema, and the third story that would have gripped British audiences at cinemas up and down the country during the summer of 1953 was the news of Randolph Turpin's triumph over the Frenchman Charles Humez before a sell-out crowd of 54,000 at White City Stadium, London, in the final elimination bout for the now vacant world middleweight crown. Despite having trouble making the weight, Turpin comprehensively outpointed Humez, but not before disappointing a huge number of his own fans with his lacklustre performance. Everybody in Britain knew that Turpin carried a potential knockout punch in both hands, yet for much of the fight he had done little more than flick out timid left jabs, much to the audible dismay of the crowd. Nevertheless, he had beaten Humez, and Turpin would now be returning to New York City, this time to fight the Hawaiian American Carl 'Bobo' Olsen for the undisputed world title in a bout that most boxing cognoscenti confidently expected Turpin to win. Two years after his close rematch with Robinson, Turpin and his party once again found themselves sailing across the Atlantic Ocean towards a New York City that Turpin claimed he was eager to revisit. He told his brothers that he missed the twenty-four-hour excitement of the city, and the attention that he had been paid, but he did not confess to them his ambivalence about having to rekindle his association with Miss Adele Daniels.

Shortly after Turpin's arrival in New York City in October 1953, it soon became clear that, unlike his previous visit in the summer of 1951, when Turpin at least maintained the appearance of being eager to train for the Robinson rematch, this time he was preoccupied and disinterested in applying himself to the task at hand. Frequently absent from the training camp that George Middleton had established in the Catskill Mountains, and distant and sometimes abrasive to those who tried to talk with him, Turpin alienated the press, his camp, and particularly his brothers. It was obvious that Turpin had no desire to fight Carl 'Bobo' Olsen, nor did he wish to be in the United States and away from 'home', and his sulking and temper tantrums quickly wore on everybody's nerves. On the night of the world title fight the inevitable ensued, and what should have been a night of glory for Randolph Turpin and British boxing ended ignominiously with a humiliating defeat at Madison Square Garden. Untrained and out of condition, Turpin nevertheless began strongly enough, taking the first three rounds against Olsen, but in the fourth he suffered a bad cut under his eye. For the remainder of the fight he was off-balance and he constantly soaked up punishment, and in both the ninth and tenth rounds an ordinary-looking Olsen pummelled him to the canvas. Clearly Turpin's mind was elsewhere, and the sell-out crowd witnessed the British middleweight take a terrible pounding before losing a unanimous points decision.

So badly was Turpin beaten that, back at his hotel, his

seconds covered him in ice cubes and wrapped him in a bed sheet in order to reduce the multiple swellings. Turpin knew that he had let himself and others down, but he was acting as though he could not care less. 'If I had been in my natural mental state,' said Turpin, 'I could have stopped him about the eighth round.' Nobody said anything in reply. *Boxing News* summed up the mood of the times: 'If ever a fighter went into the ring mentally unprepared it was Turpin. The undeniable fact is that Turpin has gone back a long way. He has things on his mind more important than boxing and when that happens a fighter has "had it", to use a well-understood expression.' Britain's *Daily Sketch*, under a head-line that blared 'He's let us down!', seemed to be clear about what had gone wrong. 'Now it has been exposed – the myth of the boxer who can train himself. Randolph Turpin made a pathetically heroic effort to justify his unorthodoxy in the Madison Square Garden ring last night.' Turpin's fans on both sides of the Atlantic were clearly dismayed by the fighter's behaviour both before, and during, the fight. But things were about to deteriorate even further.

On the morning of 2 November, 1953, the day before Turpin was due to board the *Queen Mary* for the return journey to England, the 'Leamington Licker' was arrested by New York City police officers in a milk bar opposite the Hotel Edison on West 47th Street. He was listening to the jukebox when the police stormed in and handcuffed him and then took him to the Seventh Precinct for processing. Shortly thereafter, Turpin appeared at the Upper Manhattan Magistrates' Court to answer a serious charge which had been brought against him by a Miss

Adele Daniels, who was described in the court papers as a 'Negro Clerk in the State Department of Labor'. Miss Daniels testified that her relationship with Randolph Turpin had begun two years earlier when the fighter was in New York for his rematch with Sugar Ray Robinson, and she insisted that the boxer had promised to marry her. In the two-year interim she asserted that the couple had exchanged many love letters and were planning a shared future, and that when Turpin had recently returned to New York for the fight with Olsen their relationship had picked up again from where it had left off. However, she claimed that Turpin had changed, and that even before the fight, when he should have been in the Catskill Mountains at his training camp, this newly 'troubled' Turpin was spending time with her at her apartment on Riverside Drive at 125th Street in Harlem, but she grew to be frightened of him. She alleged that Turpin had assaulted her on a number of occasions, kicking her and striking her around the face. In fact, after the Olsen contest, in which the British fighter had been badly beaten and was in need of attention, Miss Daniels claimed to have 'loyally nursed him' and in return for her troubles she was again beaten and kicked by this 'maniacal and dangerous person', so much so that for a short while the left side of her face had suffered temporary paralysis. Miss Daniels' lawyer, Mr J. Roland Sala, wanted Turpin held in custody so that he might be properly examined, for Sala claimed that Turpin was 'definitely mentally ill, psychopathologically'. He continued: 'This man is bestially primitive.'

Turpin's lawyer, Saul Straus, argued that if Miss Daniels

had received the beatings that she claimed to have done, then there would be serious marks on her body. In fact, there were none. George Middleton had already instructed Turpin's lawyer that the key issue here was to get Turpin on the boat to England, and so Straus arranged with the judge for Turpin to be released into his custody with the payment of a $10,000 bond, and a promise that Turpin would eventually return to the United States for the full hearing. In the meantime, Miss Adele Daniels withdrew the assault charge, insisting that she had not been offered money to do so, nor had she been threatened. Mr Sala remained determined, and he made it clear that a civil suit would soon be launched against Turpin, whom he described as 'anti-American'. He continued, claiming that Turpin 'should be everlastingly grateful to our American system of democracy – a system he has maligned and defamed openly and notoriously'. On the following day, the eight members of Turpin's party were able to board the ship and begin their journey back to England.

On his arrival home, Randolph Turpin was greeted by scores of reporters who wanted to know the full story of what had transpired but, at least initially, Turpin was reluctant to speak with them. News had already reached the pressmen that Turpin had been temporarily banned by the New York State Athletic Commission from fighting in the United States, and this seemed to represent a serious professional blow, but when Turpin eventually spoke he was keen to play down the gravity of the situation. He confessed to being shocked by Miss Daniels' charges, for she appeared to him to be a quiet and friendly girl, but he admitted that he had met her before the Sugar Ray Robinson fight in New York, and confirmed that over the past two years they had written to each other. He went on: 'We certainly did discuss marriage but when I came out to the United States the last time I told her it was over. I said, "Forget about me."' But Turpin could not keep his story straight. Sometimes he claimed that she had wanted to come back to England with him, and that's why she brought the charge. On other occasions he denied ever having spoken to her about marriage. However, what was undeniable was the fact that his fractious disputes with Miss Daniels had contributed to his lamentable mental state and ultimately to his losing the Carl 'Bobo' Olsen fight so disastrously. Even more disturbingly, the charges that Adele Daniels had levelled against him were, to those who knew of Turpin's past, suspiciously similar to the charges which Mary Stack had brought.

The *Empire News* was eager to get Adele Daniels' story, and they ran it soon after Turpin's return. She declared that she had 'enjoyed the confidence' of all in Turpin's camp, including his manager and brothers, but it was just Randy himself who had become difficult, strange and moody. According to Miss Daniels, Turpin would often snap at her, and she was continually taken aback by the severity of his mood swings, but those within his camp advised her to say nothing and not to challenge him. Nevertheless, she insisted that she continued to worry about him. 'I begged them to have him examined by a doctor because I thought he was a sick man. I still do. After his fight with Olsen he was worse.' Adele Daniels never explained exactly what sort of sickness she imagined Turpin to be suffering from, but she evidently regarded him as being in the grip of some kind of mental breakdown. She said that on their shopping trips together she would buy the items, for Turpin had no idea of how expensive anything was. On one of these trips, much to her surprise, he purchased a crossbow. She also claimed that she had previously sent Turpin a pair of 'I love you' nylons from New York to England, for he insisted that he had promised his sister, Joan, a present. Some time later she saw a press photograph of Turpin leaving for New York and the Olsen fight, with a girl by his side who was wearing the very same 'I love you' nylons. When she challenged him as to the identity of this girl, he maintained that she was nobody and that things between himself and the girl had finished a long time ago.

Turpin's many relationships with different women had for him always been problematic because, unlike some men who are able to put domestic disputes out of their minds and continue with their lives, Turpin smouldered internally when things did not go *exactly* the way he wanted. He was still preoccupied with Mary Stack, who had made it clear that she wanted absolutely nothing to do with him, for he felt that his former wife had tried her best to poison people's opinion of him. After the Robinson rematch, Turpin had bought Randolph Junior an expensive gold watch back from America, and he ran into Mary and Randolph Junior outside the Cassino Milk Bar in Leamington Spa. She was holding his son, but when Turpin showed the child the watch, the child spat at his father and Turpin's brother, Jackie, led Randy away. 'It ain't the lad's fault,' he said. 'It's only what they've been saying to him' — 'they' being the Stack family. Soon after this incident, the bitter divorce proceedings between himself and Mary reached court, with Mary alleging cruelty on the part of her husband, who in turn claimed that his wife had condoned his alleged cruelty. It was all an extravagant waste of time and money, but finally, on 12 June, 1953, Turpin was divorced by Mary, but Turpin was dismayed to discover that the whole sorry proceedings had cost him almost £10,000. He was granted 'reasonable access' to his son, but the reality was that there would be virtually no further contact at all between father and son.

The divorce settlement may well have cleared up some of the complications of Turpin's relationship with his former wife, but it did little to address his ongoing problems with a number of different women. Turpin liked to keep two or three different women as his 'girlfriends', and most of these 'girlfriends' understood that they were nothing more than temporary entertainment. They were generally happy to bask in the reflected glory of a champion prizefighter, but there were some who wished to be more than this. A week before Turpin departed for the United States and the Olsen fight, he was named as the co-respondent in a divorce suit being brought by the policeman husband of a twenty-four-year-old blonde woman named Pamela Valentine. The woman worked at Gwrych Castle and claimed that their relationship began there, and then continued in London. Turpin, for his part, insisted that he thought the woman was single, and it was only when she asked him for money to buy a Christmas present for her child that he realised that she was married. He was ordered to pay the costs incurred by Mr Valentine in bringing the suit.

On his arrival back in England after the disastrous Olsen fight, a bruised and battered Turpin was met by a twenty-seven-year-old Welsh hill farmer's daughter, Gwyneth Price, who was better known to him, and her friends and family, as Gwen. She was the young woman who Adele Daniels had spotted in the American press photograph wearing the 'I love you' nylons. A few weeks earlier Gwen had waved a hopeful Turpin off at Southampton, having willingly accepted his argument that it was better for them both if she did not accompany him to New York on this particular trip. However, as planned, she was there to welcome him back to England after his shocking defeat, but she was astute enough not to wait for him in plain view of the press. The Turpin party disembarked and prepared to head straight back to Warwickshire, Dick Turpin having answered the journalists' somewhat probing questions about what exactly had gone wrong in New York. Randy took a taxi to the Royal Hotel to rendezvous with Gwen whom he had first met the previous year, in March 1952, when he was training at Gwrych Castle. Her sister Mona had persuaded Gwen to come with her and get the boxer's autograph. A grinning Turpin had charmed the girl into a date in exchange for his signature, and throughout the course of the subsequent year they had both tried to keep their 'friendship' reasonably discreet. Turpin's family cared little for this fiercely loyal Welsh girl from Axton, Flintshire, but Turpin was happy for he seemed to have finally found somebody who he thought understood him. The following day the young couple left Southampton and hid away from the world in a hotel in Devizes, for Turpin was clearly in no frame of mind to submit to the judgemental scrutiny of the world, nor was he ready to resume his responsibilities as a boxer. A vulnerable, and emotionally scarred, Turpin began to increasingly lean upon Gwen for support, and a few days later, on 15 November, the couple checked into the Greyhound Inn in Newport, Wales, and decided to marry without inviting any of the Turpin family to the ceremony, or even informing them of their intentions. Turpin's mother, in particular, was hurt, all the more so as she had still not come to terms with the fact that her youngest son had divorced Mary Stack and, if rumours were to be believed, possibly mistreated her.

However, the biggest cloud hanging over Turpin's head, and one that was potentially far more damaging than his mother's disapproval of who he had married, was the ongoing situation with Adele Daniels. The case was not only proving to be prohibitively expensive in terms of legal fees, but there was also his reputation to defend and the fact that until this dispute was resolved he was effectively banned from fighting in the United States. Adele Daniels' civil case against Turpin reached the courts in late 1954, and the serious allegation of rape was added to the assault charges. Turpin's American lawyer led the fighter to understand that should Turpin lose the case then the settlement was likely to be a payment in excess of $100,000, and this would effectively ruin Turpin for life. Eventually, in

November 1955, a somewhat worried Randolph Turpin
returned to New York City and began to tell a slightly
different tale. He conceded that, back in 1951, if it were
not for the fact that he was still married to Mary Stack,
then he would have married Adele Daniels at the time of
the Sugar Ray Robinson rematch. He admitted the existence of a substantial number of love letters between them,
which included proposals of marriage on his part, but he
was adamant that on returning to New York for the Olsen
fight he had made it very clear to Adele Daniels that
marriage was no longer a possibility. Miss Daniels did not
dispute Turpin's claim that he said he no longer wished
to marry her, but she insisted that one moment he said
that this is what he desired, and the next he would retract
his statement. Clearly his deep ambivalence about marrying
her had served only to inflame her anger. Miss Daniels'
attorney, Mr J. Roland Sala, asserted that Turpin was clearly
unstable, angry, and out of control. He characterised the
defendant as 'a jungle beast in human form, and a dangerous
killer' and said that Miss Daniels had wondered if his
condition had been made worse by the beating that he had
taken. Miss Daniels repeated, and stood by, her claim that
she had suffered blows from Turpin's fists and boots that
had left her psychologically scarred.

On the fourth, and last, day of the trial, the case was
eventually settled after a long discussion between the two
sets of lawyers. Turpin insisted that he had paid Miss
Daniels money for food and rent, and he furiously denied
ever raping or assaulting her. Miss Daniels was adamant
that he had not only done so, but he had said that she

was like all Americans, 'trying to push me around'. She insisted that Turpin had continued and told her in no uncertain terms that, 'I am the master, and in England when I say move they move.' According to Miss Daniels he once assaulted her and then said, 'If you make one step to call the police I'll break your neck and if I don't others will.' When she pressed him as to what exactly he meant, he pointed to his connections in the boxing world. The lawyers listened to their clients' claims and counterclaims, and sensing that these unsupported allegations could go on being made and denied for a long period of time, the potential six-figure settlement was reduced to $3,500 which a frustrated Turpin quickly agreed to pay, thus accepting culpability for some wrongdoings. Miss Daniels had decided to settle for this lesser amount against her lawyer's advice, but like Turpin she too was tiring of these proceedings. Turpin's lawyer quickly attempted to seize the moral high ground, and he issued a statement suggesting vindication for his client. However, a relieved Turpin was by now totally indifferent to any more legal posturing, and he was simply happy to be able to finally put the United States, and the memory of Miss Adele Daniels, behind him.

But what did he have to return to in England? The truth was, in 1955 Turpin was facing serious problems both in the ring and out of it. Two years earlier, after he had returned from the Olsen debacle, George Middleton had encouraged his fighter to undergo a full medical check-up. The doctors soon discovered that not only did Turpin have an enlarged liver, his hearing had grown worse, and his eyesight was deteriorating. In fact, during the voyage to New York for the Carl 'Bobo' Olsen fight, his brother Jackie had noticed that while they were doing their road-work running around the upper deck of the *Queen Mary*, Turpin had a tendency to drift a little and sometimes even run into him. A medical examination soon determined that Turpin could see straight ahead, but his peripheral vision was restricted, which could have serious consequences for a fighter as he would not be able to see some punches coming. On 2 January, 1954, Turpin was fined two pounds at Abergate Magistrates' Court for being in possession of a rifle without a firearms licence, and the gun was confiscated. It was extensively reported in the press that during the court proceedings the fighter's hearing appeared to be impaired, for Turpin was often struggling to hear what was being said in the courtroom, but the British Boxing Board of Control, who could easily have withdrawn his boxing licence, chose to do nothing. In late January 1954, Turpin was charged and convicted of dangerous and care-less driving and fined fifteen guineas, but his driving licence was not confiscated and he continued to drive recklessly. In fact, during the two years between his return from the loss to Olsen, and the Adele Daniels trial in New York, Turpin experienced great difficulty holding his life in order. His worries over his deteriorating relationship with his family, the impending court case in the United States, and his increasingly desperate financial situation, continued to trouble him. But what concerned others was not only what they considered to be his increasingly erratic behaviour, but his declining abilities in the ring.

After the loss to Olsen, Turpin began to lose to men who he should have comfortably beaten. In May 1954 Turpin suffered a first-round knockout in Rome and lost his European middleweight title to a light-puncher named Tiberio Mitri. This was a bout he should have won with ease, and this shocking loss marked the end of any further world title aspirations. Turpin's heart seemed to have gone out of fighting, and on those few occasions when he did muster the energy and focus to take a fight seriously, the press observed that this was clearly not the same fighter who, only a few years earlier, had fought so gallantly against the great Sugar Ray Robinson. His brother Jackie, who during this bleak period continued to spar with Randy, noticed that one moment his brother could be jovial and ready to joke around, and the next moment he could become extremely angry. These sudden and unexpected mood swings were now often accompanied by blinding headaches, but Turpin refused to seek any medical help. The defeats became embarrassing, particularly a fourth-round knockout loss to a 'nobody' named Gordon Wallace in October 1954, a man who managed to floor Turpin four times and embarrass him so badly that Turpin temporarily retired. However, although Turpin's box office status began now to rapidly decline, he needed to fight to make money. In November 1956, Turpin did manage to defeat Alex Buxton and retain his British light-heavyweight title, and he was eventually able to claim a Lonsdale belt outright when he defended his light-heavyweight title for a third time in June 1957, winning a turgid fifteen-round decision over the little known Arthur Howard. But even this no-hoper managed to knock Turpin to the canvas three times during the course of the fight. There was little further glory in 1957, or during the first half of 1958. The half-dozen victories that he was able to accumulate were all achieved against woefully inadequate opposition, yet the cost of these 'triumphs' involved Turpin taking a great deal of physical punishment. The end came in Birmingham on 9 September, 1958, when Turpin was pummelled by a Trinidadian named Yolande Pompey who easily knocked him out in two rounds. The correspondent for the *London Evening Standard* summed things up. 'No doubts now – Turpin is just another fighter . . . the whiplash punch and the split-second timing that once gave him world supremacy have gone. And Turpin must not blame us for noting their passing – with infinite regret.'

It was clear, even to Turpin, that in order to protect his health, and his dignity, he should hang up his gloves. The business of boxing had begun to eat into his body, and although he remained a handsome man who had avoided the hammered spread of a boxer's nose, there was no longer any point to his continuing for he had no title to his name and there was little hope of his ever winning one again. His eyesight was damaged, his hearing was in danger of deteriorating even further, and he no longer had the stomach for the rigid discipline of training and preparing for top-class fights. His professional record of sixty-four wins (forty-five by knockout), eight losses, and one draw was something that he could be proud of, but Turpin was financially destitute, and he had no idea what had happened to all the money that he had earned in the ring. With no other sources of income open to him, he reluctantly accepted George Middleton's offer of employment in his Leamington Spa scrapyard. Turpin began working a nine-to-five shift, driving around picking up old car engines and bits of metal, then taking them back to the scrapyard where he would let loose on them with a sledgehammer. His take-home pay varied between two and four pounds a week, which was a world away from his days of first-class travel, five-star hotels, and custom-made clothes and shoes, but it enabled him to make some kind of a living and afford a small house and a car. But there remained huge debts to the Inland Revenue, and Turpin had no idea how to begin to deal with these issues. He had survived twelve years as a top-class fighter and all he had to show for it were arrears that day and night weighed heavily on his mind. However, one thing he was sure of was the fact that he was finished with boxing. A few years earlier, while trying to forget yet another shocking defeat at the hands of a lesser man, he had written a poem for his manager, George Middleton, expressing his feelings about the sport that had both made him and was now breaking him.

THE COMEBACK ROAD

The comeback road is hard and long
The boys I'll meet will be hard and strong,
But my patience is good,
And my willpower strong.

I'll hear the bell
Which means time to go
But I'll do my best, and I'll have a go
Cause I've got someone to back me.

The manager I've got
Is the one for me
As I know he'll stick
In a real rough sea.

They say I've finished
But I'll prove 'em wrong
And I'll have a go
Cause my patience, willpower, and heart
   are strong.

If I make the grade,
On that one big day
We can look at them all
With a laugh and say,

We've done our best
For the game we love
Now there's no more kicks
And that's real good.

So we'll leave this game
Which was hard and cruel
Then down at the show, on a ringside stool
We'll watch the next man, just one more fool.

The money that Turpin was earning driving around looking for old cars and engines, and then cutting up the debris for George Middleton in his scrapyard, was barely enough to support Gwen and their growing family. Already there were two daughters, and Gwen was pregnant with a third child. Turpin was also finding it difficult to deal with the humiliation of such a public fall from grace. On 15 February, 1959, the *New York Times* ran a story entitled 'Turpin: A Story of Riches to Rags'. It reported that, 'Today, the one-time world champion, who earned more than $500,000, is a junk man. He drives about little Leamington Spa in an old truck picking up scraps of iron, derelict motors and hunks of metal nobody else wants. He takes the collection to the junkyard, batters it and sells the scrap. Turpin, now thirty, does not own the sledgehammer, the truck or the business. But once he was paid $200,000 for a single fight. In those days Turpin wore Savile Row suits and bench-made shoes. Today he wears grubby work clothes. At the peak of his career, he traveled around Europe and America living in the best hotels. Usually he had a few hangers-on. Now his home is a small house on a back-street of an unlovely section of Leamington.'

Being a relatively fit coloured man, who was still a household name in England, there *was* one profession that would welcome Turpin with open arms – the burlesque of wrestling. The bouts were fixed, often crudely so, and the fighters divided into 'good' and 'bad', heroes and villains, with the coloured wrestlers – who fought under pseudonyms such as 'Johnny Kwango' or 'Masambula' – little more than novelty ring-fodder to be thrown around for the comic entertainment of the masses. Turpin began to travel around the country and 'fight' for cash payments which averaged about twenty-five pounds per bout. The money was not great, but the risk of injury was, and Turpin soon began to pick up leg and back injuries, which only added to the ignominy of his present situation and began to depress him even further. By the early sixties, the former world boxing champion began to develop a reputation in wrestling circles for being late, or sometimes forgetting about engagements altogether, and there were rumours that he had started to drink. Friends and family began to notice that his speech was sometimes slurred, and that he was beginning to display a number of signs that he might be growing 'punchy' from his many years in the boxing ring. However, given Turpin's current difficulties, his income as a wrestler was important to him and so, despite his own reservations and his evident discomfort, he persisted with the charade knowing that at some level at least these fight people were 'his people', and wrestling was certainly preferable to making pennies labouring in George Middleton's scrapyard.

Turpin continued to be hounded by the Inland Revenue for taxes that were payable on money that the authorities claimed he had earned at the height of his boxing career. In July 1962 he was formally declared bankrupt with assets of £1,204 and liabilities owing to the taxman of £17,126. This was a sum that had already been considerably reduced from a figure nearer to £100,000 by the tenacity of Max Mitchell, Turpin's accountant. Mitchell had detailed the unorthodox accounting procedures of the promoter Mr

Jack Solomons, and he had drawn the Inland Revenue's attention to the fact that his client had assumed that income tax was being paid by his promoter and his manager. Furthermore, the sums that the Inland Revenue claimed had been paid to Turpin were, according to Mitchell, nowhere near the amounts that Turpin actually received. While Mitchell could not deny that Turpin had made a series of spectacularly bad investments, including the property at Great Orme (which, following an unpleasant split with Leslie Salts, had now been purchased by the Llandudno Urban Council at a loss to Turpin), he pleaded that the Inland Revenue should take into consideration the fact that Turpin was both naïve and somewhat innocent. For instance, everybody knew that Leslie Salts was a con-man, and Turpin was the last to realise that the staff at the Great Orme complex, including John Beston, his brother-in-law, were 'on the take'. In fact, Turpin's belated discovery that Joan's husband had been swindling him prompted him to break the man's nose. Part of Max Mitchell's plea to the Inland Revenue contained the following statement: 'As time goes on, the punching power of a boxer is enfeebled the longer he pursues his profession. His brain through constant pummelling becomes bemused. His eyes are affected. Deafness overtakes him. And in effect he is lucky if in the prime of his manhood he doesn't turn into a two-legged vegetable.'

Aside from bad investments and questionable payment practices, it was apparent that the main reason for Turpin's financial hardship was his propensity, at the height of his earning powers, to give away his money to people who were almost complete strangers. He helped those who claimed that they wished to start taxi companies, or buy pubs, or pay off their mortgages; almost any hard-luck story might well be concluded by a soft-hearted Turpin putting his hand into his pocket and pulling out a bundle of cash. But despite his almost reckless generosity, a part of Turpin remained practical, and after his bankruptcy hearings, Turpin, together with a few friends, began to search out those who had 'borrowed' money from him. He threatened more than one man in an attempt to retrieve his cash, but while some fearfully agreed to reimburse him with a weekly payment, most claimed that they had either lost the money, or it had been stolen from them. Somewhat bitterly, Turpin reflected, 'It cost me bleeding money every time I shook hands with somebody, didn't it?' Keen not to compound his present circumstances by ending up in jail on assault charges, there was little that Turpin could do beyond threaten, but by the mid-sixties most people were no longer in awe of the 'Leamington Licker'.

Back in 1959, Turpin had bought a run-down café in Russell Street, Leamington Spa, called Harold's Transport Café. The place was in a terrible condition, and most people could not understand why Turpin would want to invest in such a low-class, and decidedly unglamorous, business. However, they knew enough about Turpin to know that whatever reservations they might have about this venture would be ignored by him. What made Turpin's acquisition all the more puzzling, and illogical, was the fact that the property had already been condemned for demolition to make way for a car park. Obviously there was no long-term future to this purchase, but Turpin nevertheless went ahead. He renamed the café for his loyal wife, Gwen, and his mother joined the new Mrs Turpin, the two of them working behind the counter serving mixed grills, bacon sandwiches and mugs of tea to lorry drivers and labourers, while upstairs there was a room to rent out should anybody require lodgings. Although his mother was by now almost blind, she enjoyed the work, but her son soon grew to despise Gwen's Transport Café. The income dribbled in as loose change, and the money did absolutely nothing to alleviate his debts, while the customers were often rude, abrasive, and had stopped by merely in the hope of achieving a glimpse of the once famous fighter who had now fallen on hard times. There were those who wished to arm-wrestle him, or even challenge him to mix it up in a fight, but Turpin generally made his excuses and withdrew to the family's small flat above the café where he would read one of his comic books. The half-dozen plain tables were seldom full, but at least the place kept Gwen and Mrs Turpin busy. Sadly, Turpin's mother aside, the rest of his family did not feel welcome in the café. Their relationship with Gwen was, at best, cool, and should any of her husband's brothers or sisters wander in then it was more than likely that Gwen would charge them for their cup of tea. She sensed that as an 'outsider' from Wales they somehow held her responsible for taking Randy away from his close-knit family, but to her way of thinking they were, at the height of his fame, as happy as anybody else to accept his money and exploit his success. She felt that now, when he had little left, they should be made to pay like everybody else. On the wall of their transport café, Randy and Gwen hung a sign which read: 'That which seldom comes back to him who waits is the money he lends to friends.'

Between his wrestling, the meagre income from the café, and labouring, Turpin managed to earn a living in the early sixties, but he continually worried about his mounting debts and his unpaid bills. He was also tormented with concern about the effect that his predicament was having upon Gwen and his daughters, who formed the loving centre of his life. He worked hard to hide his distress from them, and he was largely successful in maintaining the image of a trouble-free, happy, loving father and husband. However, his anxiety over his debts was compounded by the frustration of knowing that he had foolishly allowed others to take advantage of his generous nature and, to some extent, the present situation was entirely one of his own making. Turpin was well aware of the fact that he was hardly the first boxer to fall into financial hardship once his career had concluded. He knew that his own hero, Joe Louis, was struggling with similar problems in the United States, and that he too had taken up wrestling as a way of paying his bills. Joe Louis' wife, Rose, once commented that 'watching Joe Louis wrestle is just the same as watching the president of the United States wash dishes,' to which her husband replied, 'Well, it ain't stealing.' But these problems were not confined to the United States, for back in Britain there were countless examples of once well-known boxers who were now destitute. However, no British boxer had ever risen to the financial and professional heights of a Randolph Turpin, so his fall from grace was spectacular for others to witness, and for Turpin it was excruciatingly painful to endure. In a state of desperation he made two brief, and somewhat embarrassing, returns to the ring, winning a sixth-round knockout over Eddie Marcano at Wisbech, Norfolk, in March 1963, and then a second-round knockout in Malta in January 1964 over Charles Seguna, but neither opponent could really box, and Turpin collected mere loose change for a fee. Both fights were an exercise in humiliation, but at least Turpin finally acknowledged that he could never again fight seriously, for his eyesight had deteriorated to the point where it would be utter folly to fight even an exhibition bout.

In December 1965, Turpin was invited to New York, with all expenses paid, to be part of the extravagant celebrations at Madison Square Garden marking the retirement of the five-time middleweight champion Sugar Ray Robinson. Together with Carl 'Bobo' Olsen, Jake La Motta, Carmen Basilio, and Gene Fullmer, the other men who Robinson had beaten to claim his five titles, Turpin had the opportunity to enjoy one final night in the spotlight. A photograph of Turpin in the ring with the other fighters that evening tells its own story. While everyone gazes at Robinson, Turpin's face is frozen in a half-smile and he stares into the middle distance. His mind is elsewhere, perhaps wondering why he is even present, and he stands awkwardly to one side as though not really a part of this celebration of boxing history. This is particularly ironic given the fact that Robinson made no secret of his admiration for Turpin the man and the boxer, and went to great lengths to make sure that his old adversary would be present on this special occasion. Later that evening, Turpin joined Sugar Ray Robinson and the other dignitaries, including the mayor of New York City, John Lindsay, and a young Muhammad Ali, at a sit-down dinner at the famous Mamma Leone's restaurant on West 48th Street. This would be Turpin's last glimpse of the glamour and celebrity that a decade earlier had been an integral part of his life.

Late in 1965, a now financially desperate Turpin wrote to Jack Solomons and asked the promoter to help him sell his cherished Lonsdale belt. Turpin hoped that the belt, plus his other trophies, might raise somewhere in the region of £10,000, but Solomons was either unable or unwilling to help. Early in 1966, Turpin turned to another promoter, Alex Griffiths, and he begged Griffiths to help him sell his Lonsdale belt, but although Griffiths tried to attract interested buyers nothing ever came of this effort. The sense of anxiety was palpable in Turpin's actions, and photographs of the former fighter from this period show a man who has visibly aged and whose face is tramlined with streaks of worry. Some thirteen years earlier, in May 1953 as he prepared for the Charles Humez title eliminator fight, the *London Illustrated News* had run an extensive feature on Randolph Turpin and the opening of his Great Orme complex. It began, 'When Randolph Turpin ducks under the ropes at London's White City stadium on 9 June, he will be the first big-business man to fight for a world title ... The all too frequent story of the ex-champion who dies in poverty, or falls on hard times, is not likely to be applied to Turpin.' Sometime in the spring of 1966, Turpin changed his mind about selling his Lonsdale belt and his boxing trophies, and in a letter to his wife he wrote, 'They are yours. As long as you keep them, you have a part of me. Don't ever sell them.' Those around Turpin, including Gwen, could see a quiet desperation beginning to descend upon the 'Leamington Licker' as he withdrew into introspective silence.

At Randolph Turpin's funeral, the Revd Eugene Haselden spoke loudly and passionately about what he believed was the principal contributory factor to the death of this man who, only a few years earlier, was Britain's most celebrated sporting hero. 'At the height of his career,' he began, 'Randolph was surrounded by those who regarded them-selves as friends and well-wishers. But he was deserted by many as he lost his position and money. The fickleness of his friends and the incompetent advice must have weighed so heavily upon him that he was forced to desper-ation. Randolph was a simple man, a naïve man and he needed friends to protect him from the spongers. To our shame he was let down. The tragedy is not his failure alone, but the failure of the whole society.' At the conclusion of this blunt and unapologetic sermon there was silence inside Leamington Spa's Holy Trinity Church. The newspaper reports claimed that there were nearly 2,000 people present, but the truth is there were maybe 500 people inside the church. However, as the mourners began to spill out into the weak light of this gloomy day their numbers were augmented by passers-by, and by those who had decided to brave the rain and just come and pay their respects. Turpin's grief-stricken family were present, including young Randolph, his son from his first marriage, and many of the friends with whom he had grown up in Leamington Spa made an appearance. The promoter Jack Solomons sent neither words of condolence nor a note of apology for missing the funeral. Shockingly, nobody from the British Boxing Board of Control in London made the trip to the Midlands as one might have reasonably expected for a holder of a Lonsdale belt, and a former British, European, and World boxing champion.

Some time after the interment the Warwickshire coroner, Mr S. Tibbets, concluded his findings by suggesting that Randolph Turpin appeared to have been an impulsive and generous man who had given away a large part of his earnings in the ring, and in some way this had led to the present tragedy. Turpin's one-time business partner, Leslie Salts, went further, describing Turpin as 'intelligent in some respects but childish in others. You can tell people what is the best for them,' he said, 'but they don't always take notice.' This, of course, was somewhat ironic coming from a man who made a handsome profit from Turpin, and who had enjoyed the most successful and lucrative years of his life because of the efforts of the now deceased boxer. The coroner read aloud part of a note that Turpin had written and left pinned to a bedroom door before his death. In the note, Turpin made it clear that he felt that he was 'having to carry the can for money owing to the Inland Revenue'. He continued and insisted that his mind was clear and not disturbed. As it transpired, the verdict of the Coroners' Court agreed that this was most likely the case. The entry on the death certificate of Randolph Turpin records that the cause of death was as a result of:

Gunshot wounds of the heart
Self-inflicted
(Suicide)

On 14 May, 1966, three days before Turpin's death, yet another letter from the Inland Revenue had arrived at the transport café in Leamington Spa, this one claiming £200 that was due as a result of non-payment of tax on the income from some of Turpin's wrestling engagements. The latest demand seemed unnecessarily harsh to Turpin and this news, together with the increasing likelihood that the local council was about to exercise the compulsory purchase order on the café, and thereby render Turpin and his wife and four daughters homeless, caused the former fighter to slip into an even deeper trough of depression. By now Gwen was used to enduring her husband's moods so she knew that there was little that she could do beyond wait and hope that his anxiety might soon subside. Three days later, on 17 May, Turpin was working in the café with his wife. After lunch the two older daughters, eleven-year-old Gwyneth and nine-year-old Annette, went back to school, while Turpin went upstairs to check on four-year-old Charmaine, who was suffering from a cold. After a few moments Turpin came back down and told his wife that the child was sleeping, and then he went back upstairs.

Their youngest daughter, Carmen, who was almost two years old, followed her father. Shortly after 2:30 p.m. a curious Gwen went upstairs to check that everything was fine. She saw her husband on the floor between some packing cases and the bed, and she noticed bloodstains on the blanket. Her motionless husband looked as though he had tumbled from the bed, and her daughter, Carmen, was sitting on the floor beside her father, but the crying child was surrounded by a pool of blood. Gwen snatched up Carmen and ran with the child to Warneford Hospital where the authorities informed her that her daughter had been shot. Back at the café neighbours had already called the police, but the word on the street was that Turpin had shot himself twice with a .22 calibre revolver, once to the left side of the head and then fatally in the heart. He had used the same weapon to shoot his youngest daughter twice, and one bullet was lodged near Carmen's brain and the other had punctured her lung. Their local hero was dead, and his youngest daughter was fighting for her life.

Two weeks after Turpin's suicide, Gwen Turpin sold her story to a Sunday newspaper. Carmen was now out of danger, and it was clear that she was going to survive, but Gwen was still trying to find some justification for what her husband had done to their child. In the newspaper she said, 'I think he wanted to take her with him because he had begun to look on the world as a place not fit for her to live in.' But Gwen knew that this was a world that she and her children would have to continue to live in, and she was now determined to protect her four children from any scrutiny and, if truth be told, from the Turpin family with whom, Turpin's elderly mother aside, she wished to have no further dealings. Never wishing to set foot again in the transport café, and realising that she could only stay with friends for so long, once it was safe for Carmen to travel Gwen took herself and the girls off to Prestatyn in North Wales. Gwen went home, remembering that her late husband had told her that she should always try and visit the Great Orme, for that's where they had been happy. In many respects, it was her love and support, and Turpin's devotion to his daughters, that had enabled him to survive the years of debt and anxiety that followed his retirement from boxing. His love for his family had meant that he persevered even when he could see no future, but in the end life's pressure finally defeated this proud warrior. But in Gwen, who was anything but a shy, retiring Welsh Valley girl, he had found a sustaining love, and after his death she deeply mourned the loss of her beloved husband. Eventually, short of cash, Gwen sold her late husband's Lonsdale belt for £3,000.

In 2001, exactly fifty years after Turpin shocked the world and defeated Sugar Ray Robinson, an imposing 8'6" statue of Randolph Turpin in boxing pose, on a five feet high stone plinth, was unveiled in the centre of Warwick. On the bronze plaque below his feet are inscribed the words:

In Palace, Pub, And Parlour The Whole of Britain
Held Its Breath.

And beneath this *'Celer Et Audax'* – Latin for 'Swift and Bold' – the motto of the King's Royal Rifle Corps with whom Turpin's father served during the First World War. Thirty-five years earlier, in 1966, Gwen Turpin had already chosen her own memorial words and had them inscribed on her husband's headstone. Randolph Turpin may have ruled the world for an extremely brief sixty-four days, but whatever his troubles she wanted this stubborn, often naïve man to be remembered as an English hero.

TO

THE DEAR MEMORY OF

RANDOLPH ADOLPHUS

TURPIN

DEVOTED HUSBAND OF

GWYNETH

AND FATHER OF

GWYNETH, ANNETTE,

CHARMAINE & CARMEN

WHO PASSED AWAY

17 MAY, 1966. AGED 38

World middleweight
boxing champion 1951.

✻

Annette is the older of the two Turpin girls sitting before me. Both Annette and Charmaine are now in their forties, and there is a joy to their faces and demeanour which immediately challenges any notion of seeing the story of their father as a tragic one. Charmaine's eleven-year-old son Ieuan sits to her side. Opposite him, and next to me, sits sixteen-year-old Rachel. She is Carmen's daughter, and both she and her cousin are quiet and conscientiously polite. It is now forty years since Randolph Turpin died, and on this hot July afternoon we are having lunch at an Italian restaurant on London's South Bank, only a few hundred yards from the National Film Theatre where some twenty-one years ago I watched a poignant documentary film about Randolph Turpin. Annette smiles. She informs me that she too was in the audience that day, and she liked the film about her father. But that is all that she says; that she liked it, nothing more. We decide to order lunch.

Annette lives in South London, where she is a psychiatric nurse working with children and adolescents in a hospital outpatient department. Charmaine has travelled down with the two children from Prestatyn in North Wales, where she is employed by a company that manufactures military equipment. She is planning on spending the weekend with her sister. Carmen was due to accompany her, but she has recently found another job and so she has decided to stay behind in Wales. Gwyneth, the oldest sister, died of Hodgkin's disease in 1987, and their mother Gwen died in May 1992. She never remarried. As Annette and Charmaine study the menu, I look closely at the sisters and can see that they both have something of the Randolph Turpin twinkle in their eyes. They lay down their menus and then break into charismatic smiles which remind me of the film footage I have seen of their father being interviewed as he prepared to board the *Queen Mary* and sail to New York for the first time. However, it is the young boy, Ieuan – the grandson – who is truly blessed with his grandfather's features. I wonder how much he knows about Randolph Turpin, or if he is even interested. 'HMS *Belfast* and the Imperial War Museum,' says his mother, 'that's what Ieuan likes to visit when he comes to London.' Did Ieuan know that his grandfather, and his grandfather's brothers, served in the military during the Second World War? Did Ieuan know that his West Indian great-grandfather was wounded in the First World War and suffered wounds that later killed him?

Having ordered lunch, the children now begin to talk to each other. Suddenly I feel the pressure to pose a question to the sisters, but it is Annette who asks the first question. 'Do you think my dad would have got proper recognition if he wasn't black?' I have to think for a moment for this is a somewhat blunter version of a question that *I* was hoping to pose to the sisters. 'Although,' continues Annette, 'somebody told me that there are only two statues to black men in England. One is just along the river here, the one for Nelson Mandela, and the other is of our dad. The one that's in Warwick.' For a moment it occurs to me that in a sense she has answered her own question, but she continues. 'But there should be more recognition for black people, shouldn't there? And the one in Warwick has happened relatively recently.'

Two days after winning the world middleweight title, twenty-three-year-old Randolph Turpin found himself on the balcony of Leamington Spa Town Hall with a microphone before him and being asked to make a formal speech. He began, but clearly he was not comfortable with the situation he found himself in and so he departed from the text and decided to thank the crowd in what he called 'me own language'. There was nothing pretentious or affected about Turpin. He was a working-class kid who was neither overly proud of, nor ashamed of, his roots. He was not hoping to secretly ascend through the ranks of the class system and become 'accepted' by the middle or upper classes. I suggest to the sisters that a combination of race and class probably operated against their father being fully recognised, and I ask them what they think he would be doing now were he still alive. Both are sure that he would still have something to do with boxing, probably working with youngsters as a trainer of some kind. 'How about media work?' I ask. They think for a moment, but I quickly continue. 'His face wouldn't have fit, right?' Charmaine nods. 'Yes, that's probably right.' In England issues of race and class frequently operate hand in hand, and had Randolph Turpin lived it seems clear to me that he would undoubtedly have 'suffered' as much for his class as for his race.

Annette steals a quick glance at Charmaine. 'You know, our grandmother had to deal with a lot of racial abuse after her husband died. She got it because she had black kids. Five of them, but she always stuck by her children. Mum told us that. Mum never told us anything about anybody that was bad. When we were growing up she just let us make our own minds up about things.' Charmaine nods, and then takes over from Annette. 'But if we wanted to know then she would tell us her opinion, but only if we asked. After our dad died we left Leamington Spa, but we would sometimes come back and see people. Our mum would bring us from Wales, but she didn't badmouth anyone.' Annette's eyes light up. 'For instance,' says Annette, 'I idolised my Uncle Dick.' She stops abruptly. 'Mum never said anything to me until I started to ask questions about what had happened with the family, but even then it was just her opinion. You know, you should see pictures of her back then in the fifties. She was beautiful and glamorous, just like a film star. But when it came to family and questions about our dad she just let us make our own minds up.'

Shortly after her husband's death, Gwen took her four daughters back to Wales where she once again became part of a Welsh-speaking community. But none of her daughters can speak Welsh, which leads me to wonder if they consider Wales to be home. Charmaine casts a quick glance at the two children, who are now listening carefully. 'In a sense, yes, of course, but Leamington Spa is also home. Maybe it's really home.' Annette looks across at her younger sister and picks up her cue. 'When we go there we always take flowers for the grave, and the last time we were there we went for a walk down the street we used to live on, and it felt strange. Of course, the café is no longer there as it's now a car park, but the place is full of emotions, both good and bad. It's still home, though. At least to me.' She pauses. 'Mum told us that towards the end she would have preferred to sell up and go back to the Great Orme. This was when they still had both the café and the Great Orme, but for some reason Dad made his choice and he chose the café and Leamington and Mum went along with it. But when we did go to Prestatyn after his death we were never made to feel like outsiders in Wales.'

After we have all finished eating we pause for a moment and think about ordering dessert. It transpires that only the children are interested and Charmaine begins to guide them through the choices. Annette is deep in thought, and then she looks up. 'You know what my mother's father said to my dad when he told him that he was going to marry Mum? He said, "Just take care of my daughter." That's all he said. "Just take care of my daughter." My dad was the only black man around that part of Wales, and maybe the only one some people had ever seen, but in Wales everybody accepted him for what he was. They were friendly and generous, and he didn't get any abuse. They didn't care that he was famous, and they didn't want anything from him. For the first time in his life he was free, and he was also among nature. He liked to work on the hay in the fields and do farm work on my granddad's farm, but when he was in Leamington if he had a fiver in his pocket they'd want £4.50 of it and you know he'd just give it to them. In a way he could be happy in Wales because he could just be himself, and for him it was really a big change from Leamington. I reckon things might have been different if they'd left Leamington and gone back and took over the Great Orme again like Mum wanted. But that's not what they did. They stayed in Leamington.'

Having finished their dessert, the two grandchildren run off to play by the water's edge. Annette is the more talkative of the sisters, but being five years older her memories of her father are undoubtedly stronger than Charmaine's. We order coffee, and Charmaine keeps glancing anxiously over my shoulder in order that she might keep an eye on the children. Annette remembers that when she was a girl there was another black family in Leamington Spa. 'Dad used to leave the café at the end of the day and take plates of food, stacked up high, to other poor families in Leamington, including this black family across the street. He'd still feed them even when we had nothing, but he was like that. He looked after loads of people in Leamington, poor people, old people, and he didn't make a fuss about it.' Annette pauses. 'But there was this black family, and years later I met a guy who was a kid in the family and he remembered my dad bringing them food. I think my dad made a lot of black kids in England realise what it was possible to achieve, so his story isn't just gloom. I'm always meeting people who remember Dad, and whenever they talk about him they always smile. Nobody has a bad word to say about him, isn't that right?' Charmaine nods her head somewhat sadly, and then she picks up the thread of what Annette has been saying. 'You see, Dad lost a lot, but he always had dignity and he was good to people.' Suddenly Annette remembers. 'He made that trip to New York near the end, and Mum said that it made a big difference to him because he was really down.' I mention to them both that Muhammad Ali was a fan of their father, and he talked extensively with Turpin at the dinner that followed the Sugar Ray Robinson celebrations at Madison Square Garden in December 1965. Both sisters' faces light up. The children have now returned from the river and Charmaine turns to them. 'Did you hear that?' They both look blankly at her. 'About your granddad and

III

Northern Lights

I remember he always used to wear a big black coat, and he was kind of hunched over. But not like life had beaten him down or anything. He just had this big black coat that seemed a bit too heavy for him. In the evenings I'd come out of where I lived on Mexborough Drive and walk down to the main road – Chapeltown Road. I'd be on my way up to my sister's place to look after her twins, and I'd meet him around about Button Hill. Near where the library and the business centre are now. Somewhere between these two. The fact is, Button Hill isn't much of a hill. Or much of a street really, more like a little alley that leads down on to Chapeltown Road. But this is where I'd meet David.

I was fourteen. Back then, we were taught that you always had to be kind to your elders and betters. We lived a sheltered church life, and so I always acknowledged David and he'd just say, 'Take care, behave yourself.' That's all. 'Take care, behave yourself.' But it happened regularly enough so that we sort of got to know each other. I thought David was something to do with the university. He had that kind of attitude about him. Like he was a very intelligent man.

Judging by the way he spoke, he didn't seem to me like he was a vagrant or anything. And underneath that big black coat I think he had on a dark suit. He tended to have his hands in his pockets and he looked cold. His face used to worry me. His face always looked bruised, as if he'd been scratched. It must have been 1968 or 1969, and you know he wasn't standing upright. He was a little hunched over.

I remember one night when the police were out on the street in numbers. They had come to move David on. I asked a policeman, 'Please, what has he done? He has done nothing. He just stands here.' But there was something about the policeman — about how he looked at me — that frightened me and so I ran off. That night the police arrested a lot of people and put them in Black Marias — you know, the big black vans. That's what we used to call them, Black Marias. The police took a load of people away, including David. They'd only come to get David, but people stood up for him. The people on the street were protecting David and objecting to the police. While the police were trying to move David on and telling him, 'You shouldn't be here,' the young people gathered all around him. I mean, he wasn't *doing* anything, he was just standing by the wall like he always did. I thought he was such a humble man. He was polite. I couldn't see anything that was wrong with him. He just used to stand there with his big black overcoat. But, I don't think he had the same relationship with everybody. He didn't speak to other people, but he spoke to me.

After the night of the disturbance, I saw him maybe a day or so later. I could see that he had been beaten for his face was all mashed up. He wasn't standing at the bottom of Button Hill, he was walking up Chapeltown Road as if he was in pain. I was fourteen. I never saw David after that. There was no other exchange after the night of the disturbance on the street. When I saw him that final time he was dragging his feet. Something had changed. I didn't know what it was, but I knew that something was different.

I remember crying when I heard that he'd died. I felt it hard. Like I'd lost a true friend. All we'd done was exchange a few words over a period of months, but I would never dare say anything to anybody about having talked with a man. I was a Christian and I knew that it was taboo for a young girl like me to talk with a man. When I heard that he'd died I wrote a poem about David. All the feelings were locked up inside and I couldn't tell my parents. I remember that I did find a way to tell my sisters, and they understood. But I could never tell Mum that I knew somebody who'd been in trouble with the police. I could never admit anything to her about what was *really* going on out there on the streets, and so it was like I began to live two lives. I was angry. At the time of David's death everybody was angry. Here was a black man and you tell me, what was he doing in the river? We knew that the police were always trying to move him on, but something else was wrong. What was he doing dead in the river?

In the early seventies, the London Black Panthers began to infiltrate Chapeltown. They kept telling us that things were possible. They insisted that things could be changed, but they made it clear that we couldn't do it openly. They kept mentioning David, and they were very aware of him. Somebody put graffiti about him on a wall. It was near where we would all meet. It just said 'Remember Oluwale'. And we did. We knew that we had to have a strategy, and so we became even more angelic during the day, and then at night we'd go out and do things. His death made us brave. It made us more militant, and it gave us an increased sense of wanting to tease the police. We no longer felt the same about them. We would shout at them. We would throw stones at them and then run off down the back-streets. We knew which houses had cellars that we could dive into and hide, and nobody ever knew what we'd done, or what we were doing. But we couldn't take this rebelliousness back into our homes. It really was like being two people. Once the head of my school called me in and asked me if I would meet with the police as they were trying to become more community-oriented. I went home and told my sister and she looked at me and said, 'No way, absolutely not.' So I had to go back to school and tell the headmaster no. The police were trying to mend the community, but they'd already shown their hand and done something which let us know that our community didn't matter to them. That was how they felt about us. We'd always known it, but now we knew it for sure. We had evidence.

But David wasn't a West Indian like us, he was a West African so his death didn't galvanise the community in the way that it might have. There would have been even more trouble if he'd been a West Indian. But he wasn't. The area around St Mary's Close had a lot of African students living there. I would sometimes see him on Chapeltown Road walking from that direction down towards Button Hill, and maybe that's why I thought that he was a student. My sister lived at 276 Chapeltown Road. That was when I would see David by Button Hill. At the time she was married to a Nigerian, and he was studying in Liverpool. My brother-in-law used to take the last train to Liverpool and at nights my sister needed help with the twins, so that's when I would go up there, usually between ten and eleven. That's when I would see David. He didn't seem West Indian to look at, so I must have known that he was African. In this period we thought of most of the Africans as people who carried briefcases and who studied hard before getting ready to go back home to Africa. We, the West Indians, were mainly workers not students, and of course we also said that we were going home. But in reality we weren't going anywhere. Few of us ever went back home.

I called him David, I remember that much. I knew his name. Somebody must have told me his name, but I don't know how I knew it. He struck me as highly intelligent. Not crazy at all. You could see that he had a depth to him. Whatever it was that was inside of him he just kept it to himself. I can remember him looking at me. He had a powerful stare, but I have to admit he did look poor. I thought he was a poorer person than all of us, but as a devout Christian girl I just wanted to give him respect.

David, do you remember this girl? The fourteen-year-old girl who would walk up Chapeltown Road and see you near the bottom of Button Hill. She knew your name.

Your history you kept locked up inside of you. Shut tight, out of sight. But your name, David. She knew your name, and it felt good on her tongue. She smiled and looked into your eyes, and you told her to take care of herself. You waited for her and basked in her smile, and exchanged your few words, and then you watched as she disappeared from view. And then what? She didn't know that you had nowhere else to go. Once she'd passed out of sight you didn't linger for too long. You moved on your way. Perhaps you wondered how you could ask the girl her name without the full weight of the question frightening her away. But in your heart you knew that you would never ask. Did she remind you of somebody? A sister? Your mother? Back home, a long time ago before this nightmare descended upon your young shoulders. Back home, where you spoke of your life in the future tense. Back home, this girl with fine manners and good breeding might have been your wife. You studied hard at your school under the guidance of Christian missionaries. You worked with a burning desire to escape to your future as soon as possible. Your parents loved you, but they recoiled in shame for they knew they could no longer protect you from your ambitions. In their hearts they were proud, but the books that you studied had already carried you beyond them and to a crossroads. They took their place behind you, for history had chosen you and your future was calling. You turned and said farewell to your parents, and then set out on your journey. 1949. Yoruba boy. Going to England to make a life for yourself. Eighteen-year-old Yoruba boy stowing away in the dead of night, trying to make yourself invisible in the belly of a ship bound for England. Leaving home for the rich white man's world. Dark black night. You felt the heaving and creaking of the cargo ship, the *Temple Star*, as it laboured away from the Lagos quayside and out into the waters that were slick with spilled oil and clogged with debris. You felt the ship rising and falling as it moved beyond this tumult and into the clearer waters of the Atlantic Ocean. Leaving home. Yoruba boy. With your dreams of being an engineer locked up in your young heart. You were unable to come out of hiding and take one final look at the line of lights that illuminated the coastline of your vanishing world. You were unable to wave to your mother. Unable to stand straight like a small, thin man-boy and bid farewell to your Nigeria. Unable to promise the wind and the moon and the stars that one day soon you would return as a successful man with a twinkle in your eyes and with England tucked away in your jacket, ready to produce and display it to any who might wish to glimpse your pocketed jewel. You lay, instead, hidden in the bowels of the ship listening to the roar of the malevolent water as the Atlantic Ocean asserted its authority over the clumsy vessel, tossing its rusty bulk high and then abandoning it so that it crashed back to the watery earth with a loud slap. Yoruba boy. Young lion leaving Lagos, Nigeria, in the oil-rich heart of the British Empire. Cold and tired, chilled in your young bones, curled up like a newborn babe. A hand reached down and pushed you. You opened your eyes and saw your saviour glowering at you, disgusted that he had discovered a nigger on his ship. Yoruba boy travelling to meet his future. Please, do not look at me in this way. I desire only to reach England in safety. To travel across this terrifying water to England, and thereafter to continue with my life. But he stared down at you, didn't he, David? As though he was eager to throw you into the water that frightened you so much. Toss you away into the open mouth of the sea. But he did nothing. You uncurled your tight, stiff body and stood uneasily. Water. You asked him for water to drink. Water. But the man said nothing. He simply stared at you and watched your mouth moving like that of a fish. Water. And then many days later the water came to an end. There was no more water, there was only land, and an arrival in a moribund grey coastal town in the north of England, among a colourless clutter of wharves and barges, and cranes and container boxes. Your eyes feasted upon the grey vista of Hull at the mouth of the River Humber on the east coast of England, and you held your breath. Yoruba boy in England with a whole life in front of him. But first, prison. The policeman handcuffed you and led you down the plank to the shore while hostile eyes burned a hole in your thin body. You had imposed yourself upon them. Your heart sank, and for the first time it occurred to you that these people might cast you back upon the water and attempt to send you home. But they said nothing. They simply locked you in a cell and told you to wait. Wait. Their food would not stay in your stomach. You did not enjoy the contempt with which the guards looked at you. In fact, there was no joy to these men, to this country, to this prison, but it was too late for you had crossed the water and arrived. However, if only they would allow you to remain in their country then you felt sure that one day you might find joy. Eventually they bullied you into a courtroom and imposed twenty-eight days in prison upon you, after which they promised you that you would be permitted to enter British life. Twenty-eight days only. Twenty-eight days to freedom. But they did not take you from the courtroom and accompany you back to the familiar cell. They put you in a van and turned inland, away from the sea, away from Hull, and they travelled for fifty miles with their Yoruba cargo in the back of their vehicle. They furrowed their way towards the centre of England. Leeds. In Leeds the jail is Victorian. Its high Gothic walls are imposing and frightening. An extremely narrow gate. Armley jail. Your twenty-eight days would be spent here, away from the sea, in the heart of England. And after twenty-eight days of misshapened dreams that presented themselves as nightmares, they released you into this city of Leeds. To go back to Hull would be to suggest a return. No. You were cold. A teenager. Already a veteran of an Atlantic passage and prison. But now you were free and ready. But that was a long time ago, David. It would be nearly twenty years before you would meet the nameless girl at the bottom of Button Hill. Twenty years in which to live a life in Leeds in the heart of England. David, do you remember the girl? She did not know your history, but she knew your name. You waited for her and bathed in her smile, and exchanged your few words. And then you watched as she disappeared from view. Yoruba boy from Lagos who, on arriving in Leeds, thought only of himself in the future tense. A teenager at home in Leeds. Alone.

I will stay in Leeds. No more water. No water. You decided. And then later. Imagine, a fourteen-year-old girl with manners from the Old World who showed you respect. And after she had passed you by it was time for you to leave Button Hill. You walked down Chapeltown Road towards the heart of your city. The language of hope no longer sat on your tongue. It was difficult to speak in the future tense. But the appearance of the girl gave you hope. The girl seemed to know who you were even if your city misunderstood you. But after twenty years you refused to leave your city.

The history of Leeds begins with the river; without the river Leeds would never have come into being. Thirty miles to the north-west of the present-day city, a thin trickle of water dribbles through the massive limestone cliff of Malham Cove, which is part of the brooding Pennine range that forms the knobbly spine running up the middle of England. The thin trickle of water falls and becomes a stream, and soon after the stream bursts and becomes a river named Aire. The river flows quickly, to the south and to the east through the Aire Valley and in the direction of the much mightier River Humber. When the Romans laid out a road from York (Eboracum) in the east to Manchester (Mancunium) in the west the River Aire was an obstacle that had to be crossed. Eventually the Romans decided that the road should cross the River Aire at a place near the present-day Leeds Bridge.

For 400 years the Romans occupied Britain, subduing sporadic uprisings, civilising the local people, and educating them in the ways of bathing, heating, and construction. However, before the coming of the Romans, tribal Celtic people had cleared the lush woodland of the Aire Valley. Having done so they grew oats and barley, and raised sheep, pigs, and cattle on both banks of the River Aire. They lived in circular stone huts, and ground their corn and flour in handmade pottery. Although their 'civilisation' progressed from stone to bronze, and then from bronze to iron, this evolution could not disguise their essential warlike tribal nature. They built ramparts and defences against each other, and they fought with habitual ferocity, slaughtering families and livestock. However, when the Romans arrived, under the command of Julius Caesar, and began their regimented, disciplined march through the foggy island, the tribal people soon capitulated. The Aire Valley, and the people contained therein, submitted to the iron-fisted authority of Roman rule, but the invaders knew that in order to ensure no further nonsense from these Britons it would be necessary to build roads along which Roman troops could quickly move through this uncultured land. And so Leeds was born, for one such road crossed the River Aire.

Roman Leeds (Loidis) is memorialised only by occasional discoveries of shards of pottery, or old coins. Roman Britain soon became Christian Britain, and although the Romans continued to rule they were forever battling marauding Pagan tribes who were determined to overthrow them. In AD 410 the Eternal City of Rome was herself sacked, and Anglo-Saxon tribes seized this opportunity and invaded the island of Britain. Eventually, the exhausted

Romans let it be known that it was the duty of the Britons to protect their own land, including the river settlement of Loidis, and thereafter the Dark Ages descended upon Britain as the Saxons and the Jutes and the Angles swarmed across the chaotic land. Pagan tribal kings killed Christian tribal kings who in turn killed pagan tribal kings. Leeds was a Christian region which possessed a ninth-century church of some size and importance, and when the Vikings eventually invaded Anglican Britain, and set up their capital at York, they were aware of the important township to the west over which they immediately proceeded to exercise their Danish law. Leeds was growing in size, and although much of the land beyond the manorial settlement remained heavily wooded, there were some clearings that included, north of the river, such villages as Headingley, Seacroft, and Alwoodley, and south of the river the villages of Armley, Bramley, and Beeston.

The settlement of Leeds suffered the misery of being visited by the plagues that swept Britain in 987, in 1001, and again in 1046, and the population of the township was decimated. In 1066, the Normans, under the command of Duke William of Normandy, crossed the Channel, killed the new English king and imposed their Gallic rule, but the north of England objected and rebelled. Three years later, in 1069, a frustrated William led his army on a mission to sack, destroy, and forever subdue the northern population, a campaign of action which became known as the Harrying of the North. Almost half of Yorkshire's 1,900 settlements were totally destroyed, and a significant number were cripplingly damaged, but Leeds was spared the might of the Norman hammer. The evidence of her good fortune is made clear in the Doomsday Book of 1086 which recounts that, during this period, the value of the township of Leeds, with a population of approximately 200, actually increased.

The township's simple structures were dominated by the manor house, the parish church, and the mill, and agriculture was the means by which most people made their living. The tilling of the soil, and the breeding and slaughter of beasts, took place in accordance with the changing seasons. Norman Leeds, like other settlements in the kingdom, developed a cyclical pattern of life. Nestled in the Aire Valley, and located at an important river crossing, under Norman rule Leeds quickly began to develop and dominate the surrounding villages both economically and in terms of the grandeur of her vision. Throughout the twelfth and thirteenth centuries, as Norman England gradually gave way to medieval England, the township by the river crossing continued to grow. It adhered to a model of feudalism in which land was held by the king, who stood at the apex of the system, with barons and noblemen, down to the peasants, ranged beneath him in an orderly fashion. All offered the king some form of service in exchange for their right to occupy their particular station in society.

Medieval life centred around the manor house, with its communal oven, and there was a tightly organised taxation structure so that all monies flowed back towards the lord of the manor, who owed his allegiance directly to the king. However, the manorial township of Leeds, whose manor house was located near Kirkgate, was not generating enough money to satisfy the lord of the manor so an extension of the town, centring on Briggate, was established. In this new town the freeholder of the land had no political rights, but they were permitted to build workshops and establish crafts and industries which, it was hoped, would eventually generate more income for the lord. By the fourteenth century the new town and the old manorial township had fused as one, and the influence of the old system was declining as the actual manor house itself began to fall into disrepair. Profits from usage of the land began to fall sharply, and it was becoming clear to residents and visitors alike that Leeds was an increasingly dilapidated town. This situation was made worse by the arrival, in July 1348, of the bubonic plague. However, compared to the damage visited upon other English towns, Leeds escaped quite lightly.

After the plague, Leeds sought to arrest its decline and develop an industrial base. Blacksmiths were encouraged, coal mines were sunk, mills for the grinding of corn were constructed, but most notably, the woollen industry began now to dominate the economy. Having an advantageous position on a river, and a major road connection, the burgeoning woollen textile industry was able to rapidly develop. The wool was delivered by local farmers and then sorted into proper grades, washed, and the matted fibres straightened. The straightened wool fibres were then spun into thread, and the threads woven into one continuous cloth. The cloth was wetted so that it would shrink, and then trampled upon so that the fibres would mat together.

Thereafter, the wet cloth was placed on frames and stretched, then dyed and finished, which often meant raising the pile by brushing it. Leeds cloth was known as 'northern dozens', and cut to about four metres. It was taken to the Monday market in Leeds where this quality product soon developed a national reputation. Leeds men were known to be well-dressed individuals in good wool cloth, and the townspeople, including those who in the future would dress in long black coats and stand at the bottom of Button Hill, were smartly attired. The sheer quality of the cloth on the back of the town's population would ensure that this small northern town began now to swell in size, wealth, and renown.

And after twenty-eight days of darkness they released you, David. No longer a stowaway. No longer a prisoner. You had endured your punishment and you were free in your new city, and surrounded by strange white faces. It was nearly winter. You were cold, but you were determined, and you found yourself a place to sleep. Beyond Woodhouse Moor and behind the university. 209 Belle Vue Road, a tall three-storey terraced brick house, handsome in its proportions, easily divisible into living units. A room in a house. A room in an overcrowded house full of working men, but none of them African. Lonely David, all by yourself. And at night when you lay on your single mattress and listened to the sound of doors banging and voices being raised, and lovers calling out to each other with passionate indifference, you understood that you were in a new country. You curled your small shivering body tightly into a ball in an attempt to trap some heat and survive the night. And in the morning you took the bus to the central bus station, and then walked over Crown Point Bridge to the far bank of the River Aire and past the factory that made engines for trains that would soon be dispatched to India and other far-flung corners of the empire. You followed the hundreds of workers who flowed down Black Bull Street and in the direction of the bleak factories that choked the lanes and alleyways between Hunslet Road and the River Aire, and you walked briskly towards your job at West Yorkshire Foundries. You generally had to have some sort of skill to find employment in Hunslet, particularly if you worked at West Yorkshire Foundries for this was a place that made mouldings, but only for top-of-the-line cars. Smart cars, like Triumph. However, in this factory there was some low-skilled work, and they employed you, David. And then, at the end of the day, you would hear the hooter and walk out on to the windswept streets where you crossed paths with those flooding in to do the night shift. Up above your head, you could see the chimneys which continued to pump out soot and smoke into the grey sky. Aside from the one row of back-to-back houses on Sayer Road (whose occupants were always the last to arrive at work for they would not roll out of bed until they heard the hooter) you passed nothing but factories on your walk back to and over Crown Point Bridge. Row upon row of factories. Once you reached the bus station you'd wait for the bus that would take you home. To 209 Belle Vue Road and your room in a house full of foreigners with their strange food, and their strange music. The English you were already used to, for they were a part of your world in Nigeria, but many nations lived in this noisy house. If it was not a night when you had to attend college you might walk up the hill and then across Woodhouse Moor towards Chapeltown and the pubs that would accept you; pubs in which you might reasonably expect to find those in whose company you might pass some time. And once there, in a pub, you would stand with your half of beer (because you were not much of a drinker) and listen to the talk and the laughter until the man behind the bar rang the bell ('Time, ladies and gentlemen, please'). Because everybody was grateful to the man for not running a pub that operated a colour bar all drinks would be drunk quickly and then, as a group, everybody would leave the pub and you would turn to the right by yourself and begin the long trek back across Woodhouse Moor, which often involved enduring the hostility of young louts who idled on benches, or beneath trees, smoking cigarettes and eager to embrace trouble. But you ignored them and pressed calmly on your way, although sometimes you were forced to flee in your suit and collar and tie, but being young and fit you were able to fly away from your enemies and go home to 209 Belle Vue Road and pass quickly up the stairs to your room. And then you disappeared, David. And then you just disappeared.

I first saw him in the Cambridge pub on North Street. He was part of a group of coloureds who were drinking. Mainly Africans, I think. I noticed him because he was so smartly dressed. This must have been about 1950 or 1951.

The Cambridge didn't have a colour bar, unlike most of the other pubs in Leeds. Most of them had big signs in the window that read 'No Coloureds, No Dogs, No Gypsies', that sort of thing. Either that, or they'd have a quota which meant they'd only let a certain number in so as not to 'spoil' the English atmosphere. Nightclubs nearly always had a quota, apart from the Mecca Ballroom in town where anybody could go and dance. But in most cases pubs just preferred to have an outright bar on coloureds. The Cambridge on North Street was different, and they didn't give anybody any hassle. That's where I first saw him. The pubs closed at 10:30 p.m. in those days, and when we all came out of the pub everybody turned to the left. David was the only one who turned to the right and he began to walk off by himself. I asked one of the others where he was going to, and they said that he lived over by the university so I assumed that he must have been a student. In those days there were two groups of Africans in Leeds. The first group were the students, and most of them lived around the university area. The second group were the working Africans and they mainly centred around the Chapeltown area. In fact, some of the workers also studied at night. During the day they might be employed in some form of engineering, but at nights they would study. But, you know, as time went by a lot of them stopped studying and they just concentrated on making money. But there were always the two groups, the workers and the students. The two groups would often converse together in the pubs without any problems, but when we all left the pub they would go their separate ways. On this particular night, the first night that I met him, the working group turned left towards Spencer Place, which was the neighbourhood that they all lived in. David turned right.

The Booma Boys

The Nigerian warriors came home from the Burma war filled by the same impatience with the past that flung their English comrades into Clement Attlee's grim embrace. Among them was a residue of restless souls whose misconduct in Lagos won them the name of 'Burma Boys'. When the late forties raced into Nigeria (as they never did to war-sodden, static, 'welfare' England), this name became 'Booma,' and the 'Boys' really boys: for a new generation of good-bad lads sprung out of the Lagos pavements, who were too young to have fought overseas but old enough to demand that the future happen quickly now. Many of these vivid scamps, innocent as rogues under twenty-three can be, were suddenly gripped by a deep urge to know the world; and as swallows do, they took off from Africa for England with nothing but a compelling instinct as their baggage, stowing away, signing on and deserting, sometimes cajoling minimal fares from rightly reluctant families. Their landfall was in the big English dock cities, and they loped ashore blithely confident that the world loved them and owed them a treasure.

Colin MacInnes, 1960

My second memory of meeting David was at a dance at the Jubilee Hall in Chapeltown. Today the place is some kind of a media centre, but it was originally built in the thirties as a Jewish social centre back when the Chapeltown area was rather grand and somewhat Jewish. The Jubilee Hall would allow us to rent rooms for dances and here, as in the pubs, the African students mixed with the African workers. With the West Indians there were actually more workers than students, but it was the other way around with the Africans. However, I do seem to remember that quite a few of the Trinidadians were doing medicine, dentistry, law, and accounting and so on. The second time I saw David was at the Jubilee Hall dance and I noticed him because he was smarter than most in his dress sense. David always wore cool suits, always a collar and tie, and when he began to dance he danced as though he had music in his soul. In fact, when David walked he did so as though he was walking to music. There was a great rhythm to his steps. The kind of music they played at Jubilee Hall dances was Hi Life and Steel Pan, and David was in his element. I noticed him that first time because he turned the wrong way. I noticed him the second time because he was such a great dancer.

I never saw David standing alone by himself either in the pub or at a dance. Aside from his living arrangements, which meant that he lived a little way off from all the others, he appeared to me to be fully integrated into the African group. In fact, sometimes the university held dances and I saw him there, and again I noticed his skill at dancing. This would have been around 1951. He was very bouncy, and very young and slim. David wasn't really a political type and he never joined in with any of that. I tried to talk to him about the racial situation, especially as I had just formed the Chapeltown Commonwealth Citizens Committee. This was a difficult time for a white woman to be seen with a group of coloured men. I would be at risk, but the greater risk would be to them. People would often say things to me – nasty things – and naturally the men would want to defend me, although I'd try to encourage them to say nothing. But it wasn't easy. The Labour Party wouldn't officially support us in our work with the coloured immigrants; some individuals within the Labour Party, yes, but not the Labour Party as a whole. We – the members of the Chapeltown Commonwealth Citizens Committee – leafleted places and tried to make them take down their discriminating signs. We postered offices and pubs, and we also went to estate agents and tried to convince them that property prices actually went up when coloureds moved in. We told them that initially some whites might want to move out, but we reminded them that the housing demand from coloureds was such that the prices would inevitably rise back up. We also tried hard to get coloureds registered to vote, and we were forever dealing with the nuisance of the police. David was interested in what we were doing, but he didn't take part. He would always ask how we thought we were going to change things, and I would try to convince him that it was worth collecting evidence of systematic racism and challenge it head-on. However, David preferred to talk about what he was doing then, which was working in engineering across at a foundry in Hunslet.

*

It was called West Yorkshire Foundries, not because of the county of West Yorkshire (which actually didn't exist back then), but because the owner was a certain Mr Wallace West. The company began in the Second World War making castings for aircraft, then it eventually got involved in car manufacture. I was the personnel officer and I remember David as a short man who smiled all the time even though he didn't seem to have much to smile about. People in the factory used to call him 'Alliwalli' and he was known for reading educated newspapers. He spoke with a thick West African accent, I remember that, and it was sometimes difficult to understand what he was on about. But I was the one who led him from his formal interview to his department in the foundry itself. We put him in Department 87, which was then run by Percy Chainey, whose employees were required to help out with any department that had a labour shortfall. If no shortfall existed, Department 87 members were expected to sweep and clean the factory in general. Oluwale would have been among the first of hundreds of immigrant workers who eventually passed through the foundry's doors. They used to queue outside the interview room, three or four deep, and the line would often stretch right down the street. We attracted immigrants because the pay was competitive, but the conditions were terrible and safety was non-existent. We always had Lithuanians, Hungarians, and Poles, then Asians and West Indians, but Oluwale was the only West African I remember. In fact, in those days we had multilingual signs in the factory, but I'm not sure it helped anybody. The day used to begin at 7:30 a.m. In fact, the hooter sounded three minutes before work was to start, and that's when the men would assemble in the streets and begin to clock in. They had an hour for lunch and worked right through until 5:30 p.m., but it wasn't easy. In fact, to many it was worse than being down the pit. Mr West liked his employees to wear 'whites', like he'd seen workers wear in India. Well, they might look nice, but they were useless as protective gear. And there were no safety shoes or anything. In the aluminium and iron foundries you'd walk in and it would be completely black except for the light of the molten metal, a white light which was dazzling. Things were pretty bad back then, and even the area around the factory was rough with no grass in sight. The river was black, like oil. You sometimes see fish in it now, but back then the only living things in it were leeches. No, it wasn't a great job with all the heat and the sheer physical graft involved. But when overtime was available hours could easy double from the forty-four-hour basic.

And so there you were, David, working in the white-hot heat of the foundry, without protective clothing, vulnerable to spills and accident, hard grown men's work that only the strong and the skilled could survive and then, at the end of the day, out again, away from the filthy black river, out on to the windswept streets lined with redbrick factories. 'Hey you, nigger boy. Did you come out of your mam's arse?' A slow journey back in the direction of Belle Vue Road and a room called 'home', and the next morning back to work where the company doctor gave you your lightning-fast check-up. After he tapped your chest and looked quickly into your mouth, he had a suggestion. 'Cheer up, sunshine. Perhaps you should try going to the cinema. That'll make you feel better. Everybody's the same colour in there.'

I arrived in England from Nigeria as a stowaway in January 1951. Takoradi to Middlesbrough. There was one foot of snow on the ground and all I had were tennis shoes and dungarees, that's all. And a shirt with Sugar Ray Robinson drawn on the back of it. It was winter and I was freezing. I'd never been so cold, and to me it was like living in a freezer. But eventually I made my way to Yorkshire and that's where I met David. The way I see it, Yorkshire people are friendly, hard-working men. Socialists. You get the occasional problem here and there but they're generally okay. There were not many of us coloureds in those days. It was like you could basically count the number of blacks in Britain on one hand back in 1951. The only West Indians we really knew were a few ex-RAF guys with half-caste children, but there were no West Indian or African women there. We didn't mix much with the West Indians to start with; that came later. Eventually I got a job working at William Graves Foundry. We made shipping equipment. Then, around about this time, I met David. David was short and stocky-like. He looked like a jockey. He wasn't really a drinker or smoker, but he loved to dance. However, he was mostly by himself. Always alone. I never went to David's flat because I never knew where he was living. He'd say, 'Goodnight, I'll see you tomorrow', and then he'd be gone. He never invited anybody to his place, but you didn't ask him about it because you knew it would be an argument. The problem with David was he didn't understand the colour-bar situation and he would get very wound up. 'I'm from a British colony and I'm British,' he would say. 'So why do they call me "nigger"?' This was the attitude David couldn't deal with. He wasn't able to think around a situation and do something else. He was always in trouble and in conflict with the police. He wasn't crazy, he just didn't understand the system, that's all. He was a good guy. He'd never fight anybody, never draw a knife, but verbally he could be very abusive, especially against the police. He was always telling them to 'fuck off'. The only time David would cool down was when he was with his mates. On his own he couldn't handle these situations. David needed somebody to sit down and tell him what was happening to him. Some of us nearly went mad in England because the environment was new. We spoke the same language and we thought everything would be okay, but we soon found out. David really was a smart cat who could always think fast if he had to, but he was a loner who wanted to do everything by himself. The guys tried to help him, because we knew the situation, which is why we always walked out in twos or threes or fours. On your own you had to be very careful. However, David was never a troublemaker. He could be very foul-mouthed, but he wasn't a troublemaker. We knew that the police were against us because we could see it, and we had to work around them. But not David. He was determined. He never discussed his ambitions or any idea of going back to Nigeria. But then again, the majority of us didn't want to go back to Africa again.

And then David just disappeared and that was that. At first nobody thought it was unusual, for we were used to people leaving or just moving on. But after a while I remember asking people, 'Has anybody seen David?' And then I was told, 'Didn't you hear? He's been arrested.' A lot of my own work with the Chapeltown Commonwealth Citizens Committee involved having to deal with the police, who were very much in the habit of picking up people just because they were coloured. The word on the street was that one night, while walking home and minding his own business, David had been arrested and he had been sent to Armley jail. I thought okay, this is not good, but I suppose we'll see him when he comes out. But we never did. He just disappeared.

> There they stand, majestic, imperious, brooded over
> by the gigantic water-tower and chimney combined,
> rising unmistakable and daunting out of the country-
> side, the asylums which our forefathers built with such
> solidity.

> The Rt Hon. J. Enoch Powell, Minister of Health,
> 1961

You can see it from the road; a large Gothic building and a sprawling estate of outbuildings. Built in 1888, this is a deeply depressing complex. The West Riding Pauper

Lunatic Asylum; a place of grim, Victorian nightmares set in 200 acres of land. Once you turn off the road, and pass the sign that reads 'Treatment Centre', the gloom deepens. Another sign reads 'Welcome to High Royds Hospital'. The asylum. Thereafter, the sheer scale of the place soon becomes apparent. The buildings begin to multiply and it is clear that High Royds Hospital (as it became known in 1963) is the size of a village. In its heyday over 2,000 people could be 'treated' at any one time in the dark stone buildings which huddle together beneath the sinister turrets and towers. Lights are burning in the windows but there is nobody in sight. Imagine. Inside. Dirty rooms with plastic armchairs and filthy carpets. Walls and windows stained with years of nicotine, burn marks on the floor, ashtrays overflowing with crushed fag ends. Inside ex-patients sleep in the corridors for they have nowhere else to go. Some wear daisies in their hair and bluebells for earrings. *(My friend, you spent eight years from 1953 to 1961 in this asylum. Doing what? What were they doing to you? Were there any others like you?)* The main building resembles a large stately home. Above it there is a clock tower which, somewhat cruelly, serves only to remind you that in this place time no longer matters. Your time has been taken away from you. Farewell time. *(What were they doing to you? Were there any others like you?)* Inside the front door one tiled corridor leads into another. One wing quickly gives way to another wing. A crazed maze. Neither dignity nor privacy. Eating with spoons. Male and female wander abroad. Through a double door there is a huge ballroom with a mirrorball nestled high in the ceiling. On Monday nights, the cinema. On Friday evenings, between seven and nine, the weekly dance. Male and female mixing. Just after Christmas the Annual Asylum Ball. The social event of the season. On New Year's Eve, the patients' Fancy Dress Ball, where the staff present a music-hall-style pantomime, and the asylum band play on and on. (*Did you dance, David? Or did they simply sedate you into submission?*) Beyond the immaculate lawns, and through the trees, one can glimpse the small Yorkshire village of Menston. Civilisation. In the grounds a truck trundles into view. The driveway curves around the bend. Deliveries? Of food maybe, or perhaps towels? Or medicine? Or needles? Or straps? Cruelly sedated and now ready for electro-convulsive therapy. One man remembered. 'It was like going to the gas chamber, you walked in and saw this horrendous cap that they put on your head and this bed that they asked you to lie on and the injection, to this day I can taste and smell it, and that was to me horrific.' (*Did they sedate you into submission?*) The tranquil picture must not be disturbed. Cruelly sedated. Perhaps the screams of the patients are too high-pitched for the human ear? (*What, my friend, were you doing here for eight years? Really, were there others like you?*)

The growth of the woollen industry, and the development of cloth manufacturing, meant that despite occasional visitations from the bubonic plague Leeds continued to expand. By the early seventeenth century, buildings now lined both sides of the River Aire and the town's leading citizens were vociferously complaining of overcrowding. In fact, according to contemporary reports, Leeds Parish Church could no longer accommodate the hordes of people who 'resorted thither every Sabbath'. This expansion was somewhat checked by the Civil War, during which Leeds was idly batted forward and backward by the Royalist and Parliamentary armies; growth was also interrupted by a particularly violent mid-century outbreak of bubonic plague that swept away a fifth of the town's population. However, by 1660, with the monarchy restored, and a new charter granted to the town, which included permission to appoint a lord mayor, things were once again looking buoyant for Leeds.

In 1700 the population was 7,000, with another 3,000 in outlying townships. In the same year, the opening of the Aire-Calder Navigation Canal allowed cloth to be transported by barge out of Leeds and directly to the port of Hull, and thereafter to London or to the large markets of Europe. As Leeds began to develop a direct relationship to the world, her sense of her own importance deepened accordingly. Around 1720, Daniel Defoe visited Leeds and described it as 'a large, wealthy and populous town, it stands on the North Bank of the River Aire, or rather on both sides of the river, for there is a large suburb on the South Side of the River, and the whole is joined by a stately and prodigiously strong Stone Bridge ... [T]he High-Street, beginning from the Bridge and running up North ... is a large, broad, fair and well-built street ... the town of Leeds is very large, and ... there are an abundance of wealthy merchants in it.' At the time of Defoe's visit the banks of the River Aire were already full of warehouses and mills, and the main street of Briggate held a twice-weekly market where everything from the town's famous cloth to pigs or fruits, vegetables or shoes, might be bought.

The Industrial Revolution of the eighteenth century transformed Agrarian England into Industrial England, and even greater wealth began to be accumulated by the upper classes of society. These social changes saw the poorest of Leeds' citizens became poorer, while the richest became increasingly accustomed to, and smugly proud of, their material assets. In 1760, John Colliar, a schoolmaster from the neighbouring county of Lancashire, compared Leeds to 'a cunning but wealthy, thriving farmer. Its merchants hunt worldly wealth, as eager as dogs pursue the hare; they have in general the pride and haughtiness of Spanish dons . . . the strong desire they have for yellow dirt (gold), transforms them into galley-slaves, and their servants are doubly so; the first being fastened with golden, but the latter with iron chains.' With a link to Hull in the east already established, work began on the construction of a canal that would link Leeds with Liverpool to the west, and thereby provide opportunities for exporting directly into the new markets of the Americas. Although it took until 1816 to complete, the Leeds-Liverpool Canal placed Leeds at the hub of an extensive water-borne transportation network. With rail transportation having been introduced, and the town's roads being continually improved, Leeds began to develop a reputation for ease of communication, and she was able to move her cloth swiftly both nationally and internationally.

In the eighteenth century, larger and more impressive

cloth halls began to be constructed in Leeds. Public libraries, reading and assembly rooms, concert halls and theatres were also built to cater to the wealthier classes, while the working people continued to live in squalor and entertain themselves with bull-baiting, cockfighting, bare-knuckle fist fights, or drinking and variety entertainment. Working-class standards of health declined, and living conditions for the poor deteriorated; inevitably, the disparity between those who had and those who had not grew ever wider. By the end of the eighteenth century this town of 30,000 people, with a further 23,000 in the outlying townships, had already developed the practice of establishing a soup kitchen for the indigent, and handing out blankets to those who could not provide for themselves. Fines levied for drunkenness and other abuses were used to help the needy, and food which was 'sold light in weight' was confiscated and given to the poor. This charity was motivated as much by goodwill as by a general fear of civil insurrection and disease.

Hundreds of poor left Leeds in the early nineteenth century and migrated to the United States in an attempt to escape ruin, while others turned to crime and prostitution. The Leeds Workhouse was always full, as was the prison. As machines began to replace men with increasing frequency, the poor and unemployed became more vocal and expressive in the manner in which they made known their discontent. After all, the daily reminders of widespread poverty and starvation meant that they had little to lose. Those who *did* work were always in danger of being injured in the mill, or factory, or mine, and the worst abuses were often visited upon young children who were habitually pressed into service. However, despite the travails of the working people, and the prevalence of vagrants and paupers on the streets, the town *was* wealthy. The mistreatment of oppressed workers who laboured intensively in dangerous conditions, and the exploitation of child labour in factories and mills, guaranteed that industry would prosper and the wealthy become increasingly affluent. Meanwhile, the area of Mabgate, which was located down by the river beside the parish church, witnessed the greatest concentration of misery, and although social problems of poverty and prostitution were neither confined to Mabgate nor to Leeds, the town was eventually forced to acknowledge that it was confronted with a serious situation.

Victorian Leeds boasted an extraordinary number of alehouses, which exacerbated the atmosphere of misery, and although many temperance societies grew up in the wake of this excessive drinking, neither church nor local government could arrest the decline in the social fabric of the town. These were dark times for Leeds, and not even the air was pure, for the toxic industrial soot blackened the lungs of the high and the low alike. By the middle of the nineteenth century the population, including the townships, had surged to 150,000 and overcrowding was endemic. In 1836 the Leeds police force had been formed and, shortly thereafter, they were armed with cutlasses and heavy batons. It was understood that the police were obliged to defend the rights of the mill owners and prevent the 'mobs' from attacking the mills, and soon after the establishment of the police force their numbers, and powers, were extended in order that they might deal effectively with growing working-class resentment. In 1847 a new borough jail was constructed at Armley to cope with vagrants and other undesirables, and during this period of rapid urban growth, the wealthier citizens quickly learned that they must vigorously monitor the underclasses for these people were not, under any circumstances, to be allowed to gain the upper hand. Aside from wealthy mill owners and industrialists, by 1845 there were over one hundred stockbrokers in Leeds, and the town enjoyed its own stock exchange. There were, in effect, two towns of Leeds, and although Mabgate bore no relationship, social or otherwise, to cosmopolitan Leeds, the underclass also wished to participate in the success story of their town. They too wished to belong, and be a part of this miraculous adventure in growth and development which had witnessed a small river crossing grow to the point where it now stood ready to make a magical transformation into a city. The disenfranchised of Leeds were refusing to go anywhere. They insisted on being heard, and they demanded that they be allowed to participate. They would not disappear. Nobody disappears. People don't just disappear.

Surname:	Oluwale
Christian Name/s:	David
Unit No:	2726
Status:	Informal
Address:	NFA
Sex:	Male
Marital Status:	Single

Admitted From:	St James's Hospital, Beckett St, Leeds 9, Town Hall, Leeds (2)
D of B:	8.8.30
Religion:	C/E
Nat. Ins. No:	ZK 45 03 60 C
Admitted:	11.6.53 Section 26
Status:	C (Certified)

I never saw him and I never knew him, but it's a big place. Massive. In fact, I never saw no coloured people at all. But then again it's difficult because of the drugs. They affect your memory. The medication, as they like to call it, it can make you scream and then they just look at you and that's when they remind you that you're mad and that you'll not be going anywhere. I would find myself walking up and down corridors, talking to myself, thinking who the hell is this crazy bastard in my head, and then before I knew what was happening the nurses would be all over me, holding me down, forcing more stuff down my throat. They used to talk to me like they were my friends, then suddenly they would turn on me and that would be it. All men, never any women nurses, and they would trick you into thinking that everything was fine and okay, but it wasn't like that. And slowly, you know, I think I began to get the idea of what was going on. You'd see people coming in who looked alright, like you could go up to them and ask them how things were on the outside. Then the next time you'd see them they were zombies and they didn't know you, and that's when you realised that something was seriously wrong. But like I said, I didn't see no coloureds.

I didn't see anybody like David Oluwale. I decided I had to get out of High Royds, but it wasn't that easy. I must have been getting better because I saw a doctor one day, and you didn't get to see them that often. But I saw this doctor and he even smiled, and before I knew where I was I found myself in an open ward. I thought to myself, you know, this is your big chance so you better take it. And so I absconded, but they caught me in the next village, or so they said, I don't remember. In Guiseley, I think it was. They brought me back and this time they locked me in a room by myself with only a bucket for a toilet. They let me out in the morning, but kept an eye on me. I went to Occupational Therapy, which everybody called OT, and I learned a bit about printing. The females did sewing and knitting, or they made baskets, but they gave the males different things to do. I used to wish I was back in prison, because you have more freedom in prison. Also, they don't give you medication in there, so you don't twitch as much and there's less nightmares. There's plenty of coloured blokes in prison. I might have seen this Oluwale fellow in there. At night they'd take me from OT back to the room with the bucket, and they'd lock me in. After I'd gone down the drainpipe and absconded the first time I thought, I'm not doing this again. But they weren't going to take any risks now. They watched me like a hawk. I never really did see how big this place was, but it was huge, I knew that. But by now all I wanted was to get out of there. It had been years, and nobody visited anymore, and I was sick of seeing old men picking up tabs from off the floor and shuffling around like they didn't know their name or care anymore. I didn't want to be like them. They were in their seventies some of them, and I didn't want to end up like that. If somebody gave them a sweet they were so grateful they looked like they might cry, but they were the ones who gave me the will to get out. It wasn't the doctors, for I hardly ever saw them. In fact, there was nobody to talk to about how you really felt about things, so you just kept your mouth shut and pretended to behave and hoped that the drugs wouldn't make you any more mad. Eventually it worked for me because one day they didn't take me back to the room and lock me in. They put me in a Nissen hut type of place which was a more open kind of ward, and I slept in there for a while. Maybe a year, I don't know. You never really knew much about time in High Royds. This place was better, but I'd still rather have been in Armley jail, because there you definitely knew about time and you've got your wits about you. But it's hopeless once they put you in the loony bin. It's hopeless trying to hang on to anything. Before you know what's going on they turn you into a bloody zombie and there's nobody to talk to. The nurses have got their jobs to do, but they're more like guards or prison officers. And the guys in OT, they some-times told you straight out that it would be easier training chimpanzees. Basically, you've lost control of your life, but I was lucky. Luckier than most of them, because I got called into the doctor's office and he told me that I was going to be discharged. I said nothing because I didn't believe him. Then I realised that I didn't want to go because I didn't have any connection with the world anymore. Not since I'd gone down the drainpipe then been dragged back again. I didn't know anybody. I didn't know anything about life out there and it was frightening to me. The thing is, not only had I not seen any coloureds in High Royds, I don't know if I'd ever seen any at this time, apart from when I was in prison. I was more of a country person, not a city type, and we just didn't have any. But he could have been there and nobody would have known as the place was so big. But when they eventually said to him 'You're discharged' he'd have had the same worries as the rest of us. I mean, where are you supposed to go?

I look over the low fence of 209 Belle Vue Road. The garden is a riot of overgrown weeds and shrubbery. A blue minivan lies derelict in the yard. Beyond the minivan, at the end of the long narrow garden, stands the three-storey house. There are six neatly spaced windows on the top two floors, three on each. The ground floor boasts a bay window. The curtains are variations of white and green, and they don't match. The curtains that hang in the bay window on the ground floor are white, but their dignity is compromised by the fact that not only do they hang askew, they are also badly twisted. Traditionally, curtains block out all light. They block out the day. The world. But not these curtains. To the side of the front gatepost somebody has hand-painted '209'. Blue string holds the brown gate shut, but much of the fencing to either side of the gate has collapsed. The gate serves little purpose. This was David's home. The place he hoped to return to when the High Royds doctor said, 'You're discharged.' This large three-storey brick house with a crushed Marlboro packet lying discarded by the gate; a place that boasts no television aerial on the roof. Back in the thirties this must have been a highly desirable neighbourhood for the street is broad and the houses suggest grandeur and affluence. But by David's time – by the fifties – this area was full of transients and prostitutes; and little has changed. Today a woman (Miss Dorton-Smith) lives here alone, but she will not answer her door. The door remains closed. I walk around to the side fencing. The labyrinth of jungle hides two more minivans, one red and one white; and the skeleton of a motorbike. The house, the garden, the vehicles, have all been 'let go'. Abandoned.

The next time I saw David must have been six or seven years after the dance. I was walking down towards the university and he was walking up. I hesitated for a moment because he had changed. He'd put on an awful lot of weight and the bounce had gone. It was just no longer there. And the light had also gone from his eyes. David was a man who was in the habit of making strong eye contact, but I looked at him and saw that the light had definitely gone out. And then he told me that he'd been in hospital, and I thought 'oh shit'. Around this time people were beginning to become conscious that Armley jail wasn't the only place that could brutalise these men. We stood together by Woodhouse Moor and talked for a while, and I just assumed that he still lived at Belle Vue Road where he'd been living before. But it was only later that my husband explained to me that David probably appeared strange because he was so pumped up with drugs. After this meeting by Woodhouse Moor I met him next at a dance at Jubilee Hall where he was a bit more talkative, and I seem to remember he was mixing in quite a lot. And then one of the Ghanaians confirmed everything for me, and he told me that David had been drugged while he was in the mental hospital and that's why he'd been behaving a bit strangely of late. And then after a few months or so, David disappeared again into Armley jail. By this stage I'd already decided that I was going to watch out for him. Armley jail had a fearsome reputation, for the wardens and officers often had fascist pins on the inside of their lapels, and they'd flick them at you if you were visiting a coloured prisoner. But they didn't frighten me. I wouldn't let them.

When David came out we started seeing a lot more of him, especially around Chapeltown. But the truth was although he still wore a suit and tie he was beginning to look a little unkempt. He had a bit of a wispy beard, not like the straggly one he had towards the end, but he wasn't really holding it all together as well as he'd done in the past. The Hayfield pub in Chapeltown was now our regular hangout, and he'd sometimes come into the pub, but David was never much of a drinker. I mainly saw him in the street, and he always gave me the impression that he knew where he was going. However, it was only after two or three years that I realised that when David left us after a night in the Hayfield he was, in fact, going to sleep in shop doorways. Things were getting worse for David, and in those days he was always getting himself arrested, but mind you it was never his fault. I would go to the cells and try to get him a solicitor and arrange for bail, but it was clear what was going on. Once I went to court and David was in the dock with a bruised right eye, yet they were convicting *him* of assaulting a police officer if you can believe it. I mean, you only had to look at the size of the police officer and then look at the size of David to see how ridiculous this was. The other charge that they habitually brought against David was that he had been drunk, but everybody knew that David was not a major drinker, but the situation was hopeless. The police did whatever the police wanted to do, particularly when it came to vagrants, and especially when it came to coloured people. David, being the only coloured vagrant in Leeds, was in a bad situation.

My husband and I always looked out for him, and if we ever heard that he was in a particular shop doorway we would always go out and try to find him. The white vagrants slept in the city centre underneath the railway arches, but whenever I went down there looking for David they would say 'He's not here' and 'We don't want that type around here'. I mean, the cheek of them. We tried to get David into the shelter at St George's Crypt, but they said that he was a drunk and that he was too loud, but what they didn't say was that he was too black. The Salvation Army would often take him in for a couple of days, but then he'd get racially abused and he'd answer back and that would be the end of that for they'd want to get rid of him. You know, that was half the problem, that David wouldn't take any abuse from anybody. And he was an easy target. In the early days, the lonely walk back home across Woodhouse Moor from a night's drinking in Chapeltown, or from the Mecca, always left him exposed. I'd never realised just how much of an easy target he was, but he'd never take any abuse from anybody, including the police. They would always tell me that David had failed the 'attitude test', but that was because he wasn't prepared to be anybody's victim. Some of the other Africans tried to help him, but you know it was a very busy time with lots of activism. People's energies were being used up all over the place. It was, after all, the beginning of the Black Power movement for one thing, and the local community were actually succeeding in their efforts to close down racist pubs. People were busy and so they didn't always realise that David was no longer on the scene.

I think David suffered a lot in silence. I'm sure that the first time they took him into Armley jail he wouldn't take any abuse from the screws, and that's why they sent him to the asylum where they treated him like a schizophrenic and tried to drive him mad. Oh, they have their stupid reasoning, telling you that he gets aggressive and that they can't understand him, but it's a cultural thing for heaven's sake. Rather than add another adverb or clause, West Indians and Africans tend to raise their voices or use their hands to speak. Jews do it as well, and that's not madness that's culture. But by sending him out of Armley jail and to High Royds they deliberately made David 'slow' when he was never, ever, slow before. I mean, when he emphasises with his hands they say he's aggressive, and so they pump him full of drugs. Like anybody, David could be lippy if you insulted him, but ninety-nine per cent of the time he was extremely gentle and polite, and very protective. I remember that once when we were out somebody swore in a pub, and David just looked at the offender and said, 'Ladies', meaning, 'Stop that because ladies are present.' After David came out of the hospital he was very, very quiet. On a few occasions the police actually phoned my house. Not all the police were bad apples. There were some good ones, and if they found him sleeping rough anywhere near my house they might call me up and David would come here and spend the night. In the morning he'd wake up, read the *Guardian*, then have some breakfast and go off. Before David left the house my husband would often ask him, 'David, shall we go and look for a flat for you?' but he would always say, 'No, I'm fine. I'm going to meet somebody.' He never wanted help. He was too proud. In fact, as soon as I even got close to saying that I'd get him a flat, or a rented room, he didn't want to discuss it. He was a man of great personal dignity. He used to have such high hopes for his future, but the sad thing was he came to recognise that all of that had gone. In the old days he used to wonder what he'd do once he qualified as an engineer. That's all he used to think about. But this new David didn't want to be pitied. Not by anybody. But I should also say that there were others who helped a lot more than I did. Other Africans were always looking out for him. If they saw David wasn't doing well they would offer to give him money, or help him in some way. I remember one Ghanaian who sold crockery, and who had a crockery warehouse. This man always left the side door of his warehouse open in case David needed somewhere to sleep, but David didn't want to bother anybody. He didn't want to be a burden or cause trouble for anybody. This was his way.

These days the typical black admission is young, in his twenties, loud, paranoid, resisting strongly – you need to get him sedated to restrain him, and the doctors don't know what's going on – he's usually brought in by the police, therefore the doctor hasn't got a clue as to his history – and as with men generally they would be more aggressive, you would be more frightened of them and you would put them on more medication.

National Health Doctor, 2002

In 1858 the Empress of the British Empire, Queen Victoria, came to Leeds to open the newly constructed town hall. Boasting Corinthian columns, and guarded by large stone lions, Leeds Town Hall was one of the largest civic buildings in Europe. The words around the vestibule – 'Europe – Asia – Africa – America' – reminded the people of Leeds that, only one year after the Indian Mutiny had been put down, the globe remained Britain's true sphere of influence. Leeds was perfectly positioned to take advantage of this fortuitous fact. Clothing was no longer the town's main business, and Leeds was becoming better known as the 'workshop of the world'. Hundreds of factories produced bicycles, cranes, nails, sewing machines, bolts, train rails, locomotives, axles, bricks, and much more. There were scores of furnaces burning every day, and the sky was choked with chimneys and pollution. Glassworks and tanneries, skinworks and breweries, every type of industry was represented. Leeds was a hive of productivity and entirely dependent upon the labour of the poor and the young.

Thousands of little children, both male and female, but principally female, from seven to fourteen years of age, are daily compelled to labour from six o'clock in the morning to seven in the evening, with only – Britons, blush while you read it! – with only thirty minutes allowed for eating and recreation. Poor infants! Ye are indeed sacrificed at the shrine of avarice, without even the solace of the negro slave; ye are no more than he is, free agents; ye are compelled to work as long as the necessity of your needy parents may require, or the cold-blooded avarice of your worse than barbarian masters may demand! Ye live in the boasted land of freedom, and feel and mourn that ye are slaves, and slaves without the only comfort which the negro has. He knows it is his sordid, mercenary master's interest that he should live, be strong and healthy. Not so with you. Ye are doomed to labour from morning to night for one who cares not how soon your weak and tender frames are stretched to breaking! You are not mercifully valued at so much per head; this would assure you at least (even with the worst and most cruel masters) of the mercy shown to their own labouring beasts. No, no! your soft and delicate limbs are tired and fagged, and jaded, at only so much per week, and when your joints can act no longer, your emaciated frames are instantly supplied with other victims, who in this boasted land of liberty are hired – not sold – as slaves and daily forced to hear that they are free.

Richard Oastler, Letter to *Leeds Mercury*, 29 September, 1830

During the nineteenth century, cloth continued to occupy a special place in the Leeds economy, and with the onset of Jewish immigration it achieved something of a revival. The first Jew arrived in Leeds in the 1820s and was listed as a voter in 1832. By the late 1840s a small community of middle-class German Jews had established themselves in Leeds, but the Jewry that followed in their wake was largely comprised of poor Jews from Eastern Europe, often Polish or Russian in origin, who were fleeing pogroms, particularly those that followed the murder of Tsar Alexander II. They would arrive at Hull and make their way west to Leeds in the hope of finding some kind of occupation in the clothing industry, for many were skilled tailors. As their numbers increased they settled in their own ghetto near North Street in conditions familiar to most working-class residents of Leeds. But this was now their city – their new home – and they had no intention of going anywhere else, despite the well-displayed signs that let them know that Jews were not welcome. By the end of the nineteenth century, the vast majority of the 8,000 Jews in Leeds were employed in one of the 98 Jewish tailoring sweatshops where the conditions were often indescribable.

The thousands of Irish immigrants to Leeds, who arrived in the wake of the great famine of the 1840s, lived in conditions at least as intolerable as those of the Jews. They congregated in the east end of Leeds in slums of unimaginable depravity where crime and prostitution were rife, and these Irish Catholics often embarrassed their English co-religionists with their supposed debauchery. However, what was beyond dispute was the fact that conditions for the poor in Leeds were among the worst in Britain. The water supply was putrid and contaminated with effluence from the sewers, and hundreds of people were often forced to share one privy. Disease was rife, and these overcrowded places were devoid of either daylight or fresh air. Understandably, life on the street was, for some, a much more palatable option. With the introduction of horse-drawn, and then electric, tramways, by the end of the nineteenth century some workers were able to move out of the centre of Leeds and they began to commute to work from the suburbs. However, the vast majority of the poor were trapped in squalor and therefore unable to enjoy civic improvements in education, transport, and the opening up of public spaces for parkland.

At the end of the nineteenth century, Leeds formally became a city and it boasted a population of nearly half a million. However, despite the city's affluence, problems of pollution and overcrowding continued to blight the lives of the working population. Fears of contagious diseases such as tuberculosis were real, as were Jewish concerns about anti-Semitism. Despite the fact that over 2,000 Jews volunteered for service during the First World War, Jews continued to be regarded as 'foreigners'. In 1917 fighting between Christian and Jewish men in the city escalated into a full-scale riot which resulted in many Jewish properties in the Leylands area being destroyed. The city's resistance to perceived 'outsiders', no matter how long they have been resident in the city, has always bedevilled Leeds. This antipathy easily crossed over into the twentieth century, and its virulence was fuelled by the well-known capacity of the people of Leeds for drinking and gambling.

The economic depression of the early twentieth century meant that there was no shortage of people to fill the poorhouses and workhouses of the city. Although new council-owned houses were being built to house the working classes, those who lived below a certain economic level had little choice but to live in slums that remained mired in a depravity reminiscent of the early Victorian years. During the great depression of the twenties and thirties it was once again the clothing industry that saved Leeds. Firms such as Burtons, Hepworths, John Collier, and Jackson's began to corner not only the national, but the international market in ready-made 'smart' clothes. Employment opportunities began to grow, and eventually slums began to be cleared. By the Second World War, Leeds was becoming surprisingly progressive in her civic attitude towards ongoing difficulties in housing and education, but the city's often hostile attitude towards 'outsiders' continued to be a deeper and more impenetrable problem.

In 1933 the Leeds Jewish Refugee Committee began to

help German Jews escape from the brutal anti-Semitism of their own country, and by 1939 some 700 German Jews had found refuge in Leeds. However, upon arrival they soon discovered that local golf clubs banned Jews, and that the tea rooms and dance halls openly advertised their 'English only' policy. Jews were treated as pariahs and often subjected to physical attack, or swastikas being painted on their shop windows. But this was now their home; modern Leeds. A city of half a million people with one of the most robust economies in Britain; a city made up of migrants who had all come to settle on the banks of the River Aire. Like the Irish before them, the Jewish population of Leeds refused to move on. They were going nowhere. This was their home. And then others arrived.

In fact, these 'others' had been appearing in Leeds for some time. In 1791, the famous African writer Olaudah Equiano visited Leeds while promoting sales of his influential autobiography, and he later wrote a letter to the *Leeds Mercury* under his adopted name, Gustavas Vassa. In December 1859, Frederick Douglass delivered a speech in Leeds Town Hall at a meeting of the Leeds Anti-Slavery Society, and the third edition of his autobiography was actually printed in Leeds. And later still, in 1901, the black composer Samuel Coleridge-Taylor composed a choral cantata for the Leeds Triennial Music Festival. However, aside from these visitors, there is precious little evidence of a significant black presence prior to the Second World War. The occasional individual does turn up in the records, such as Abraham Johnson, who was born in Zanzibar in 1848 and who, during the second half of the nineteenth century, worked for a while at John Marshall's Flax Mill in Leeds. Or Pablo Fanque, a black man who owned and operated a circus in late Victorian England, and who is buried in Leeds. The small pre-Second World War black population in Leeds consisted almost entirely of domestic servants, theatrical performers, or industrial workers, and they existed as isolated individuals in an otherwise homogeneous white society.

After the Second World War many 'demobbed' colonial soldiers, aircrew, and seaman from Africa and the Caribbean 'stayed on' in some English cities. In 1945 the black population of Leeds largely consisted of such persons but, in common with the rest of the country, the numbers were negligible. However, by the mid-fifties the nation had begun a programme of massive recruitment of Caribbean labour in order that the post-Second World War infrastructure of Britain might be maintained, particularly in health and transport. As a result, dark strangers began to appear in far greater numbers on the streets of Leeds. According to the 1951 census, there were 107 West Indians and 45 Africans living in the city. Ten years later, in 1961, there were 2,186 West Indians and Africans, which included carpenters, masons, tailors, mechanics, painters, and electricians. These newcomers of African origin were visible and vulnerable on the streets of Leeds, but they no longer needed to think of themselves as being isolated. A community was being formed.

Chapeltown's history is written into its architecture. Its huge semi-detached and terraced houses, built for the prosperous, Christian new middle classes in the early 1900s, its two parks and its wide, tree-lined streets are now interspersed with buildings which were once synagogues, and Asian-owned mini-markets selling the produce of the world. Halfway up Chapeltown Road there's a wall which, throughout the seventies, bore the inscription REMEMBER OLUWALE in huge white letters. Near that wall there's an ugly vacant lot which, until recently, was the site of the elegant country club built in the twenties for those prosperous Christians. The club became Chapeltown's most notorious pub. White Leeds imagined that inside the Hayfield every type of black sinner was making mischief. A curious corollary of this fantasy was that the Hayfield became a kind of 'black space', where whites only entered if they accepted the rules laid down by the black men who played dominoes, drank, sold a little weed and checked the ladies. Since these rules were easy to accept – mutual respect and toleration, whatever status the outside world conferred upon you – lots of adventurous whites found themselves at home there. It's said that David Oluwale frequented a similar place in Chapeltown, a nightclub called, in his day, the Glass Bucket, but I'm pretty certain the early evening would have found him in the Hayfield. The Hayfield was erased from the map around 2004 – yet another sign of the city's inability to deal properly with its black citizens.

Dr Max Farrar, Leeds Metropolitan University, 2006

The Chapeltown Enterprise Centre stands at the bottom of Button Hill. The centre features the Best Fade Unisex Salon. Across the road is the Silver Tree Club which, these days, is a bricked-up, burned-out building. Chapeltown has changed. Chapeltown no longer boasts good manners. It is becoming derelict and infested with drug dealers. Garbage lies piled up in the streets, and there is a paucity of civic pride. Modern Chapeltown is home to a lost generation. A young woman shouts at me. 'Hey you, black man.' Her voice is raw and flat. A broad Yorkshire voice. As she crosses the street and walks toward me I can see that she is swathed in a big black coat. 'Hey you, black man.' Her eyes are wet with drugs, and she promises me that she will do anything. 'Black man.' I quicken my steps. I glance back at the Best Fade Unisex Salon. I want to tell the people in the enterprise centre that they are right to try, but they should look around themselves. There is no real enterprise. No real business, beyond survival, in this faded Chapeltown. And across the street, where the Hayfield pub would have stood, there is now nothing. Nothing at all. It is gone. (*Like you, David. Gone.*) The bottom of Button Hill is empty.

The dark 'others' began to arrive in Leeds in the fifties. But what kind of a city was this that expected these newcomers to live like animals in abandoned bombed-out slums? The emigrants had heard rumours that the English often set fires in their houses, but until they reached England and felt the sharp bite of their first winter they did not fully understand. But they soon learned. However, what they never learned to understand, or accept, was the racism which confined them to filthy rooms. Landlords, including Leeds City Council, seemed intent upon extracting money from them in exchange for rooms in which it was barely possible to turn around; rooms which one had to share with mice and fleas and rats, where water ran down the walls when it rained, and thereafter snails crawled up them; rooms where the nearest bathroom was your handbasin, and your one toilet bowl was in the next street and had to be shared with 200 others. The mother country was welcoming her citizens at the front door, and then quickly ushering them out through the back door crying, 'No Blacks', crying, 'No Coloureds', crying, 'Go back to where you come from'. And David heard these shouts, but he wanted an education in order that he might make something of himself in England, and so he redoubled his polite efforts to learn. He worked harder, and studied harder, but still they took him to Armley jail, and then on to the asylum where they changed his personality. And when they released him back into the world, David soon discovered that he had lost his damp, cold room at 209 Belle Vue Road. Even this dismal place had slipped through his fingers, but he still possessed his city of Leeds on the banks of the River Aire. David still had his city.

I have to say that by the later stages I believe some fatalism had begun to creep into David's spirit. He expected to be arrested, so he didn't bother to try and hide. He just kept going back to the heart of the city centre and staying there where he knew that he would be very visible. It was as though he was challenging them to remove him from the city. They would beat him and arrest him, but his attitude was clear: 'I'll just do what I want to do and I won't disappear. I won't be invisible.' It was all very rational to him. He knew the consequences, but he continued to defy people. As I said, he could have slept every night in the back of his Ghanaian friend's warehouse if he'd have wanted to. He could have had a flat, or he could have been safe and invisible in different parts of the city, but he didn't want to disappear. He wanted to be seen, and Leeds was his battleground – his home – and he wasn't going to leave his home. In the later stages he sometimes gave the outward signs of being a shambling, slow-witted, slow-walking man, but he always knew where he was going. He knew Meanwood, Hyde Park, and Chapeltown; he understood the streets. He knew the safe areas, but he also knew that if he took Step A then Step B would follow. He made a rational decision to take Step A, which was to go back into Leeds city centre and claim his right to be in the city. Step B was to be beaten, arrested and then carted off to Armley jail. First Step A and then Step B, but he wouldn't give up. During this time there was, to my memory, no other black person from Africa or the Caribbean who was homeless and on the street. In the sixties, David was the only black man sleeping rough on the streets of Leeds.

My father was a military-minded man. Being an army sergeant, he was dominant in the family and he was difficult. My joining the police force was his idea and he said it would make a man of me. My mother was silent on the matter, as she was on most things. She was ten years younger than my father, and she didn't get a look in when it came to decisions. At the age of nineteen I thought I'd give it a crack and join the Leeds police force and see if I could get my father on my side. Initially I liked Leeds, and I liked the life on The Headrow. I was stationed in the centre of Leeds. Millgarth Station covered a non-residential area. Issues at Millgarth were mainly to do with crime, vagrancy, revellers in the pubs, drug users, and there was supposed to be a 'problem' with students. I was very friendly with the tradesmen on my patch, but what I didn't do was make friends with anybody in the force. Not one single person. This caused me problems because the police service in Leeds was like a closed club. I remember being told to choose my friends from within the force, and not from outside it, and this was a sticking point for me. I had been seen by someone in a pub in Wetherby with my old school pals and I was on the carpet for that. I was up in front of an inspector and he said, 'Who are you mixing with outside duty hours?' I remember thinking this wasn't actually going to work for me. On duty or off duty, you had to stay within the group of officers, but I didn't really have any friends in the force. But, at least to begin with, I did enjoy working in the centre of Leeds. There *were* some black people that would turn up in the centre, and they didn't have an easy time. You might find somebody who'd been out drinking and hadn't caught the bus home, or somebody who was trying to get into a hotel, or somebody who was separated from their group of friends. But generally speaking, black people and mixed-race people were rare sights in Leeds city centre at that time in the sixties. I patrolled mainly around the area of Vicar Lane, The Headrow, and then going down towards the river area and around the open market. The business people – café owners, restaurant owners, shop owners – they all regarded the police as people who could do no wrong. And the police were fiercely proud of this and so there was a very strong feeling that the police were there to serve the incumbent business people. I befriended quite a few café owners, you know, people that you could go and chat to, and who made you feel that you were part of the community. Now in the daytime, that was all very nice and it was all very cosy. In the night it was a different place. The streets were deserted, people had gone home, and the police, what were they to do? What was their job then? Well, it was to check property. To scour about and make sure that they didn't find broken windows around entrances at the rear of properties. At night the city centre, instead of being the business people's place, became very much the Leeds of the authorities and of the policemen. And that's really an important thing – the change of the city from day to night. On my patch I befriended quite a few dossers and I used to go and chat to them. There was a tea stall in the open market which may or may not still be operating, and it used to open at about five in the morning, and I would always drop in. And you'd get a mixed bunch of people and they accepted me. I used to take my hat off and chat with them. In fact one officer said that I had the attitude of a social worker to the job, which was not thought to be a good thing. But I did, I used to take my hat off. I was in a very difficult position. Life with my father was greatly improved, but I soon realised that I didn't like some of what was going on in Leeds. I was very concerned because it was becoming obvious that there were some difficulties for a certain individual. I was in a terrible state of moral dilemma. If anybody was still about in Leeds city centre after the late night taxi queue it was very rare. A couple of times I did find a drunk, but it was very rare. In the two years I worked the patch, I can't remember finding a person at say four o'clock in the morning. I never did. Only David. I never found another dosser sleeping out anywhere. The other dossers might have had somewhere they knew they could go; to the crypt or whatever. I can't remember exactly *when* I first saw David, but I know I saw him on my foot patrol in the Millgarth area. He would go into the deep shops. I know the Bridal House was one that he went into. Yeah. He'd be in there. But he'd be in other ones on Vicar Lane as well. He tried to get into the deep shops. The ones which have got two entrances. He was always alone. I never saw him with anybody, and he wouldn't be at the café in the morning. Some of the other dossers would be at the café, but not him. I used to wonder where he got his food from. I saw him quite a lot, but he never ran away from me. He wouldn't enter into a conversation with a policeman, he just wouldn't talk. But he didn't run away. Whereas, if he saw Inspector Ellerker or Sergeant Kitching he would run, and he would shout. But he wouldn't run from me.

＊

The prison sits on the high ground of Armley, its massive Victorian exterior and castellated towers dominating the horizon like a medieval fortress. Constructed in 1847 of stone from local quarries, its purpose was to both punish and to intimidate. Ninety-three people have been hanged at HMP Leeds, the last in 1961; the gallows were eventually dismantled in 1965. Today, the prison is no less intimidating. I stand in the reception area and look at the noticeboard. On the wall there is a picture of the Race Relations Management Team. Three white faces, including the governor of the prison. 'HMP Leeds is committed to the elimination of harassment and discrimination in all areas of work.' Times appear to have changed. 'No single racial group will be allowed to dominate any activity to the unfair exclusion of others.' I enter the prison itself. The chapel is now the multi-faith centre. On all four wings I see different races, and out in the exercise yard the faces are an advert for multi-racial Britain. The warder smiles at me. 'Today we cater for all different religious foods and practices, except Jewish. Roman Catholic and Muslim are the main ones.' I look again at the prisoners sprawled on the ground trying to soak up the weak rays of the sun. 'Back then they had to walk in circles for an hour. But it's different now.' The warder thinks for a moment. 'Easier for them, I suppose.'

I saw Oluwale on a number of occasions and I note, by looking at the hospital case papers, that when I saw him on 25 October, 1965, he complained to me about the police and I asked him what he was in prison for and he said, 'Fighting with the police.' After further questioning I deduced that he had been fighting with the police in Albion Street on 13 October, 1965, he said, 'A policeman removed his hat and grasped his [*sic*] throat.' He alleged that this had occurred because he had been sleeping in an empty house in Albion Street and was about to enter the house at 7:30 p.m. when two policemen accosted him and he added, 'They took me to Leeds Town Hall.' My assessment of Oluwale's intelligence is that he was a 'dullard'.

Denis Power, Senior Medical Officer at HMP Leeds 1962–7

The last time I saw David was a few months before he died. It was dark and wintertime, and my husband and I were coming back from some university dance. David was by the public lavatories at Hyde Park Corner. There were shrubs and bushes there, and a bench. It was the sort of place that was used for 'cottaging'. Well, David was sitting on the bench, and my husband went over to the chip shop and got him a bag of chips, which he took. David said that he didn't want to go home with us. He insisted that he had somewhere to go, and so we left him sitting by himself on the bench. At the dances that David used to come to after he first arrived, he never paired off or chatted up women. He was very solitary. But, as I said, he was a marvellous dancer. And he liked church singing. You know, he used to look in the papers to see if any West Indians had died so that he could go to the funeral, but it had to be in a church that would accept black people. The Anglicans discriminated against the blacks, but the Methodists were cooler. David wasn't a practising Christian, but he was educated by Christian missionaries, that much I do know.

As far as I remember he just called at the hostel and asked for accommodation. [Between 17 April and 4 July, 1968] I do not think he was sent there by any social-work organisation . . . He did not mix with the other men in the hostel and he had no friends that I knew of. As far as I can remember he left the hostel of his own accord. About May, 1969, nearly a year later, the police . . . asked me to identify a body that they had found in the River Aire. I was unable to make a positive identification as the face was badly distorted. As far as I know, Oluwale never attacked anybody in the hostel and certainly never attacked my wife. He did ask my wife to live with him in a room away from the hostel, but she told him not to be stupid and ignored his remark. I never spoke to Oluwale about the suggestion he made to my wife. The type of man we usually get in the hostels are capable of making such suggestions and my wife and I have learned to ignore them.

Raymond Bradbury, officer in charge of Church Army Hostel, 53 The Calls, Leeds

I heard the word on the street that David had drowned. I knew that he had been systematically badly treated by the police over a number of years, but I didn't put two and two together even though I was still running the Chapeltown Commonwealth Citizens Committee. Then, over a year after we lost David, Austin Haywood, who was the new chief constable, took me into his office and said that two of his officers were going to be charged and tried for manslaughter. I nearly fell over, but in my heart I knew that it made some kind of sense. It was almost unbelievable, and it produced a rising tide of anger, not just in me, but in everyone. We all felt that we should have done more, for we *did* know some things. However, everybody also felt that David had a right to live his life as he pleased, and that he should be able to exercise the dignity of deciding if he needed our help or not. But there *was* a feeling of responsibility. After all, I'd made many, many complaints against the police. In fact, over 400, but there was no getting away from the fact that it was a nightmare in this city for young black men. The police were out of control. It wasn't just a hard-core minority of people in Leeds who didn't want foreigners, it was also the police. With David's death it became obvious that if things didn't change in Leeds then David was simply going to be the first of many dead black men.

To me, David was a fighter for freedom. He was *not* another victim. You see, his life and death affected a whole generation. His life led to the full emergence of the Black Power movement in this city, and to black and white people finally saying 'enough'. David made it possible for a demonstration to be a thousand people, not just two or three. His death was a warning to all society, including white society. I wanted all the white institutions to wake up and realise that there *was* danger around them. That there was no such thing as a racist joke. If it's racist then it's not a joke. In the wake of David's death the police invited citizens in to help them with the training of the police in this sensitive area. And I became one of the teachers.

He would always hide in doorways so he was easy to find. I mean, as a young policeman, I knew little back alleyways and ginnels that he could have gone up. But he didn't do that. He just went in the doorways, which left him vulnerable. But I don't remember exactly which ones. They were down Vicar Lane as well as The Headrow. Inspector Ellerker and Sergeant Kitching had a fascination for David. He would always run away from them, and yet he would sleep in those doorways on their patch. Why? God knows. Sometimes he would go away for a while and things would calm down. We would hope, well I would hope, that he wouldn't come back. But then he would come back. Ellerker and Kitching always wanted to find him, but if I saw David I did not report that I'd seen him. This is the only good thing that I did. So I think that in some ways by always coming back he was actually just being courageous and not letting them have what they wanted. Because he never used to plead with them. He would run away but he never pleaded with them. He actually remained a problem for them. It was as if he was pushing them, you know. As if he wasn't going to let them have the satisfaction. I was inside the van when they did have a go at him. And it was terrible, it was just unbelievable. Absolutely dreadful. I was driving the van. They would look for him, and they would find him. Then they would go through the motions of arresting him. And then, when he was inside the van, they would beat him, but he kept his dignity. He never asked them to stop or pleaded with them, or anything. It was as if they were machines, and it was just a job of work. It was like that, and they would beat him. There was one occasion when it was like this, and then there were other occasions when I saw them chasing him, but I actually didn't see the business. Once they beat him with a rubber torch and the torch all fell apart. All the glass – merciless, merciless. I remember when they were hitting him they were very careful not to hit his face, because then there would be no evidence when they went into the court. They had ways of doing stuff, and the ethos of rank was very, very strong. Some of the police officers at that time had come in from the army, and they were what was known as old school. They were people who had been sergeants or privates or whatever. I can't say for definite, but I believe that Kenneth Kitching had been somebody who had come in that way. He was an older man. My experience was that a young PC could not approach a senior officer for any reason. He would only take orders, and that was the job – to take orders and not ask questions.

Personally, I didn't know what Oluwale did. I was a West Indian community leader then, as I am now, but I couldn't say that I knew him that well. However, it did create a very bad feeling in the West Indian community when we found out that he had been killed. You see, the David Oluwale that I remember was a man who used to keep himself to himself, but he was present at most of the functions that we used to have. Social dances and so on at the Astoria Ballroom. Oluwale liked dancing and he used to go to the African Hi Life dances. The music and the singing preserved us, and I think that without it we'd have been wiped out. At that time West Indians had pride in their dress and wore three-piece pinstripe suits, and Oluwale was the same. He liked to dress. But later on I remember seeing him just standing by the side of the road crying. It was very painful when we heard how he was hunted like a fox by the police. Apart from the colour angle, you just couldn't believe what you were hearing in a British courtroom. That kind of treatment of a human being was unacceptable, and the truth was it just made things go worse with the police. We used to tell them right out, if they wanted another Oluwale then they were not going to get one from us. We now knew exactly what we were dealing with when it came to the British policeman.

We heard about it at the station, obviously. And I remember at the time that when the other police officers talked about it they didn't talk about it as a tragedy. It was talked about as 'the balloon's gone up'. You know, it's out now. It was that kind of conversation. It wasn't talked about from the point of view of David Oluwale's position at all. It was just, you know, 'Oh well, we're in for trouble now' sort of thing. I'd go home. My father and mother must have seen the information about the trial on the television. In fact, I was on the television. I was there and they included remarks that Ellerker had made about me on the television to try and discredit me as a witness. My mother and father would not discuss this matter with me. My father didn't want to know. He would hear nothing said against the police force. So I got no support there. My relationship with my father went back downhill, ice-cold again. I was very confused about the situation. I was feeling isolated, and I was also thinking about David's isolation. I found myself thinking a lot about what had happened to him. And since then I've had these flashbacks about that. The worst feeling of all is that the tragedy was predictable, and no one, including myself, prevented it. Obviously, I left the police force. When I went to the court I met some other officers who had left the force as well, and who'd been giving evidence. So I realised that I wasn't alone. I had a feeling of guilt then and I've got it now. We shouldn't have let it happen. I'd even thought about getting David in my car and driving him away myself. You know, doing something like that, and trying to get him away from it. But I had my own trouble with Ellerker and it was all terrible. I didn't speak to anyone about it, but I hoped that it would be a conviction for manslaughter. I didn't know what had happened on the night David died but I thought that there must have been other police officers around at the time. There wouldn't have been just the two of them, so I wondered about that. And I thought that the evidence given by witnesses to assaults on David must have been powerful, and that my own evidence must have been powerful. So I thought that manslaughter was the best we could get.

The trial concerning the death of David Oluwale took place in November 1971. It opened on 11 November and lasted thirteen days, concluding on 24 November. The judge was Mr Justice Hinchcliffe (seventy-one). Prosecuting for the Crown was Mr John Cobb (forty-eight) and the barristers for the two defendants were Mr Gilbert Gray (forty-three) representing former Inspector Ellerker, and Mr Basil Widoger (fifty) representing Sergeant Kitching. The jurors included two women and one coloured man. The first defendant, Sergeant Kenneth Mark Kitching (forty-nine) of Blakeney Grove, Hunslet, was born in 1922. Sergeant Kitching had joined the police force in August 1950. He was married, but without children. He was described as an 'old time' sergeant who was proud of the fact that he chose to wear a helmet as opposed to a peaked cap. He stuck to a regular routine, which usually involved rising at lunchtime, having a few pints of beer in a 'police' pub, returning home for a meal and some sleep before reporting to Millgarth Station for the night shift. He was known to be Ellerker's right-hand man and confidant. His co-defendant was former Inspector Geoffrey Ellerker (thirty-eight) of Church Lane, Horsforth. Born in 1933, former Inspector Ellerker had joined the police force in December 1956. He was married with two children, a boy and a girl. He was made a sergeant in 1964, but in April 1968 he was promoted to uniformed inspector and put in charge of the night shift at Millgarth Station, overseeing the south section of the city centre. Between 10 p.m. and 6 a.m. he was the highest-ranking officer on duty, but he harboured a well-known ambition to be a non-uniform inspector and was somewhat frustrated in his career. Both men were, at the time of the alleged crime, serving in the A Division of the Leeds City Police Force. Both men were charged with the manslaughter of David Oluwale. At the time that the charges were brought in April 1971, Geoffrey Ellerker was in Lincoln jail. In December 1969 a seventy-two-year-old lady was knocked down and killed by a car that was driven by a superintendent of police. Ellerker attempted to cover up for his fellow officer, claiming that he could smell alcohol on the breath of the victim. It later transpired that the victim was teetotal. Ellerker was found guilty of misconduct as an officer of justice and he received a nine-month prison term. Already discredited as a former police officer, the David Oluwale case would thrust Ellerker, together with the middle-aged sergeant, back into the lime-light for it was claimed that the pair of them had 'hounded and tormented' Oluwale before he drowned in April 1969. They enjoyed, what they called, 'tickling' the Nigerian vagrant with their boots, and on one occasion it was alleged that Oluwale was actually lifted off the ground, within the confines of Millgarth Station, when Ellerker kicked him hard between the legs. It was claimed that such incidents were habitual pastimes for the two officers who made it their business to terrorise a defenceless man.

The case had come to light because a little over a year after the death of David Oluwale in April 1969, an eighteen-year-old police cadet, Gareth Galvin, overheard rumours of what had *really* happened to the Nigerian vagrant. He informed his sergeant at the cadet training school, who in turn passed on young Gareth Galvin's concerns to his own superiors. Eventually police headquarters at Scotland Yard in London became involved and the 'Oluwale Squad' was set up on the third floor of Leeds' Westgate Police Station. The squad was established with great secrecy, and under very tight security, with the investigation being led by Detective Chief Superintendent James Fryer and Detective Chief Inspector Len Shakeshaft, both of Leeds Criminal Investigation Department. They set about interviewing every policeman and woman, and every traffic warden in Leeds; in the end they interviewed 1,170 men and women, including Kitching and Ellerker. During interrogation, Kitching denied giving anything other than the odd slap to David Oluwale, but he went on and said, 'I can only describe him [Oluwale] as a wild animal, not a human being.' As the concerns of the 'Oluwale Squad' deepened a new post-mortem was ordered. A Home Office pathologist travelled from London to Leeds, and it was shortly after he had completed his work that Sergeant Kitching and former Inspector Ellerker were charged with manslaughter.

At the trial the defendants' lawyers sought to 'characterise' David Oluwale. They presented him to the jury as a man born in Lagos, Nigeria, in 1930 as a member of the Yoruba tribe. He was, according to them, possibly a fisherman. He had stowed away to England in 1949 and arrived as an illegal teenage immigrant in Hull. He was sentenced to twenty-eight days in jail for this crime, and he began his sentence at Armley jail on 3 September, 1949. As far as the defence was concerned, Oluwale was 'not quite educationally subnormal', but he was certainly not 'bright'. Variously known to the police as 'Ollie', 'Ali', 'Uggi', or 'Lone Duckie', he was a loner with not many friends. His mental health problems allegedly began in 1953, and he entered High Royds Hospital in Menston where he was a patient for the next eight years. The defence called Dr Richard Corty, who was the consulting psychiatrist at High Royds. The doctor stated that, 'at times [Oluwale was] completely withdrawn and inaccessible and on other occasions aggressive, noisy, violent, and disturbed . . . He was hallucinating – he saw animals, lions with fish's heads and said these animals were going to kill and eat him . . . He bit people, spat, but his condition gradually improved so that he was no longer giggling and talking to himself in a confused or childish manner. Originally he would defecate and urinate in the ward. He had two jobs but lost them through fighting and stealing.' The defence then called a staff nurse, a Mr Eric Dent, who described Oluwale as 'built like a miniature Mr Universe and [he] could take more punishment than Cassius Clay'. Mr Dent went on to assert that Oluwale was 'like a savage animal'.

The defence claimed that during his twenty years in England, Oluwale had been imprisoned on numerous occasions for assault on police, disorderly conduct, and 'walking abroad'. He had often been picked up under Section 4 of the Vagrancy Act, 1824, which empowered the police with the right to stop anyone they suspected of committing an offence. According to the police, Oluwale had often been violent to those who had crossed his path, and he habitually used newspapers for sheets and a duffel bag for a pillow. He was no more than a 'dosser' who didn't work, and he was not acceptable as an inmate of a hostel. All Ellerker and Kitching wanted was a 'clean city' and, with this in mind, Oluwale was a problem. The defence argued that this was a man who drew social security payments so that he might simply spend them on alcohol. According to former Inspector Ellerker, 'Oluwale was a small, chunky man, filthy in his personal habits. He was not the sort of man one wanted to grapple with too long or too close . . . His language was dirty, and he was fluent in the use of four-letter words . . . when Oluwale became excited he would set up a high-pitched screaming noise – although nothing was happening to him. He would scream and shout before being spoken to.' Chief Superintendent Leonard Barker appeared for the defence and reminded the court that Sergeant Kitching had recently been presented with a Humane Society Award for rescuing a man who had fallen into the River Aire.

The prosecution presented a somewhat different version of events. They spoke of the continued harassment that Oluwale had been subjected to since arriving in England as a teenager, and how this harassment became more systematic and malicious between August 1968 and his death in April 1969. During this eight-month period David Oluwale was relentlessly hounded by Sergeant Kitching and former Inspector Ellerker. On 27 September, 1968, David was jailed for six months for alleged assault on the police and Sergeant Kitching told a colleague, Police Constable Yeager, that he could not wait for Oluwale to come out because 'there wasn't another one like him'. David was released from prison on 10 April, 1969 and eight days later, on the morning of 18 April, he drowned in the River Aire. The court was told that Sergeant Kitching and former Inspector Ellerker had made it clear that they did not want David Oluwale within the boundaries of the city of Leeds. Any sighting of David Oluwale was to be reported directly to them, and an officer was once reproved by them for dealing with Oluwale directly.

> It became well known at Millgarth Station that if ever Oluwale was sighted within the town a message had to passed through for them [Kitching and Ellerker] to go out and deal with him. They were off in quick pursuit as soon as the message was received.

John Cobb, Crown Prosecutor

The prosecution called Police Constable Cyril Batty who testified that in May 1968 he had witnessed Sergeant Kitching urinating on David Oluwale in Lands Lane in the centre of Leeds. Former Inspector Ellerker was holding a torch, but at the time Police Constable Batty chose to say nothing in order that he might protect his career.

> Kitching and Ellerker were pushing Oluwale like a plaything, backwards and forwards, with the flat of their hands. Oluwale was clasping his duffel bag, containing all his worldly possessions.

John Cobb, Crown Prosecutor

They told him [Oluwale] to get up. He was on his hands and knees and the sergeant and the inspector kicked them away, causing him to fall. The inspector started to beat him about the head and shoulders with his duffel bag.

PC Seager

On another occasion, on 7 August, 1968, the two defendants radioed a call to Police Constable Keith Seager. Upon arrival, Seager was instructed by Sergeant Kitching and former Inspector Ellerker to drive them, plus David Oluwale, to Bramhope village on the outskirts of Leeds. Once there Police Constable Seager was instructed to stop outside of the Fox and Hounds public house and David Oluwale was ordered to get out and knock on the door of the pub and ask for a cup of tea. It was four o'clock in the morning. Police Constable Seager drove his fellow officers back to Leeds city centre and left David Oluwale in Bramhope.

The entry [in my notebook] which Ellerker told me to make was not true. I told him I did not like the idea.

PC Seager

The prosecution asserted that on other occasions David Oluwale had been driven by the defendants to Middleton Woods in South Leeds and left there in the middle of the night. Police Constable Phillip Ratcliffe and former Police

Constable Hazel Dalby both saw the defendants kick Oluwale so hard in the groin that he was lifted off the floor. They saw David Oluwale crying silent tears of pain and emitting no noise.

I have never seen a man crying so much and never utter a sound.

PC Phillip Ratcliffe

Police Constable Kenneth Higgins testified that the defendants made David Oluwale bump his head hard against the floor. He heard Sergeant Kitching claim that both he and former Inspector Ellerker made David Oluwale bow down before them, and he heard Sergeant Kitching say, on reading the report of Oluwale's death, that 'it looks as though we shall have to find a new playmate now'. When Oluwale's body was found, PC Seager remembered Sergeant Kitching reading a teleprinter message about the death. 'He looked at me and said: "I wonder how he got in there." It was in a jovial sense; he was smiling.' Police Constable Frank Atkinson fainted after giving evidence that he had seen Oluwale beaten up at the police station.

I have made a search of prison records in respect of a man named David Oluwale or Oluwole or Uluwale or Oluwuala or Uluwle.

Marjorie Whitaker, Executive Officer in the Discipline Office at HMP Leeds

1. **Admitted** 2.9.49 Sentence Stowaway — 28 days imprisonment. **Discharged** 30.9.49
2. **Admitted** 27.4.53 Sentence 1. Assault Police — 2 months imprisonment. Sentence 2. Wilful Damage — 1 month imprisonment concurrent. Sentence 3. Disorderly conduct — 28 days concurrent. **Discharged** 6.6.53 to St James' Hospital.
3. **Admitted** 22.9.62 as Oluwole. Malicious Wounding — 6 months imprisonment. Transferred to Hull 25.10.62. **Released** 2.2.63
4. **Admitted** 13.4.64 Disorderly Conduct — 28 days. **Discharged** 6.5.64 (fine paid)
5. **Admitted** 16.10.64 Drunk and Disorderly — 14 days. Plus 28 days on Lodged Warrant for D&D. **Discharged** 16.11.64
6. **Admitted** 13.10.65 Hospital Order, transferred to Menston 11.11.65
7. **Admitted** 29.8.67 as Olowuala. Wandering Abroad. **Discharged** 23.9.67
8. **Admitted** 27.10.67 Wandering Abroad. **Discharged** 1.12.67
9. **Admitted** 26.12.67 1. Wandering Abroad. 2. Indecent Exposure — 3 months imprisonment. Transferred to Preston Prison 3.1.68. **Released** 29.3.68
10. **Admitted** 4.9.68 Assaulting a Police Officer. Transferred to Preston Prison, 10.1.69
11. **Admitted** 13.1.69 Disorderly Conduct. **Discharged** 23.1.69
12. **Admitted** 27.1.69 Disorderly Conduct. **Discharged** 5.2.69

13. **Admitted 24.2.69** Disorderly Conduct. **Discharged 8.3.69**
14. **Admitted 12.3.69** Trespass Railway. Disorderly Conduct. **Discharged 10.4.69**

On 10 April, 1969 I was on early reception duty. One of my duties would have been to restore personal clothing, property and money to prisoners being discharged . . . One of the prisoners discharged on 10 April, 1969 was a coloured man named David Oluwale. I can say that he was handed the following items of property and clothing: one blue shirt, one plastic cup, two reels of cotton, one hymn book, one form U/140, one leather purse, one form EC4, one leather wallet, one form P45, two photos, one out-of-date bank book, one rosary and one ballpoint pen. All these items were in a plastic bag. I can verify when released, Oluwale was wearing the following clothing: one brown check cap, a green check single-breasted overcoat, a grey striped check waistcoat, a green fancy necktie, pair of brown suede rubber-soled shoes, black fancy socks, green check trousers, elastic braces and a plastic belt . . . Most of his clothing was in poor condition.

William Edward Swapp, Prison Officer, HMP Leeds

Records state that on 10 April, 1969 I interviewed
David Oluwale . . . and he was later paid £4 cash.

Phillip Davies, Executive Officer at DHSS

Date of discharge: 10.4.69.
Private cash: £1. 17. 1
Discharge grant: −
Offence: Trespassing, disorderly conduct, times two.
Sentence: 30 days.
Last discharge: Leeds 8.3.69
Address: Living rough.
Any relevant reports (Probation, Children's Officer);
   any domestic problems: states nil.
Notes and comments of Prison Welfare Officer,
   13.3.69
Several prison sentences. Released 8 March. Had
   not worked for some time. No job on release.
   Single, NSA. Nowhere to go on release. Will
   probably go to a hostel or some furnished
   accommodation. Rapidly becoming a social
   problem (so reports).
Pre-release interview.
This man has been released after a sentence of 30
   days. Latterly he had been coming to prison every
   month or so. It is increasingly obvious that he is
   completely unable to function on the outside.
Mr Hoyle was present during the interview and it was
   quite impossible to get through to him. He seemed

schizoid to me, one wonders whether or not he was capable of knowing what the discussion was all about. It is certain, however, that he had nowhere to live and no job to go to.

It is doubtful if he is capable of making a sustained effort at any job. He was told that if he reported to Mr Hoyle on discharge he would be given every assistance possible.

Plan: Will go to Leeds to look for lodgings. Will sign on at Ministry of Labour. May contact probation and/see officer.

Clothes: –

(Signed) W. H. Halla, Prison Welfare Officer

The Leeds Probation Office.
The Leeds Probation Service, 10.4.69.
At the Office.
Discharged from Leeds Prison today.
He was not excitable, and it was almost impossible to understand him. He said that he had £1. 19. which was his own money and that he would have no difficulty in finding an address if he gets some more. Gave him a letter to the MOSS at St Paul Street and told him to go straight there. Phoned the manager, Mr Denison, and explained the situation, and he said they would do what they could to help him so that he will have some money to put down for lodgings.

Letter written by a senior probation officer to Mr W. Hoyle at the Department of Health and Social Security, 10 April, 1969.

Dear Sir,

Re David Oluwale. This man was discharged from Leeds prison this morning. I understand that he has £1. 19. He had lived in lodgings in Leeds previously and said that he would have no difficulty in finding lodgings again if he has the money.

He is a somewhat difficult man to place in lodgings and I see no alternative but allowing him to find his own.

I should be obliged, therefore, if you will take an application from him for assistance so that he can find lodgings.

As I said, I was a young police officer, but I remember. He seemed to be very small. I saw him when he was sleeping and I didn't wake him up. I saw him when he was walking about, and I saw him when he was dealing with Ellerker and Kitching. I did not see someone who was weak and all sort of jellyish. I saw somebody who was doing his business. He was going about his routine, despite the harassment, and he would still choose to go into that same Bridal House. He would still be there. And so, what I saw was somebody with some sort of courage. But, I mean, weird. I did sense that he'd got mental health problems. Because the other dossers generally were drinkers, and you know, they'd be drunk, very drunk sometimes, but not David. I sensed that his issues were different from that. I guessed that he'd been in some sort of psychiatric care. Yeah I definitely guessed that, and that's one of the things that makes it so poignant. It was the isolation, the fact that he didn't seem to be a user of any sort, and that generally speaking he was just a mild, quiet person. And I just thought, why does this have to be happening to him? The injustice, you know, that it had to be him. Somebody who didn't have anybody to help him. But I saw that the man had some dignity. I think he was really pissed off. That's what I think. He was absolutely pissed off. That's what I believe, but that's only a feeling. I think he was really, really pissed off with what had gone on.

At 3 a.m. on the morning of 18 April, former Inspector Ellerker and Sergeant Kitching found David in the doorway to John Peters' furniture shop on Lands Lane in the centre of Leeds. They 'moved him on'. (*'I heard the sound of blows being struck. I saw Oluwale run out of the entrance [of the shop] covering his head with his arms . . . I have not seen Oluwale since that time.' PC Seager*) A little over an hour later the two policemen discovered David elsewhere in the city and they chased him. (*'We dragged him to his feet and I booted his backside. I did not kick him too hard, just enough to wake him up. He screamed but then he always screamed when I dealt with him.' Sergeant Kitching*) David ran down Call Lane and in the direction of Warehouse Hill. David Oluwale was never again seen alive. He entered the River Aire at the foot of Warehouse Hill, just by Leeds Bridge. On 4 May, 1969, Leeds police frogman Police Constable Ian Haste recovered David Oluwale's body from the River Aire some three miles east of the city centre at a point near Knostrop Sewage Works.

> I received a telephone call from the Information Room, to the effect that there was a body in the River Aire at Knostrop and that I was required to go there and recover the body ... the body appeared to be lodged on some obstruction. I put my frogman equipment on and swam to the body. I saw that it was the body of a man, who appeared to be coloured ... I pulled the body from the obstruction by its feet and pushed it downstream ... I returned along the bank ... PC Sedman turned the body over and I recognised it as a coloured man called David Oluwale who I knew from my police service in the city centre ... a vagrant who used to doss down in John Peters' doorway in the city centre. I used to move him on when I worked from Millgarth Street but I have never arrested him for anything. He was just another of the city characters. I can never remember him causing me any sort of trouble.

PC Ian Haste

Police Constable Francis Sedman helped to recover the body from the river. He noticed a large lump on David's forehead, bleeding from an eye, a bruise on the right upper arm, and the fact that David's lips were cut. Inspector Leonard Bradley was also at the scene, where he searched Oluwale's pockets, providing the following list of items:

National Health Medical Card
2 Photos
Income Tax Form (P45)
2 After Care forms
2 Leeds City Magistrate Receipts
6 Forms 103
Irish Information Centres in England card
A Blue bead necklace with a crucifix on
A felt pen
2 ballpoint pens
A toothbrush
Comb
Post Office savings book

I accepted the body into the mortuary and cut the clothing from it because it was rotten ... I put the number '451' on the legs and the name 'Oluwale' on the body, and put it in the refrigeration unit ... Later, some uniformed officers came to the mortuary and identified the body to me as Oluwale. There was no conversation other than someone saying, 'It's Oluwale.'

Reginald Fricker, mortuary attendant at St James' Hospital

Dr David John Gee, Senior Lecturer in Forensic Medicine at Leeds University, examined David Oluwale's body on 5 May, 1969. He concluded death by drowning, and observed that David Oluwale had received a blow to the forehead before entering the water.

> In the case of the deceased, Oluwale, diatoms were found in the lungs but not beyond them and therefore the tests do not provide conclusive proof that he met his death by drowning, but in the absence of any gross injuries or natural disease I formed the opinion the death was due to drowning . . . The bruise on the forehead of Oluwale was purple and swollen. The purple colour indicates that the bruise was sustained within about one or two days before death or a similar period after death. The fact that the bruise was swollen indicates in my view that it is most likely that it occurred during life though it is possible but less likely for such a bruise to be caused after death in a body immersed in water . . . I did not see a large bruise on Oluwale's upper right arm . . . Oluwale's lips were swollen and the skin in parts of the face were separating due to putrefactive change. These putrefactive changes could give the inexperienced eye the appearance of injuries such as cuts and bruises especially when in the body of a coloured person such as Oluwale . . .

Dr David John Gee

David Oluwale was buried in a pauper's grave at Killingbeck Cemetery – plot B5850A – courtesy of Leeds Corporation's Welfare Department. He was buried with nine strangers.

✻

Before the last day of the trial, Justice Hinchcliffe ordered the manslaughter charge to be dismissed. He concluded that there were no witnesses to the charge and therefore no evidence. On 24 November, 1971 the jury returned a verdict of guilty of three charges of assault against Sergeant Kitching, who received a twenty-seven-month sentence, and a verdict of guilty of assault relating to four charges against former Inspector Ellerker, who received a three-year sentence. Justice Hinchcliffe's summing-up contained the following plea: 'Policemen are members of a fine and splendid profession, and without them there could be anarchy and chaos. But you must not allow the fact that the two accused were police officers to influence you one iota. You do get black sheep in every flock.'

The way I see it, the legacy of Oluwale in this city is that a man had to lose his life to get people to sit up and notice what was happening. It's a high price to pay, especially when things are worse now than they were then for my West Indian community. Today there is still a high percentage of black people in prisons and mental homes. The one with the briefcase is a smokescreen. And people still care if they have to sit next to you on the bus, and we can't walk some streets without feeling like a novelty, and the concept of us is still low. Mr Oluwale paid a high price, but sometimes when I drive down Chapeltown Road and see the lack of discipline, and children having children, and what we've allowed ourselves to become, then I feel bitter. Parents have lost control of their kids and

England has taken them. David Oluwale paid a high price to get people's attention, but for what?

27 Church Lane, Horsforth, Leeds 18. By a church. A small estate of respectable semi-detached and detached brick homes. Built in the sixties for the upwardly mobile middle classes. Safe. Neat. Shrubbery. Trees. The estate oozes civic pride. I watch an old man edge slowly out of a door on his Zimmer frame. Another old man, a neighbour (with his shirt off), puts the hose over his plants and trees. They've all worked and lived together. Now they are retired together. Closed community. Protecting each other. There is a blue saloon car parked outside number 27. Neat white net curtains in the windows. The house overlooks the church. Quiet peaceful house. Net-curtained respectability. A TV aerial on the roof. Two teenage schoolboys in white shirts and long black trousers, ties flying in the breeze, backpacks hanging off one shoulder, lollop by with cans of Coke in their fists. There is a burglar alarm to the side of the house number. It is yellow. From the back of the house there is a spectacular view of the Aire Valley. A panoramic view over the city of Leeds. Enjoy your retirement, former Inspector Ellerker. Black sheep.

Middleton Woods. South Leeds. Beyond Hunslet and Beeston. Close to Belle Isle. David was dropped in wilderness and found himself surrounded by dark, inhospitable nature. The nearest one might approach to a jungle of untamed land on the southern edge of Leeds. Go back to nature, black boy from Lagos. Go back to the jungle. Come, let me take you there. And today, thirty-five years later, one can see houses decorated with Union Jacks on the fringes of these same dark woods. And a church which flies the cross of St George. Smashed cars litter the streets. Unmarried teenage mothers push babies in second-hand prams around the perimeter of the dark woods. Houses sprout satellite dishes of various sizes. When I walk down the street, parka- and trainer-clad youths stare hard at me. They bare teeth that are a gated yellowish entryway into their spotted faces. Ten o'clock in the morning and already these youngsters are waiting for the pub to open. They have nothing else to do with their time except loiter around the boarded-up off-licence. In the daytime this is a zone of deprivation and depression. Every other house displays a 'For Sale' sign. At night, to be dumped and abandoned in the heart of the woods. Imagine it. No 'For Sale' signs. No humans. No light. In the heart of the woods. A terrifying hell, to be lost in a wood whose expanse is the size of a small town. Nothing in Middleton Woods is really tamed or sculpted. There is no human hand. Sergeant Kitching and former Inspector Ellerker taking the nigger back to nature, depositing him in fascist South Leeds. Sometimes they would take him deep into the heart of Middleton Woods and abandon him. Sometimes.

The Fox and Hounds is a stone building; the type of building that is imitated by those who insist on 'stone-cladding' their otherwise ordinary homes. The inscription '1728' by the door suggests the pub's vintage. The village of Bramhope is a well-to-do suburb of Leeds, some ten miles beyond the city centre. Stone detached houses with neatly trimmed lawns. Closed minds. The pub itself is in the village square at the top of a short steep hill. The monitor for the car park CCTV is in the bar so that the barman can stand behind the bar and, as he pulls his pints, he can watch what is happening outside. Clearly there has been a recent problem with hooligans. In the bar itself there are neatly framed pictures of hounds and horses which suggest history and tradition. This is England. Hand pumps. Slate floor. Old clocks. Policemen might drink in a pub like this on their day off. Older policemen might be lucky enough to retire to a village like Bramhope and occasionally come to this pub for Sunday lunch. I sit and look around. I am sure that Sergeant Kitching and former Inspector Ellerker had a quiet contempt for this village and its people. Its 'well-to-do' people. By the back door there is a low stone wall. On the wall there is a sign which reads 'For Patrons Only'. It refers to the car park, but it could be the village motto. Smug village, with its small village square, and its proud little Village Bakery. Four o'clock in the morning. Go on, Sambo. Knock on the door and ask for a cup of tea. They've never seen anything like you. They'll be furious. They'll abuse you. And then you'll have the problem of trying to get back to Leeds city centre where we don't want you, understand? David had to walk back through the village. Then out into the open countryside. Miles to walk before the houses began to once more congregate by the side of the road. They laughed at David. 'Go on, nigger. Knock.' In the Fox and Hounds everybody is asleep. Four o'clock in the morning. Where are the hounds? The dogs on two legs. The animals in blue trousers. A lonely fox harming nobody.

Underneath the arches. Huge Dickensian arches beneath Leeds City Station. The river rushes right through the arches with a loud cascading roar. On stepping out again into the bright light one can hear the announcements of the train station. Once upon a time this was a vast filthy cavern full of homeless people. It's different now, underneath the arches. They have been 'redeveloped' (and renamed – Granary Wharf) into a pleasant new shopping complex, featuring Afrodisia – an Afro-Caribbean and French cuisine restaurant – and the Casablanca bazaar, which sells pots, bowls and baskets, and a stripped-pine furniture shop. All huddled underneath the arches, but the truth is this place cannot be reclaimed. It remains dark and forbidding. It resists redevelopment, and whispered stories linger in this dank air. Today, pedestrians use the arches of Granary Wharf as a short cut through to the city centre. They hardly ever break step for the place still reeks of abandoned lives and quiet desperation. They hurry through these arches, which once rejected David. 'He's not here and we don't want that type around here.'

By the Knostrop Sewage Works. Here the River Aire and the Aire-Calder Navigation Canal move side by side. The river rushes with a strong current, and flows away from the city centre. The canal lazily swirls and eddies. I watch swans floating on the canal. They have no desire to pursue a journey and travel through to Hull. Around nine o'clock in the morning the sun suddenly breaks through the clouds and casts a blinding light into my face. Still rising in the east. Don't look too closely. Don't look. I walk the narrow path between the river, with its fast-flowing water, and the languorous canal. The river bore you out of the heart of the city that you made your own. It carried you past the tall brick mills that stared in your direction; it carried you away from Leeds Parish Church and out towards the sewage works. The canal continues to lap quietly. A peaceful place where one can hear both the odd cry of a bird and the low hum of traffic somewhere in the distance. And then church bells begin to peal. On the hour. And then the stripe of sunlight on the water widens as the clouds part further. The glare is too much to bear, but the swans don't mind. They simply upend themselves and fish. And then one swan tries to rise in a gawky pantomime of flight that betrays the gracefulness of their residence on the water. These canals attract weeds. The shoreline is choked with effluence; empty pop bottles and abandoned packets of crisps. The washed-up scum of bad eating and living. Rubbish. Effluvium of an ignorant city. Back then, all those years ago, the hot machinery of Leeds stamped out brand-spanking-new goods for colonial use and dumped the waste into this water. Small-gauge trains to transport sugar cane in the Caribbean. Larger engines to India. Waste into the water. Back then, during the final spasm of empire. Back then, when it was still considered acceptable to furiously burn both industrial fuel and human dreams. White dreams and black dreams. Flat caps and woolly hair. Pull of a cig. Knock back a pint. Tuck the paper under your arm. Tramp your way to the bookies. Go home to the missus. Have your tea. What's the divvy? Go down the pub. Go on, go down the pub, dreamer. No colour bar in here, mate. I have come to your country to work. Go down the pub, mister. Go on, go down the pub. The river flows quickly. Down the river towards the sewage works. Rush away from your city, David. Over the tumbling weir and down into the tranquil part of the River Aire where you will eventually become snarled up in the undergrowth. Rest with the water. Spent. Knostrop Sewage Works on the bank of the river. The end of your journey. Betrayed by the water. Carry him further beyond the sewage works. Don't stop now. Carry him beyond this place. More respect, please. More respect.

Question by Detective Superintendent Fryer; answer by Sergeant Kitching. 27.10.70

Q: Where have you kicked his [Oluwale's] behind? [In] What doorways have you kicked his behind?
A: Under Leeds Library in Commercial Street. In the dark doorway next to the Wine Lodge in Bond Street. Brills in Bond Street, Bakers in Trinity Street, in John Peters in Lands Lane. Bridal House in The Headrow, the Empire Arcade in Briggate, and Trinity Church in Boar Lane.

David, you wandered hungry and sick through the heart of a city that has now pedestrianised itself. Today there are no cars. It is all reserved for pedestrians, like you. But back then it was different. 3 a.m. 18 April, 1969. Clutching old newspapers that kept you warm on cold Yorkshire nights. You are sleeping in the doorway of John Peters Furniture Shop on Lands Lane. Sleeping peacefully in the heart of your 'clean city', and again these two men come and begin to abuse you. They shout and they kick you. They are forever moving you on from this place, and tonight they are very angry. Will they urinate upon you again? No, this time they merely shout and beat you, but you escape and run up Lands Lane towards the main street, The Headrow. Leeds' grand avenue. You turn right into The Headrow and run down the hill towards the doorway of the Bridal House where you often like to sleep. The only shop doorway on The Headrow that is illuminated, a place where everybody can see you. 397 The Headrow. Opposite the Odeon Cinema (which has now closed down). Today, in the window of the Bridal House, there are two white plastic models with silver decorations on their heads. The fully garbed female models flaunt themselves in the window, and female pedestrians stop and smile and look beyond your open-air bedroom. David, if only you had turned and gone up The Headrow and away from the city centre they might not have discovered you. But you came to where you *knew* they would find you at the Bridal House, and you squatted on your little stone step on The Headrow. The most open place in town. Fully illuminated. Just a short way up The Headrow from Millgarth Police Station, and on every policeman's route home from work. They pass by your bedroom without mirrors, and you are not hiding. Just sitting quietly in the heart of your city trying to stay warm and out of harm's way. Today the 'H' on the sign 'Bridal House' is hanging askew. But your house has not fallen down. Three doors away there is now the Housing Advice Centre for the homeless. Through the window I can see some black faces; miserable thin faces looking for shelter, people who are eager to be rescued. The window boasts a sign: 'We might just have what you're looking for.' Tracksuited, sleepless, desperate men. Asians, blacks, whites. Next door is Big Lil's Saloon Bar for broken drunks who are down on their luck, and beyond Big Lil's is William Hill the bookies. Sad new world. You did not need these places. You did not fail. You stayed in the doorway of your Bridal House. You eventually curled up next to happiness. You slept with the joyful brides, but once again they found you, and attempted to beat the life out of you, and so you ran and instead of going straight down The Headrow towards Millgarth Police Station you turned right into Vicar Lane and you ran for your life in the direction of Call Lane, but still they chased you, and you knew that this time they would kill you, and so you ran furiously, but they came closer, and closer. Twenty years in England had taken some wind out of your sail and you could hear them pounding the pavement behind you, and so you ran straight from Vicar Lane into the narrow entrance to Call Lane but they were getting closer and your legs could no longer carry you and then, as Call Lane turned to the right, you saw a narrow gap between the warehouses and you passed into this gap. It was five o'clock in the morning and you ran into the gap, my friend. You ran into Warehouse Hill. You ran towards the river, their hot, desperate, breath on the back of your neck. You ran.

Warehouse Hill is little more than a narrow gap between tall warehouses. A short cobbled hill of perhaps thirty yards that quickly dead-ends at the river. To the left is Warehouse Road and more warehouses. To the right is Leeds Bridge, where the city was born. In front of you is the River Aire. You did not jump, David. There is no evidence that you could swim. You did not jump. Today there is a safety barrier which is four feet high. A black metal barrier to prevent people from accidentally falling in. But not then, my friend. Back then you could fly down the thirty yards of Warehouse Hill, miss the cobbled turn to the left into Warehouse Road, and get very wet. But not you, David. You did not jump. Today, on the wall, there is a sign. It reads: 'Aire-Calder Navigation. Before the railway age, the making navigable of the River Aire importantly made Leeds an inland port connected directly to Hull. Cheap water carriage was vital for the successful export of the cloth marketed and finished in the town. Opened 1700.' Perhaps, David, the river tried to carry you away to the east and back in the direction of Hull. Twenty years in Leeds is a long time. Perhaps the strong current, down here at Leeds Bridge, was intent upon carrying you all the way back to Hull, and then back to the safety of Africa. Away from your home.

'*Remember Oluwale*'.
  Graffiti on the wall by the Hayfield pub on the corner of Reginald Terrace and Harehills Avenue.

*

I was living in Sheffield when the case went to trial and I thought, 'Goodness, I know that guy.' It was David. I was outraged that the police would target him in the way the newspapers said they did, and behave with such un-bridled brutality. Obviously they had a personal vendetta against him, but the David I knew was stubborn and was never a man to back down. I knew he would have refused to play second best to these people. David and I first met when we were about fifteen. We were part of the same group of about six to ten guys who ran together in Lagos. At Christmas and Easter we used to dress up in fancy dress; you know, a cowboy on a bicycle or something like that. We called ourselves the Odunlami Area Boys' Club and our dream was to escape to England, for the war had 'officially' educated us about that place. Olu had an uncle who ran a hotel called Ilojo Hotel in Tinubu Square, and sometimes we would meet there. Then eventually, one by one, we all sought out ships to stow away on and we made our way to England. I was lucky for my captain let me work my passage painting the ship, and when we docked in Birkenhead he handed me over to the immigration officer but he told the man that I'd worked my passage. Eventually I made my way to Yorkshire where I'd heard there were good jobs, and I got work at the Hatfield Steelworks. I couldn't believe it but Olu was also working there. David had the same no-nonsense attitude about him, and I was really very happy to see a face from Lagos, but I worried about him. He wouldn't let anything go. Nobody was going to do this or that to him, and his attitude was always getting him into trouble. If a foreman said something wrong to him, it would be 'fuck off' and there really wasn't any point in talking to him. I tried. I would say, 'Hey, Olu,' but he was a stubborn, fighting man who simply found it impossible to back down and work the system. I worried about Olu. We all had strong heads as youngsters in Lagos, but maybe Olu's head was a little stronger. When I heard about the case I felt sick. I was shocked to hear that he had been reduced to sleeping in the street, but I knew that Olu would never back down and let these people humiliate him. Maybe that's it; he was a little stronger and more determined. But I didn't know that he was sleeping in the street. I just didn't know.

Killingbeck Cemetery is ludicrously overcrowded. The cemetery equivalent of a ghetto. Its location opposite St James' Hospital suggests that somebody is in possession of a strange sense of humour. The cemetery sits on York Road. The old Roman road to York. On this desolate patch of land trees have been planted as though they were a hurried afterthought. To the east of the cemetery houses are clustered tightly together behind flimsy wooden fencing. Children wander through the cemetery, using it as a short cut on their way home from school. The cemetery lacks gravitas. Abandoned flowers are dying on stone slabs. The children are oblivious of the significance of what lies all about them. They laugh. And then I see it. Your tomb-stone. It stands at the crest of a hill and lists slightly to the right. You are at the top of a hill, but 'David Oluwale' appears at the bottom of a list of ten names. And why a Roman Catholic cemetery for you? Was there something in the pocket of your wet coat that suggested this? Your blue bead necklace with a crucifix? Your grave is full. There are nine others. In death you have fulfilled a promise made at birth. Here at Killingbeck Cemetery there is no more land for graves. Soon there will be no more burials in this place. Everybody can rest peacefully. You have achieved a summit, David. Climbed to the top of a hill, and from here you can look down. You are still in Leeds. Forever in Leeds.

Acknowledgements

I wrote this book with the help and assistance of a number of people. I would like to thank: Kester Aspden, Maureen Baker, James Basker, Jill Campbell, Allison Edwards, Max Farrar, Patricia Farrell, Arthur France, Vanessa Garcia, Karen King-Aribisala, Cordelia Lawton, John McLeod, Colin Mann, George Miles, Joseph Odeyemi, Gill and Tei Quarcoopome, Liz Stirling, Vanessa Toulmin, Annette Turpin, Charmaine Turpin, James Walvin, Eurwyn Williams, Orig Williams, Alex Woolliams, and Matthew Yeomans. I owe a particular debt of gratitude to David Thornton's *Leeds: The Story of a City*. Maya Wainhaus assisted me through the final stages and typed the manuscript. Finally, Andrew Warnes proved to be a wonderful researcher, source of information, and friend as I was writing 'Northern Lights'.

Caryl Phillips
March 2007